A SMALL TOWN, SECOND CHANCE ROMANCE

FOR YOU I'D BREAK

BOOK 1 OF THE PEACE FALLS SERIES

HANNAH JORDAN

About This Book

A FREAK ACCIDENT YEARS after graduation gives a former high school hottie and the wallflower who was too nervous to speak in his presence a second chance at love.

After her two-year marriage ends with a crash, Rowan returns to her hometown of Peace Falls, VA, riding shotgun in her sister's 1990 Cadillac hearse. Everything about her is damaged: her heart, her pride, her bank account, and her spine, which she injured running into a tourist on a Segway after finding her husband and her boss getting busy at the DC financial firm where they all worked. She's determined to reclaim her career and city life as soon as she recuperates and lands a new job.

Caleb "Cal" Cardoso may not have noticed wallflower Rowan in high school, but the former football star, and Peace Falls's newest physical therapist, can't take his eyes off the stunning redhead now. Too bad he's sworn off relationships. After his ex-girlfriend purposely tanked his professional reputation online, he stands to lose his job if a single patient leaves his care. Which is why he can't let Rowan switch to another practice, despite the friction between them, and why he definitely can't act on his growing attraction.

Rowan agrees to remain Cal's patient if he helps her younger brother train for football tryouts. Though Cal hasn't touched a football since the devastating car crash that killed one of his best friends, he agrees. As Cal helps heal Rowan's body, their connection begins to heal both their hearts.

For You I'd Break is a small town romance with a hefty dash of spice, a HEA ending, and a cast of memorable characters, including a goth sculptor who secretly loves to decorate cakes, a fearsome-looking felon with a heart of gold, a hothead with a sweet side, a karma-devoted barista who collects damaged pets and first dates, and a lovable dog with more emotional sense than everyone put together.

Content warning: This book contains references to self-harm.

Published by Hannah Jordan Books 2024

Cover Design: Kaytalin McCarry, Duskbound Books

ebook ISBN: 979-8-9905868-0-2

Paperback ISBN: 979-8-9905868-1-9

https://hannahjordanauthor.com

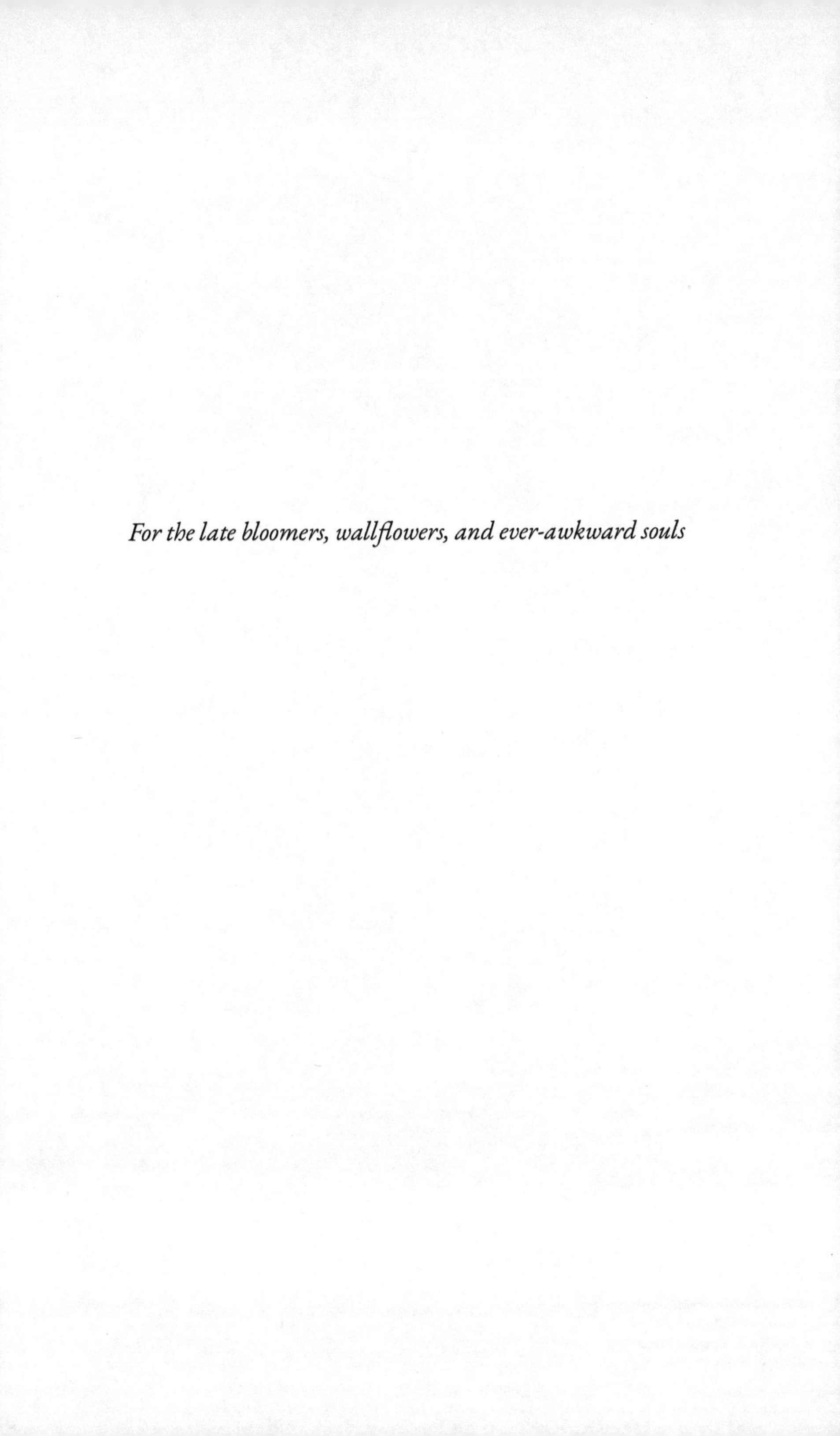

For the late bloomers, wallflowers, and ever-awkward souls

Chapter One

Rowan

Being a wallflower makes you thirsty, so parched for attention your heart feels brittle. Then after years—or in my case a lifetime—someone finally sees you. The exquisite feeling seeps deep, the attention saturating your life. So, you jump, headfirst. The red flags go unnoticed. Declarations of love tossed as lightly as petals. Maybe you marry him, like I did. Maybe you bloom in domestic bliss with a house in the suburbs and two adorable kids. Maybe a dog. Bare minimum a pet turtle.

I wasn't so lucky.

After two years of marriage, instead of house hunting in the outskirts of DC, I was riding shotgun in my sister's 1990 Cadillac hearse, headed back to Peace Falls, VA, with everything I owned stuffed where a coffin ought to be.

I'd cried so much in the past three hours, I could barely make out the foothills rising in the distance. My throat was raw. Crumpled tissues littered the floorboard, and lint covered my leggings.

"I'll vacuum in here later," I croaked.

Poppy shot me a worried glance and returned her attention to the road. She blew out a breath that ruffled her short black bangs.

For two sisters who looked so much alike, we couldn't appear more different. We have the same bright copper hair as our mother, but Poppy hadn't worn hers naturally since middle school, when she bought a box of dye at Mr. Wilson's pharmacy and applied it while our mother was at work. Mom lost it until she realized what a great job she'd done. I suspect my sister made a deal since Poppy's hair has been every color but red ever since, and Mom's grays vanished overnight.

Poppy settled on black a year ago, which matched her entire wardrobe. The color, coupled with the heavy winged liner she wore faithfully, made her green eyes pop in a way I could never make my own.

"Don't forget your drink," she said.

Had she spoken since we got in the hearse? I honestly couldn't remember, but judging by how tense her shoulders were, and the box of tissues I'd burned through, I'm guessing we hadn't talked much.

The tears surprised me. Apart from a couple of late-night phone calls to my mother after I left the hospital, I'd held it together pretty well. I was too busy tying up the loose ends of my life in DC to feel anything but stressed. The moment Poppy arrived to drive me home, the tears started and built with every box, bag, and lamp we slid into the hearse.

Poppy had stopped in Manassas to pee and fill up her gas guzzler, but I stayed in the passenger seat and cried. I hadn't touched the fountain Pibb Xtra she'd bought me, which was basically a sin. The 32oz-er had sweated in the cup holder for nearly two hours. I finally picked it up and took a long pull from the straw, letting the slightly flat, watered-down goodness soothe my throat. I drank nearly half before I put it back. I guess crying dehydrates you.

My stomach gave a loud gurgle. Understandable, since I'd been too upset to eat much over the past week and hadn't attempted anything this morning. I tried to remember the last full meal I'd eaten and couldn't. Normally, I baked when I felt stressed. Instead, I'd used the tension to speed me through my task list like I was one of those wind-up cars. Hopefully, I'd taken better care of my plants than myself.

I twisted to check how my orchid was faring, and pain shot up my spine. I shifted, but the twinge deepened into a throbbing ache. Now that I wasn't crying or dying of thirst, the pain in my back resurfaced. The doctor had warned me to take frequent breaks to stretch, and instead I'd gone most of the trip without leaving my seat.

"Can you pull over at the scenic overlook? I need some air."

Poppy swerved into the right lane, cutting off an 18-wheeler. "Don't puke in Tallulah."

Air brakes sputtered in our wake, but the truck driver didn't honk. A perk of driving a hearse, perhaps, but no amount of courtesy would have prevented us from getting flattened if the semi had been going downhill instead of up.

"What's wrong with you? I just need to stretch."

As the scenic overlook approached, Poppy flicked on the turn signal, giving the semi enough warning this time before she slowed. She drove past a few out-of-state cars to the edge of the small parking lot and shut off the engine.

"Sorry," she said, patting the dashboard. "You took down all that Pibb and then your stomach made those weird noises. I'm a little protective of Tallulah."

I glared and opened the passenger door. My back screamed as I pulled myself from the hearse and straightened. I took one painful step after another until I reached the stone wall that protected visitors from the steep drop to the valley below. I shuffled along, letting the wall hold my weight until I reached the center.

I turned to face the view and my breath caught. I'd have wanted to stop at the overlook even if my back wasn't hurting. Poppy had only lived in Peace Falls. She wouldn't understand how it felt to watch the mountains surrounding our small town disappear in the rearview mirror, to search for that feeling of shelter among tall buildings and find only a claustrophobic ache for open space.

The mountains spread before me in waves, the dips and rises worn smooth with time. Summer was my favorite season in the Blue Ridge Valley. Many people preferred the fall colors or spring blooms, but seeing everything so lush and green brought back countless memories of hiking with my dad. He'd play hooky from work a few times during our summer breaks from school, so we could enjoy the trails with fewer tourists. Our mountains were another hour down the road, but the chain began here. Waterfalls like the one that gave our town its name trickled and poured from underground springs within the mountains, visible only to those willing to weave on foot through the trails to reach them.

Whenever I came home, I always stopped at this overlook to admire the earthen giants that welcomed me back with the same pull of longing as when I left. But this time was different. I wasn't returning to visit. I no longer knew when I'd leave the mountains again. At the ripe old age of twenty-six, I was unemployed, separated, and in more pain than I'd ever felt in my life. Everything I'd worked so hard to accomplish had been obliterated in two minutes, leaving me broken in every way a person can be. When I left Peace Falls, I was determined to make something of myself. To become someone people respected, or, at the very least, mentioned on occasion without a sigh and a "bless her heart." I'd failed.

"You're still wearing your rings," Poppy said, propping herself against the wall beside me, facing the parking lot instead of the view. She crossed one combat boot over the other and examined her broken fingernails. "You're not planning to take him back? Are you?"

"Of course not," I snapped. I twisted the overpriced rings and sighed. It wasn't Poppy's fault my heart and body ached, and she'd earned serious sister points today, minus the near-death experience. "I was afraid I'd lose them if I packed them."

"You should take them off before we get to Peace Falls. Mom will notice."

"Mom will understand. She wore hers until Chris went to kindergarten."

"That's why she'll notice. And worry. Besides, you can't compare your situation to Mom's."

I wiggled the large diamond and matching band from my left hand and handed them to Poppy, who unclipped one of the chains around her neck and slid on the rings. "Good. I'd hate for you to move back in with all that dog poop."

I chuckled, despite how awful I felt. "Dog poop is a tamer nickname than I expected from you."

"Brad's a dick. I'm talking about the real dog poop."

My stomach sank. "What dog poop?"

Poppy smiled, a rare and terrifying thing in the best circumstances. "While you were saying goodbye to your super, I might have left a few parting gifts around the apartment."

I rubbed my forehead, which suddenly hurt more than my back. "Where?"

"No way. I'm not telling. You'll text dickhead a warning or call your super to clean it up. Plus, I can't remember where I put it all. Two pounds is a lot of crap to locate. I weighed it. A pound for every year you were married."

As usual, Poppy's prank was oddly poetic and over the top. "Where did you get that much poop?"

"Chris."

"Mom finally let him get a dog?"

"Nah, he walks the neighbor's. He started collecting right after the accident. It was all his idea." Poppy smiled again, a softer smile that gave a peek at the sweet person she was under all the makeup, black clothes, and heavy boots.

I get it. I do. Poppy, Chris, and I stick up for each other. We always have. My baby brother might be ten years younger than me, but that hadn't stopped him from covering Avery Peterson's convertible with tampons soaked in Hawaiian Punch after she "accidentally" spilled a carton of milk on my head senior year and told everyone I should thank her for making my hair less glaring. Poppy took the fall, of course, and high-fived Chris when she got home from yet another detention.

"Remember what happened after the tampon incident?"

Poppy's eyes widened. "Shit. You think we made things worse for you?"

"Probably." I rested my head on her shoulder. "But thank you." My back gave another twinge, and I stiffened.

Poppy sighed and wrapped her arm around my waist. "What can we do to make your back feel better? Some yoga? A couple shots of Jameson?"

I lifted my head and narrowed my eyes at her. "Please tell me you don't have an open container of liquor in your vehicle?"

Poppy stepped back and held up her hands. "Hey, I didn't know what kind of mood you'd be in. I wanted to be prepared. Plus, I'm twenty-three. I don't think there's an issue, not that I'd be drinking it. The law is a little gray. I just figured it was good to have on hand, in case you needed it. Honestly, I didn't know what you'd need. Lauren wasn't helpful. She said to 'listen with love' and suggested I grab some pastries, which I totally planned to do, but then I overslept after working on a piece too late. I didn't want you there one minute longer than you had to be, so I grabbed the whiskey and dog poop and left. Times like these, I wish Tallulah had a second passenger seat. Lauren wouldn't have forgotten the pastries or assumed you were going to hurl and almost kill us, but another set of seats would defeat the whole purpose of driving a hearse."

The corners of my lips twitched with a smile. "If we get pulled over, I'll say I'm mourning my husband."

Poppy stood taller. "Dickface isn't worth mourning, Rowan. But the Jameson's in the glove box. I even packed Dixie cups, so you could measure, or drink like a lady, or not smash your teeth on the bottle if we hit a bump."

I placed a hand on her shoulder and shook my head. "I'm not showing up at Mom's reeking of whiskey before dinner. Like you said, she's worried enough. Let me walk the length of the overlook a couple times to loosen up, and I'll be fine."

"You are, Rowan," she said, firmly, "better, without him."

My eyes burned at her confidence and lack of pity. It was the reason I'd asked Poppy, and only Poppy, to help me move. Mom would have cried right along with me, just like she had on every phone call since I left the hospital. Chris would have gotten upset the way only a sixteen-year-old boy can and done something stupider than collecting dog poop to rain on my ex. My best friend Lauren would have tried to console me with positive affirmations and 100% would have waved a burning sage stick over everything I owned before we left DC. It's the reason I begged them all not to come a week ago when everything happened. I couldn't handle their pity or their sadness. I knew Poppy would take whatever she was feeling about the situation and pour it into her art, but even she looked near her breaking point. I haven't seen her this agitated since our dad's funeral when she realized she'd outgrown her black ballet flats and refused to wear a pair of my hand-me-downs with gold sequins. Even then, she didn't cry or rage. Instead, she rambled about proper funeral etiquette with a specificity no nine-year-old should know and ended up staying at the house with a neighbor to set up the repast, missing the service. I swiped at my eyes and took a steadying breath. "I hope you got his brown Ferragamo loafers. He loves those."

Poppy smirked. "I cannot confirm or deny."

I linked my arm in hers, and we set off across the parking lot toward the hearse and the next chapter of my life.

CHAPTER TWO

Rowan

WHEN WE PULLED INTO the driveway, Chris shot off the porch steps, shouting to our mother as his long legs ate up the distance to the hearse. Mom burst through the front door moments later in a flour-dusted apron, wooden spoon in hand.

Poppy rolled her eyes as Chris yanked open my door. "Ann," he said, contorting his lanky frame into the hearse to hug me. Chris had struggled with my name as a little boy and shortened it. The nickname stuck, but whenever I heard it, I remembered the toddler with the lisp who followed me everywhere and climbed into my lap whenever I sat down. He'd grown at least three inches since I saw him at Easter. He squeezed me so hard I winced.

"Fuck, you're probably still bruised." He pulled away and gripped the back of his neck.

"Don't say fuck," Mom said, pushing him aside. "Let her get out of the damn hearse. I don't like seeing any of my children in this thing, but especially Rowan."

"Told you she's Mom's favorite," Poppy shouted to Chris from the driver's seat.

Mom waved her words away and reached in to unbuckle my seatbelt like I was two. She grabbed my hands and guided me from the hearse before squeezing me tighter than Chris had.

"I can't tell you how relieved I am to hold you. It's been torture staying away."

She smelled of fresh bread, roses, and home. My eyes burned. I took a deep breath and forced the tears down. "It's what I wanted."

Mom stepped out of the hug, but held onto my arms, scanning me from the top of my head to my feet, pausing long enough on my hands for me to send Poppy a silent thank you.

Mom's blue eyes filled with rage, and she pressed her lips so tight they went white at the edges. I'd love to be inside her head to hear everything I should have said to Brad before I left.

"You need to eat," she snapped, directing some of that venom at me. "Let's go."

I wanted to keep up with her, but my back had other ideas. I took a painful step, trying my best not to groan.

Chris looked at Poppy and she nodded, either confirming what a mess I was or that she'd fulfilled operation dog poop.

Mom brushed at her eyes, turned, and stomped back to the hearse. "You can't leave your Cymbidium in this heat. Where is it?"

Poppy opened the back and yanked out enough boxes to climb inside to the middle of the pile where we'd stowed the orchid. "Here it is," she said, handing the plant to Mom, who examined the blossoms like a doctor giving a thorough physical. She tsked and headed toward the house, focused on healing something she could.

"I'll unload everything," Chris said, bending to grab a box. "Where do you want it?"

I looked at what remained of my DC life scattered across the driveway and spilling from the hearse, and my mind went blank. I wasn't even sure where I'd be sleeping. Brad and I always got a hotel room when we visited together. On the few occasions I came alone, Poppy and I shared our childhood bedroom, which didn't seem like a viable solution long term.

"Just put everything in the living room," Poppy said, weaving her arm through mine. "We'll figure it out later."

"I didn't think this through," I said as I gripped the porch railing with my free hand and pulled myself up the steps. "I don't know how long I'm staying, but you shouldn't have to share your room with me."

"Our room," Poppy said. "Besides, I usually sleep on the futon in the studio."

"You do not sleep in the shed. Mom wouldn't let you."

Poppy rolled her eyes. "For the last time, Rowan, I'm twenty-three. A full-grown human. I only live here because I'd rather work less at the café and have more time to sculpt. Mom understands and does her best to let me be the adult I am. Besides, she's so worried about you, I could do a satanic ritual in the backyard, naked, and she wouldn't notice."

"She wouldn't," Chris added, hurrying past us with a precarious stack of boxes. "Pop?"

The two of them had a shorthand way of speaking I'd never understand, and, of course, my sister insisted he give her a nickname as well. Poppy released me to hold open the heavy wooden door and Chris sailed through. I followed him inside.

"Don't you dare lift anything, Rowan," Mom shouted from the kitchen. "Take a seat in the dining room."

"If you tell her I let you help load the hearse, I'll draw on your face with a Sharpie while you sleep," Poppy hissed in my ear.

"You let her carry stuff?" Chris shouted.

"Shut up," Poppy and I said in unison.

"What was that?" Mom asked, peering out of the dining room archway with a platter of biscuits.

"Chris was making fun of Rowan's throw pillows," Poppy said. "I agree, no one needs that much paisley, but he shouldn't kick a bitch while she's down."

"Hush, the both of you. Grab all the plants and leave the rest until after we eat. Rowan, honey, come sit."

I pointed to the small powder room, and Mom nodded and hurried out of sight. I hobbled to the bathroom and locked myself inside. I loved my family but only five minutes in, and I needed a breather. They weren't usually so aggressive with their affection or concern. I caught sight of my face and cringed. Eyes so swollen I could barely see the green, cheeks gaunt and paler than usual, and a nose red enough to audition for Rudolph. I washed my hands and splashed water on my face, then ran my damp fingers through my hair before taking the hair tie from my wrist and twisting my long locks into a bun. I still looked a hot mess, but slightly less deranged. When I opened the door, Poppy and Chris were leaning against the wall, waiting.

"Seriously, I'm fine. This is why I didn't let you come to DC earlier. Y'all hover."

"I don't," Poppy said, pushing past me into the bathroom. "I just drank as much soda as you did and need to tinkle. Though, if I were being overbearing, I'd say I didn't hear the toilet flush, which means you're either gross or severely dehydrated." She glanced at the toilet and back at me. "Dehydrated it is."

"I was just waiting to wash my hands," Chris said, "But might as well help my favorite sister to the table instead of listening for toilet flushes like a perv." Poppy gave him a one-finger salute and slammed the door. He grabbed my elbow and guided me to the dining room like I was made of glass. An armchair that belonged in the living room sat at the head of the table like a throne. Without warning, he lifted me off my feet and placed me on the cushioned seat.

"What?" he said, blushing. "I'm weight training for tryouts. I could carry you upstairs later. It looked like the porch steps gave you trouble."

"I'm fine," I said gently. "Did you put this chair here or Mom?"

"I did after Poppy texted that you were walking like an eighty-year-old. These wood chairs hurt my butt, so I figured they'd be torture for you."

"Thanks, Chris," I said, squeezing his hand. He squeezed it back so weakly I almost laughed. "Whoa," I said, taking in all the dishes on the table.

It wasn't so much a cohesive meal as a buffet of savory and sweet options with only one thing in common: I loved them all. A steaming bowl of chipped beef gravy beside a platter of thinly sliced country ham. Fried chicken with waffles. Fresh strawberries smothered in mountains of whipped cream. Hush puppies, fries, and mozzarella sticks. Flatbread pizza with homemade crust. And no less than three types of pie.

"Is Mom expecting company?"

"Nah," Chris said, popping a fry in his mouth.

I felt a stab of guilt. Mom and I both liked to let off steam in the kitchen. Something about kneading dough and measuring ingredients precisely always lowered my blood pressure, while she enjoyed anything that ended with feeding people. She'd clearly been working through some strong feelings, and it didn't take a rocket scientist to know I'd caused them.

"Oh good," Mom said, hurrying in with a covered dish. "You're settled. I made collard greens for something healthy." She plopped the dish on the table and scurried out as Poppy entered the dining room.

She looked at the table and snorted before pulling out the chair beside me.

"Don't worry, Pop, I made a garden salad," Chris said, disappearing into the kitchen.

"Since when does Chris eat salad?" I asked, taking the cloth napkin from my plate and placing it on my lap.

Poppy grabbed a water pitcher and filled my glass to the brim with a glare. She watched me gulp half the glass, then refilled it before filling her own.

"He's trying out for the varsity football team in August," Mom said, breezing back into the room with a gravy boat and an overflowing bowl of mashed potatoes. Chris followed with a large green salad and a small pitcher.

"I made the dressing myself," he said proudly.

After Dad died and Mom started working insane hours to make ends meet, I took over most meal prep while Poppy handled the dishes. Being only two, Chris's initial contribution was banging pots and pans on the kitchen floor while I cooked or baked. When he got old enough to wash up, my sister shoved that task his way and took over mowing the lawn from me. I'd never eaten anything made by my brother, and I wasn't sure my stomach was experiment ready.

He served me a heap of mixed greens and roasted veggies, and I dutifully poured the dressing on top. Mom stopped rearranging the serving dishes to watch, either to see my reaction to Chris's cooking or to assure herself I was eating.

"This looks great," I said, because, honestly, it did. I took a bite and an explosion of unexpected flavors hit my tongue. "What's in this?" I asked, going in for another forkful.

Chris beamed and shot Mom a smug look. "Curried chickpeas with a lime-coconut dressing."

"Your brother has been watching cooking videos on YouTube," Mom said, finally taking a seat. "He says we need to eat healthier."

"We do," Chris said, lifting a huge portion of salad onto his plate. "But just because it's healthy doesn't mean it has to taste bad."

"Rowan, pass me your plate," Mom said. "You can eat rabbit food later. You need real calories."

Poppy grabbed it before I could protest and gave it to Mom, who loaded on more food than I could eat in a week.

"I was able to get you a physical therapy appointment tomorrow morning," Mom said, passing back my plate.

"Is it in town?" I asked, suddenly ravenous. I bit into a fried chicken breast and moaned.

Mom shot Chris a smug look and he shrugged.

"Right on Main Street," Mom said. "I'll take you and bring you home after, unless you'd rather borrow my car."

I shook my head. "I'm on some pretty strong pain killers. It's best I don't drive."

Mom nodded. "Hopefully Cal can get you sorted, so you can get off that stuff. I hear it can be addictive."

I choked on the piece of waffle in my mouth and coughed hard enough to send my back into a painful spasm. Poppy shoved my water at me. I pushed it away, coughing until I could breathe again.

I only knew of one Cal who lived in Peace Falls, but maybe someone else with the name had moved to town while I was in DC. "Cal as in Caleb Cardoso?" I sputtered.

"Dr. Cardoso now," Mom said. "He's usually booked solid, but the receptionist fit you in at eight. I bet he's opening early as a favor."

"Why would Caleb Cardoso do us a favor?" I asked.

Mom looked at me like I'd grown a second head. "Why wouldn't he?"

"He doesn't know us," I said.

"He doesn't know you," Chris said, around a mouth full of salad. "Cal bought the Hilberts's house when they moved to Florida last fall. I walk his dog every afternoon during the week, and sometimes Cal and I run together." Chris's eyes widened, and he put down his fork. "Maybe I should ask him to help me train before tryouts. He played wide receiver, same as me."

"That's a wonderful idea," Mom said, dumping a mound of mashed potatoes onto her plate.

"You collected Caleb Cardoso's dog's poop?" I shrieked.

"Why do you keep saying his full name?" Poppy asked, narrowing her eyes.

"Of course, Chris cleans up after the dog," Mom snapped. "I haven't raised degenerates."

Chris laughed so hard he snorted, which sent Poppy into an uncharacteristic fit of giggles.

"Have you been drinking?" Mom asked her.

"No, but I think we should start," Poppy said, rising from the table. "Poop collector, help," she added, smacking Chris on the back of the head.

"Eat," Mom ordered.

I attempted another bite of waffle. Mom seemed content to sit in silence as long as I kept eating, which gave me way too much freedom to think about Cal.

Infatuated. There is no other word to describe how teenage me felt about Caleb Cardoso. Though in my defense, every girl at Peace Falls High was obsessed with him. It's true, he probably had no idea who I was. We never had a class together since he was two grades ahead of me, and our extracurriculars and friend groups didn't overlap. He was a star on the varsity football team and dated Avery Peterson. Yes, the Avery of milk and tampon fame. She was in Cal's grade, captain of the cheerleading team, homecoming queen, and a total bitch to anyone who didn't fit in, aka me and my best friend Lauren. It would have been easy to lump Cal in with Avery and hate him on principle, but he wasn't a bully like her. Whenever Cal and Avery were together, I knew she wouldn't mess with me or anyone else. She was too busy touching him or kissing him to give the rest of us any attention. Can't say I blame her. I wouldn't have been able to keep my hands or tongue to myself if he were my boyfriend. Thick brown hair, a jaw line that could cut glass, and a pair of lips so full they'd look feminine on anyone else. On Cal, they were just the cherry on top of an irresistible sundae. My stomach fluttered every time our paths crossed, and I'd go mute. No lie, I could be in the middle of a conversation with Lauren, and the words would dry up in my mouth. Just thinking about him made me ache in the only places my body hadn't over the past week.

"I'm glad to see you eating," Mom said with a small smile, interrupting my inappropriate highlight reel of Cal Cardoso sightings.

I had made a serious dent in my plate while I fantasized.

"Who's ready to get shitfaced?" Chris asked, returning with an open bottle of champagne and four flutes. "Half a glass," Mom said, pointing at him. "Same for Rowan, assuming she can drink at all while she's on drugs."

Poppy followed, carrying the most detailed cake I'd ever seen. Three stacked tiers of black fondant with gold-painted details. Each tier was edged with an abundance of red flowers: poppies, chrysanthemums, and roses so realistic I thought for a moment they were real. On top, a fondant sculpture of me, in a red dress with a wreath of Rowan berries woven in my hair, shoved a sculpture of Brad off the side of the cake. Poppy had somehow captured the moment before the fall. Brad's arms flailed above his head, and his feet hovered at a forty-five-degree angle off the cake.

"My name is not Chrysanthemum," Chris huffed.

"Only because you aren't a girl," Poppy said. "But I wouldn't have put it past Mom if you weren't born a brunet."

"It's symbolic, Chris," Mom said. "How else was Poppy supposed to represent you?"

"You made this?" I asked my sister, my eyes misting again. "You baked a cake for me?"

"Calm your tits," she said, flicking a napkin at my face. I grabbed it and dabbed at my eyes. Guess I had rehydrated enough for tears.

"You hate baking," I blubbered.

"I bought the cake. The decorations are mine, though."

"It's incredible, sweetie," Mom said, leaning over the table to get a better look. "You did all this last night?"

Poppy shrugged and pulled a massive knife from the sideboard. "Rowan, do you want to impale Brad or should I?"

"I will if she won't," Chris said.

"Get in line, son," Mom said.

I held out my hand for the knife and they all cheered, but as I served the cake, I couldn't stop imagining how Cal Cardoso would look in a pair of scrubs.

CHAPTER THREE

Cal

Skye put her front paws on the door and started whining before the bell rang. When it did, she barked and wagged her butt so hard her tail blurred.

"You got to move so I can open it," I told her. She wiggled behind me, every muscle tense with excitement. "Brace yourself," I shouted before opening the door.

Theo had his arms out and ready to catch my seventy-five-pound Weimaraner, who should have grown out of her energetic puppy phase nine years ago. Aiden stood behind Theo, a case of IPAs against his chest as a bonus barrier.

"Who's happy to see Uncle Theo?" Theo said, his deep voice raised a couple octaves. Skye licked his neck tattoos and beard.

Aiden shook his head. "The beer is getting skunked. Mind wrapping up the love fest?"

Theo put down Skye, and she rolled onto her back for belly scratches.

"Don't mind me," Aiden said, stepping over Theo as he crouched down to oblige my dog. I wished the couple who crossed Main Street last week to avoid Theo's face tattoos and piercings could see him now.

"Thanks, man," I said, taking the case from Aiden. He nodded, acknowledging my gratitude for the beer and for tolerating Skye.

"Thank fuck Aiden got your air conditioner working again," Theo said, rubbing Skye's belly in just the right spot to make her leg kick.

"We could have watched the game at his place or yours," I said.

"You know I don't have a TV," Theo said. "Aiden?"

"I'd rather fix Cal's air conditioner than let the pair of you in my house."

Theo raised his eyebrows at me and shrugged. "Worth a try," he said.

Aiden bought a huge fixer-upper just outside town a couple years back and had yet to invite us over. He claimed it's still a working construction zone, but I've imagined everything from a creepy doll collection to a BDSM chamber. Either would be a better explanation than unfinished floors or cracked tiles.

"Here comes the Goth Pixie," Aiden said, catching sight of the black hearse accelerating down the street.

Theo spun around to watch Poppy Stevens pass in her morbid car.

"I don't get why anyone would want to drive one of those unless they work at a funeral parlor," Aiden said. "Aside from being creepy, the gas mileage must be terrible."

Theo narrowed his eyes. Skye stopped wiggling and licked his hand. "It's a practical vehicle for a sculptor. Some of her pieces are very large."

"Couldn't she drive a truck?" I asked.

Theo shrugged. "I guess. But a hearse fits better with her aesthetic."

"I can see that," Aiden said, closing the front door. "The hearse does match the whole Wednesday Addams vibe your girl's got going on."

"She's not mine," Theo said, straightening. "I mean, she's just a friend."

"How many of your art classes has she taken at the community center?" I asked, carrying the beer to the kitchen. Skye followed at our heels, leaving Aiden to settle in the armchair by the couch in peace.

"Just the one that finished in May."

"That must have been an upgrade from the retirees you usually teach." I opened the side of the case before sliding the whole thing onto the lowest shelf of the fridge.

"Honestly," Theo said, lowering his voice. "She's more talented than I am. She should be teaching, not me."

"So, you haven't asked her out because you think you shouldn't date a student from a class you volunteer to teach or because she's more talented than you?"

"Neither," he said. "We're just friends."

"Cool," I said, tossing him a Hairless Dog IPA from the fridge door and grabbing two cans from the case Aiden brought. "Maybe I'll ask her out then."

"Fuck you," he said, shoving my shoulder. "She'd eat you alive."

I grinned. "Probably. Come on, we can't miss the first pitch."

I handed Aiden a beer before Theo and I took our places on either end of the couch. Skye plopped between us and yawned. We opened our cans and raised them in the air. "To Logan," we said in unison and drank.

"Who's playing again?" Theo asked, setting his non-alcoholic beer on the coffee table.

"The Washington Nationals and Charlotte Knights," Aiden answered.

"Who are we rooting for?" I asked.

Aiden shrugged. "Don't matter."

We got together at least once a week to watch a game, more during football season. I think Theo suffered through them as a form of self-punishment. Aiden and I were basketball fans as well, but the summer season bored us all.

Theo shook his head. "We could watch a movie if neither of you care about the game."

"The movies you like are depressing," Aiden said.

"Fair enough," Theo said. "Speaking of depressing, how's work, Cal?"

Skye shot off the couch and jumped at the window, barking. Aiden curled into the armchair as she passed. "For Pete's sake," he yelled.

"Skye," I said. "Come."

She gave another bark at whatever had grabbed her attention, probably a squirrel, and sprang back to the couch. She had an obsession with the bushy-tailed rodents, which made controlling her on walks a full-body workout.

Aiden put his feet down slowly, shoulders tense. The crushed can in his hand dripped, and a large wet mark spread across his chest.

"Sorry about that," I said. "You can rinse your shirt out in the bathroom and borrow one of mine. You know where they are."

He glared at my dog and walked down the narrow hallway toward my bedroom. Skye huffed and rested her head on her paws.

"Maybe we should shut the blinds," Theo said.

"Good idea." I closed the shutter blinds on the big picture window facing Sullivan Street before heading to the kitchen for more beer.

"How are things going at work?" Aiden asked, pulling one of my t-shirts over his head as he walked back down the hallway.

"You're going to stretch the shit out of that," I said handing him a beer.

Aiden flexed and the shirt pulled so tight it had to be cutting off circulation to his arms. I take care of myself, running and hitting the gym five days a week for weight training. No one wanted an out-of-shape PT pushing their bodies through the pain of recovery. But Aiden worked construction in addition to joining me at the gym.

"You didn't answer him," Theo said, taking another sip of his drink.

"Everything's fine. Do you want to order a pizza from Peppers or Door Dash something else?"

"Bullshit it's fine," Aiden said, flopping back into the armchair. "Four more one-star reviews today, and the comments, fuck."

"Don't read the comments," I said.

"Do you?" Theo asked.

"Of course not," I said. "They're all bullshit. It's just Avery throwing a hissy fit."

"Well, it's working," Aiden said. "You're down to three stars on Google."

"Has that impacted your schedule at all?" Theo asked. "I couldn't make rent if I had a three-star rating. People would think I gave shitty tattoos or spread Hep C."

"My business would suffer too," Aiden said, his eyes laser-focused on the game. The thrill of the competition, no matter the sport, always drew him in eventually. Otherwise, Theo would have us watching movies with subtitles at least once a month.

"My work is different," I said, opening my second beer. "People look for a provider in-network with their insurance. The reviews are secondary."

"And how many providers are in Peace Falls?" Theo asked.

"Four," I said.

"Plus, ten more within a fifteen-mile drive," Aiden said. "And most take the same insurances he does."

"So, he's screwed," Theo said.

"I had some reviews removed," I said, shifting to find a comfortable spot on the couch. This conversation wasn't what I had in mind when I invited them over. I wanted to drink a couple beers with my friends and relax, not detail my imploding career. "It just takes a while."

"Which means Avery can replace them faster than you can have them taken down," Aiden said.

Theo shook his head. "What were you thinking, getting involved with her again?"

"All of us can't be celibate," I said. Theo turned his attention to the game, and I felt like an asshole.

"Doesn't mean you had to go for seconds with that crazy bitch," Aiden said, stretching his arms over his head. Something ripped and he grinned.

"It was supposed to be casual. I'm too busy to date anyone for real."

"Still?" Aiden said.

That hurt. Apart from a few repeat patients, my schedule the first two weeks of June had been painfully light. My boss had started to notice, and it was only a matter of time before I had to explain that the practice, and by extension his bottom line, was suffering because of my personal life.

I knew Avery was angry when I broke things off, but I'd assumed she'd cool down after she posted a few negative reviews. I thought I'd be able to have them removed before it affected my cumulative ratings. I hadn't counted on her adding more. Aiden was right. Avery was steadily destroying my professional reputation no matter how many posts I reported. "I'll meet up with her and talk it out. I'm positive she'll help get my ratings back where they were as soon as she's calmed down a little."

"Too bad she hates dogs," Theo said and rubbed Skye's head. "I always feel calmer when I spend time with Skye."

"If Skye helps so much," Aiden said. "Why don't you get your own dog?"

"My landlord doesn't allow pets."

"So move," I said.

"You don't want to share your dog anymore? That's cold, brother."

"You're always welcomed to visit Skye, but why not get your own?"

"You know why," he said, quietly. I wanted to call him on his bullshit, but it wouldn't help. It never did.

"I could go for a Meat Lovers from Peppers," Aiden said.

"Get a tomato pie too," Theo added.

We always ordered a tomato pie, even if no one wanted a slice. My chest ached as I looked at my two best friends, and the empty armchair that should have been Logan's.

"Anything else?" I asked, my voice tight. In the months following the accident, it surprised me how grief could crash into a moment without warning. After all these years, I'd grown to tolerate the shock, even if the pain felt the same.

Theo and Aiden shook their heads and pretended to watch the game.

Chapter Four

Rowan

"Shoot," Mom said as we drove down Sullivan Street the next morning. "I meant to wrap up some pie for Cal to thank him for fitting you in. Should we go back?"

She stopped in the middle of the road in front of the Hilberts's Cape Cod, which sat on the corner of Sullivan and Broad. It had fresh blue paint that echoed the distant mountains and a new porch swing. The lawn was well tended, the sidewalk swept. I couldn't imagine Brad maintaining an entire house with such care by himself. It'd taken me a year to convince him to put his dirty clothes in the hamper and carry his dishes to the sink. I eventually gave up any expectations that he'd toss in a load of laundry or run the dishwasher.

"Does he live alone?" I asked before I could stop myself.

Mom glanced at me.

"I just meant that's a big house for one person."

"It is a lot of space for just him and Skye."

"Who's Skye?"

Mom smiled. "The dog."

"Oh," I said, clearing my throat. "If Chris walks Skye today, he could drop off the pie."

"You're right," Mom said, tapping her fingers on the steering wheel. "No sense lugging pie all over town. I'll send your brother a text later. Do you think Cal would like apple, cherry, or pecan?"

I wish I knew the man well enough to say. "I'll put together a Tupperware with a couple slices of each when I get home," I said.

Mom made a low humming sound in her throat and turned onto Broad Street for a couple blocks, then Church, which some locals called Saints and Sinners Street. The street began at the Lutheran church and passed by the Baptist, Methodist, Presbyterian, and Episcopal churches until it ended at Main Street where Church Street Brews occupied the corner lot. The bar was quiet as we passed, but every night it came alive with "sinners going to Church."

When we turned onto Main, the sidewalks were empty since most shops hadn't open yet, but all along the street, store owners prepared for the day. Mr. Wilson stopped sweeping the pharmacy entrance to wave. The small tables outside Karma, Lauren's café and bookshop, overflowed with women in running gear. Mom's floral shop, Red Blossoms, was located across the street with its cheery striped awning and twinkle lights. Unlike my life, nothing much had changed in Peace Falls.

Mom's shoulders crept closer to her ears, and her grip on the steering wheel tightened as we continued down Main. Just past Centennial Park, a four-story brick building rose above all the other businesses and shops. Everyone in town referred to it as "the Main doctors." There were other medical offices scattered across town, but the large building housed suites for different specialists. You could have your eyes examined, your in-grown toenail removed, and a Pap smear all without leaving the building.

Mom pulled up to the curb and shut off the engine. The color drained from her face, and her fingers shook as she fumbled for her purse.

I reached across the car and laid my hand on her arm. "Mom, if it's ok with you, I'd rather go in alone."

"Rowan—"

"No," I said, talking over her. "This is embarrassing enough without bringing my mom along."

Newsflash: Mom wouldn't make it any more embarrassing. Truth be told, I'd rather she come with me since I was a complete physical, emotional, and mental mess, but ever since Dad lost his battle with Hodgkin's Lymphoma, Mom avoided medical offices. The only good thing I can say about Brad was he listened when I came to on the sidewalk and begged him not to call my family unless I died. I know now that was a little dramatic, but at the time, I didn't know the extent of my injuries. Whether he didn't call because he was afraid to confess what an asshole he'd been or because he respected my request didn't matter. Either way, I was thankful Mom hadn't gone to the hospital because of me.

Her fear had gotten so bad that Dr. Evers, our family doctor, started making house calls whenever she needed him.

"Are you sure?" Mom asked, her death grip on her purse loosening. "You could barely walk into the house yesterday."

"Positive. I was sore from the drive. I'm moving much better today."

"You are," Mom said, tugging at her thumbnail. "I'll just wait in the car then."

"Aren't you prepping for a wedding this weekend? I'll call Chris or Poppy when I'm done."

"How'd you know?"

I smiled. "It's the middle of June. I just assumed someone was getting married."

"Ok, but I'm waiting until you get inside. I don't want you standing by yourself if it's locked."

The biggest crime to go down in Peace Falls in my lifetime involved a fence dispute between two neighbors that resulted in an all-out prank war. But if watching me walk ten steps through the front door made Mom feel better, I wouldn't argue.

I did my best to cross the sidewalk without gritting my teeth. Mom drove off with a wave as soon as I pulled the door open. Despite looking like the lobby of an old-fashioned hotel, the whole place reeked with that antiseptic smell that nauseated Mom. I was glad to see a few comfy-looking chairs against the wall beside the front window where I could wait for a ride later. A large sign on the back wall listed each practice by name and location. My stomach fell when I saw Peace Falls Physical Therapy was on the top floor. A wide marble staircase twisted around the lobby.

"You've got to be kidding me," I said grabbing hold of the brass railing. What kind of sadist put a physical therapy office on the fourth floor in a building without an elevator? I hefted myself up a flight of stairs and paused on the landing between the first and second floors to catch my breath. The front door banged closed in the lobby below and a young woman raced up the stairs with a to-go cup from Karma. She ran past me but paused halfway up the next flight of steps and turned.

"You wouldn't be Rowan by chance?" she asked.

"That's me."

"Halleluiah," she said, hurrying down the steps to me. "Dr. Cohen gets so mad when I'm not at the desk when the first patient arrives, no matter how early they are. His eight o'clock is always late, so I stopped for coffee, and then I remembered adding you to Dr. Cardoso's schedule. Not often we get patients from DC, and your mom was so sweet on the phone. I'm Cammie," she said, sticking out her free hand.

She looked to be Poppy's age, but the similarities ended there. Cammie was tall with long blonde hair and a sweet smile. She wore bright pink scrubs and neon-yellow sneakers that should have looked ridiculous but somehow worked on her.

"Nice to meet you."

"Are you taking the stairs because you want the exercise?"

"No, I've just forgotten how to teleport," I said. Cammie's smile dimmed. "Sorry, that was bitchy. My back is killing me."

"No, I get it. Being in pain makes me snappy too. The building has a small elevator. I think they added it a couple years back when they moved the PT office from the ground floor. I keep telling the super to put up a sign. I'm about ready to tack up a piece of posterboard. Is it easier going up the stairs or down?"

"Both hurt. Might as well go up."

"Here," she said, moving her large floral bag to her other arm. "If you don't mind, I'll help you. It'll keep me out of trouble with Dr. Cohen."

"Thank you," I said, letting her take my elbow. "Are you new to town? I grew up here, and I don't remember you."

"I moved here a year ago. I love Peace Falls. You must be so happy to be back."

I forced a smile as we slowly climbed to the next floor. Peace Falls was a great town, and I could understand why people moved here and why most locals never left. But as much as I appreciated people like Dr. Evers who made up the fabric of the community, I couldn't wait to leave. I told Lauren and my family I wanted an impressive job at a big firm and a colorful city life. The truth was more depressing: Apart from my little family and singular friend, I didn't fit in. Not just in Peace Falls, but anywhere. I always found it difficult to begin friendships, and I was so awkward with men, I'd never dated anyone before Brad. In a large city, I could blend with the crowd and didn't have to make small talk every time I stepped outside. My return to Peace Falls was temporary. I'd be moving wherever my next job took me. When we reached the second floor, Cammie led me to a small elevator tucked in the back corner of the building.

"Hope you're not claustrophobic," she said when the car arrived. We squished in together, and I was hit with the warm smell of cinnamon and coffee.

"Is that a cinnamon toast latte?" I asked.

"Yes," Cammie beamed. "It's one of my favorites from Karma. The other is the Rowan. It's this mix of Nutella and caramel and coconut milk, and oh my word, you're that Rowan, aren't you?"

I laughed. "Lauren is my best friend."

"She's an angel. Really, I can't tell you how much she's helped me. I'm not sure what I'd have done without her this year." Something dark crossed Cammie's face. I'd seen the same look on Lauren's more times than I could count, and I knew I wouldn't be asking questions about Cammie's life before Peace Falls.

"She's the best," I said, smiling.

The elevator lurched to a stop, and the doors slid open onto the fourth floor.

"This way," Cammie said, guiding me toward a large glass door.

The office was not what I expected. Several padded tables lined one wall, but the rest of the large space looked like a gym. There were treadmills, ellipticals, and weight machines facing several windows overlooking Main Street. A large mat covered most of the floor with a collection of balance balls, bands, and free weights. Cammie set her purse and coffee at the reception desk by the entrance and turned on her computer. "Your mom told me your insurance info so I could get approval, but let me grab—"

One of the two doors by the desk opened and a balding man who looked in his early sixties stormed out. "Miss Gibson," he said, glaring at Cammie.

He stopped when he saw me. "I hope you weren't waiting long."

"I haven't been waiting at all," I said, my voice tight. "Cammie helped me find the elevator. I apologize if I made her late. I'm slow moving."

Just then, the second door opened and out walked Caleb Cardoso in a pair of slate gray scrubs. Years of watching him swagger down school hallways and sprint across football fields did nothing to prepare me. He'd added more muscle to his lean frame, his broad shoulders tapering to a narrow waist. His dark, tousled hair looked styled to suggest he'd just climbed out of bed after an all-night sexfest. His jaw was sharper, his cheek bones more chiseled. When he looked at me with those rich chocolate eyes, all the air left my lungs.

"Mrs. Norris," he said, glancing at the tablet in his hands.

The sound of my married name lifted the lust fog from my brain. "Please call me Rowan," I said, relieved I'd finally managed to speak in his presence.

He studied my face, frowned, and looked back at his tablet. "Nice to meet you," he said, studying my face again. "I'm Cal. Take a seat on the first table."

Lauren would have politely told him that we were two years apart in school. Poppy would have flipped the embarrassment of being forgotten back onto Cal with a snide comment about his observation skills. Not that anyone ever forgot Poppy. I just turned my back to him and hoped he hadn't seen my cheeks burn. People often didn't remember me, but it still stung, especially when it was someone I'd spent so much time fantasizing about in my teens. As I crossed the room, I could feel him behind me, watching my every movement.

When I reached the table, I stared at it, wondering how I was going to hoist myself up. Cal pulled a stool from underneath the table, standing so close I could smell him. Thank goodness teenage me never got near enough to sniff the unholy concoction of cedar and pheromones. I would have panted like a cartoon character. I was more experienced now. I could control myself, barely. Cal held out his hand, and I took it. Then I blushed again, thinking maybe he was just motioning for me to climb onto the table.

"Can you manage stairs?" he asked as I stepped onto the stool.

"She climbed to the second floor before we got the elevator," Cammie shouted.

"That's great," Cal said with an encouraging smile. He squeezed my hand ever so slightly, and I did my best not to hyperventilate. Nope, zero self-control still. The second my butt hit the table, he let go of my hand and grabbed a rolling stool for himself. He was so tall, we were eye to eye, despite the table being a foot higher than his stool.

"Your orthopedic surgeon sent over your X-rays and your prescription, but his chart notes weren't compatible with our system. I'll try to get them before our next session. For now, it'd be helpful if I had more information about how the injury occurred and where you're in pain."

"Um, it was a stupid accident. I'd rather not talk about it."

"Most nonsurgical recoveries are," he said with a lopsided smile that made my core clench. "Trust me, Rowan. You have no reason to be embarrassed. I'm here to help you. I've heard it all, and I don't judge."

I doubt he'd had a patient get plowed over by a tourist on a Segway after catching her husband getting a blow job from her boss. I opened my mouth and closed it again.

"We could start with where you're feeling pain. What hurts the most?"

My heart. My pride.

"My back. I had a nasty bruise on my hip and a concussion, but the bruise is fading, and my head hasn't hurt for a while."

He glanced at the tablet again and nodded. "I can see by your X-ray you didn't fracture your spine. Hopefully, we're just dealing with muscular pain. If you haven't made sufficient progress after our sessions, you should have an MRI to check for bulging or excised spinal discs. Unfortunately, that's something we can't fix with PT."

"Should I get the MRI now?"

"Ready to get rid of me so soon," he said, flashing another smile.

My stomach flipped, and my face grew hot. "I don't want to waste your time."

"You can call your insurance company, but most won't approve an MRI until after you complete the physical therapy your orthopedic surgeon prescribed. Your script is for two sessions a week for the next six weeks. Even if you have an issue with your discs, the work we'll do here should improve your mobility and reduce your pain. Knowing how you got hurt would really help me design your treatment plan."

He waited. And waited.

I blew out a breath and let the words rush like water from a broken pipe. "I was texting and collided with a vehicle. And a tree." It was mostly true. A Segway is a type of vehicle and it did pin me against a tree. I wasn't texting, but the lack of attention was real since I was crying so hard I couldn't see anything. But telling him all that would only lead to questions I didn't want to answer.

"Was anyone else injured?" he asked, his voice cold.

"Um, I don't think so," I said. "I passed out for a bit, but it wasn't mentioned in the police report. See, stupid accident. I shouldn't have been texting."

"No, you shouldn't have. You're lucky your injuries aren't worse."

So much for not judging.

He closed his eyes and rubbed his forehead. "Let's test your range of motion," he said. Unlike before, the warmth in his voice sounded forced.

I nodded and followed his curt directions. I felt a jolt the first time he put his hands on my legs, but the pain that followed when he tested how far I could move zapped any pleasant tingle. It hurt. Bad. I knew he was just doing his job, but he pushed me as far as he could until the pain became too much for me to handle. He always stopped when I told him, but then he'd move on to another stretch that left me breathless with pain.

Neither of us made small talk. I wouldn't have minded a little distraction from the agony that sliced through me with increasing intensity as the hour dragged on, but as usual, I felt too awkward to start a conversation. Apart from instructing me how to do each exercise, he remained silent while he studied every movement and grimace I made.

When the session ended, he smiled like someone who'd just received a backhanded compliment. "Great work today, Rowan. Before you leave, have Cammie make you an appointment for Thursday or Friday." He walked ahead into the office he'd left earlier and closed the door before I could reply.

"You must have a complex injury," Cammie said with a small smile. "I've never seen Dr. Cardoso so focused."

Great. Apparently, I'm the only one who turns Cal Cardoso into an automaton. "I don't suppose Dr. Cohen has any openings for Thursday or Friday?"

"Between us," she said lowering her voice, "You want to stay with Dr. Cardoso. He's a sweetheart and really good at his job. Not to mention, I'd much rather have him stretching my body than Dr. Cohen."

Her eyes widened, and she slapped her hand over her mouth.

I laughed and Dr. Cohen stopped working with his elderly patient to glare at Cammie again.

"I see what you mean," I said. "What does Dr. Cardoso have available?"

"How about this time on Thursday? Does that work?" she asked, clicking her mouse.

"It does."

"Great, the address we have in our records is in DC. Would you like to update it?"

"Sure," I said, giving her my mom's address on Sullivan Street.

"We'll see you on Thursday. It was great meeting you."

And unlike Cal, I could tell she really meant it.

Chapter Five

Cal

THE SUN HAD JUST begun to rise as I stepped outside for my run. The mountains blocked most of the light, but the clouds to the east glowed, outlining the hills in crimson. As I stretched, the red faded to orange and spread across the sky.

I started running north toward the high school, taking deep breaths of the damp air to clear the sleep from my mind. As I approached the Stevens's house, a figure dashed off the steps and sprinted toward me.

"Morning, Chris," I said as he slowed to match my pace.

"Cal."

We ran for several minutes without talking while the world around us formed from the fading darkness. It was one of the reasons I liked the kid. He helped pass the time with conversations about sports or Skye but gave me as long as I needed to wake up.

"Did you leave the pie in my fridge?" I asked a half mile into our run as we approached the high school.

"Yeah, Mom made way too much food to welcome my sister home. How was Ann's session?"

I broke stride and had to do a little hop not to trip over my own feet. I knew I recognized the gorgeous redhead that came into the office yesterday. Her face and first name were both familiar, but I'd failed to make the connection with Rowan Stevens or even that Rowan was Chris's oldest sister since he called her Ann whenever he spoke of her.

The last time I'd seen Rowan, she was a scrawny thing with frizzy hair, braces, and glasses that covered half her face. We didn't have the same friends in school, and I honestly couldn't recall hearing her voice before yesterday. The Rowan I remembered did her best to disappear. She'd grown into a stunning woman who commanded attention. Without the glasses, her captivating green eyes couldn't be ignored, and she'd filled out in the best ways.

Her ass alone had made it difficult to focus on her mobility issues. I kept catching myself staring at it when I should have been watching her gait, which was incredibly unprofessional and unlike me. I've worked with attractive women before, but I've always been able to keep my focus where it belonged and never gotten involved with anyone I've treated. Something about Rowan overrode my professionalism, which was the last thing I needed right now.

"Tell your mom thanks," I said when I realized I wasn't holding up my end of the conversation. For the first time in my career, I was grateful for HIPAA. Otherwise, I couldn't avoid talking to Chris about Rowan, and what an idiot I'd been yesterday.

"How was Ann's session?" Chris asked again.

A fucking disaster. Not only had I snapped at her about texting, I'd introduced myself like we hadn't grown up in the same small town only two years apart. Her chart had listed a DC address and a different last name, but even so, I must have come across as a huge prick for not remembering her. I already felt uneasy about how tense our session became. I've had plenty of patients recovering from car accidents, many of whom were texting, but I've never reacted the way I did yesterday. Maybe I was off balance because I couldn't place why she looked familiar, or maybe it was because as soon as she mentioned being pinned to a tree, I'd thought of the accident that took Logan. Memories often resurfaced as the anniversary approached, but that was no excuse to take it out on a patient. I'd planned to apologize to Rowan on Thursday, but knowing who she was, and that she's living on my street, made my behavior worse. "Come on, man, you know I can't talk about who I treat or don't."

Chris nodded. The kid usually had an easy smile, but this morning he looked tense.

"You ok?"

Sometime in the past year, Chris decided I was the male role model he needed, and for some reason, I went along with it. He joined me for runs without asking, and I gave him advice on girls and electric razors. In exchange, his mom Rose fed me more than she should, and Chris refused any payment for walking Skye. Even Poppy had grown on me. Beneath the frightening exterior was a sweet girl who'd gone with me to the hardware store countless times after she'd witnessed my exasperation with exterior paint swatches. Seriously, the number of blue exterior paint shades and ceramic bathroom tiles should be illegal.

Chris spoke in a rush. "I was wondering if you'd help me train this summer. I'm trying out for wide receiver on the varsity team. I thought since that was your position, you might have some tips."

"No," I said. Even to my own ears, my answer sounded harsh. His eyes widened in surprise before his shoulders sagged. I hated being a dick, especially when Chris had been such a help with Skye, but I'd never touch a football again. I cleared my throat. "Sorry, it's just I don't have time. Work has been crazy."

He shot me a look but didn't call me on my bullshit. He and I both knew I'd been able to walk Skye myself lately because I don't have patients.

"It might be good for Rowan to throw you some passes. Not yet. But once we've built up her core strength, it could be a great exercise." Great. The sun wasn't up all the way, and I'd already violated HIPAA. "Hypothetically."

Chris smirked, which I hoped meant he'd forgiven me for turning him down. We talked about an action movie he'd seen, and whether Skye would ever act her age. By the end of the run, I felt certain I hadn't hurt his feelings too much, but I still felt like an ass.

The feeling intensified as we ran toward the Stevens's house, and I caught sight of Rowan sitting on the front steps, leaning against one of the large wood pillars that held up the porch roof. Her hair was piled on her head in a riot of curls that cascaded down her delicate neck. She was wearing a different pair of glasses from the ones in high school but equally hideous. The lenses had steamed over from the large coffee mug she held to her full lips. She jumped when she saw us and pulled the sides of her robe together, covering the smooth skin beneath her throat but doing little to hide her toned legs. She looked barely awake. I bet her bed was still warm. This rumpled version of Rowan was somehow even sexier. I ran Super Bowl stats through my head before I made a spectacle of myself in my running shorts.

I should have waved at her and run home. Instead, I kept pace with Chris all the way to his front porch as if my feet had a mind of their own. Music blared from inside the house, the bass far too powerful and upbeat for the hour.

"Not Cyndi Lauper again," Chris said, plopping down on the steps.

"I have not missed Mom's music selections," Rowan said. "Morning, Dr. Cardoso. Are you helping Chris train for tryouts?"

"Please, call me Cal," I said. I lifted my shirt to wipe the sweat from my forehead. When I lowered it, her mouth was hanging open. I smiled and she buried her face into her coffee mug until her glasses steamed over again. "We're just finishing our usual run."

"I haven't convinced him to train me," Chris said, flashing me a huge grin. "Yet."

"I want to apologize for not recognizing you yesterday," I said. Chris looked at me like I was the biggest dumbass on the planet, which maybe I am.

"It's fine," Rowan said, attempting to drink from her empty mug.

"Can you tell me about the session now?" Chris asked me. "That's all she said to us too. I've lived in this estrogen fest long enough to know 'It's fine' never means 'It's fine.'"

Rowan sighed. "It hurt like a mother, but my back didn't feel as tight after."

"That's good, right," Chris said, wrapping his arm around her and beaming. Her entire face lit up when he grinned at her, and I forgot to breathe for a second. The warmth of her smile and the tenderness in her eyes stole the air from my lungs.

"Ew, you're sweaty," she said, shoving him playfully. She winced, and Chris frowned.

Seeing her in pain reminded me of how many sessions we had left and how awkward it would be if I didn't clear the air. "I should also apologize for sounding judgmental. We've all looked at a text when we shouldn't."

"What text?" Chris asked.

Rowan's eyes widened. "Never mind, nosy. Go shower, so you can help me make those cinnamon rolls you like."

He gave her shoulder a squeeze and me a wave. When he opened the front door, Cyndi wailed louder about girls having fun.

Rowan closed her eyes and sighed. "Did you need something else, Dr. Cardoso?"

I should really leave. Skye was waiting for her morning walk, and I had no reason to stay. "I'm afraid we got off on the wrong foot."

She opened her eyes and gave me a polite smile. "It's fine, Dr. Cardoso, really."

"Cal," I said.

She shook her head and started to stand. I took a step forward to help her, but she held out her palm to stop me. "I can manage. I'll see you tomorrow, doctor."

I blew out a breath once the front door closed behind her and sprinted down the street toward my house. Technically, I had a doctorate in physical therapy, but unlike my boss, Adam Cohen, I preferred not to use the title. I wasn't a physician, and some people got nervous talking to doctors. I wanted my patients to feel comfortable telling me how their bodies tolerated the exercises. Hopefully, my rapport with Rowan would improve whether she used my first name or not.

Skye started barking the moment she saw me from the window. My house sat on the corner of Sullivan and Broad. Luckily, my only next-door neighbor, and former high school principal, Mr. Twillings, couldn't hear a thing until he put in his hearing aids. None of the other neighbors complained, which felt like a miracle given the number of apartment buildings I had to leave on account of my dog's enthusiasm.

I widened my feet and opened the front door. Skye leapt at me as though I'd been gone a month and licked my face.

"Are you ready for your walk?"

She dropped to the ground and ran to get her leash from the kitchen. It was the only "skill" she had and something she taught herself. After she failed obedience school the second time, I decided to embrace the chaos, to an extent. I knew her limits. If I tried running with her, I'd get dragged after every squirrel. If I left food on the counter unattended, she'd eat it. If I didn't want her to bark at things outside, I closed the blinds.

Skye ran back to the door so fast, her feet slid on the hardwood floor. She slammed into the wall but picked herself up and spat out the leash at my feet.

My phone buzzed on the end table where I'd left it charging. I hopped over Skye and ran to grab it before it went to voicemail.

"Morning, Cam," I said. Cammie was the only twenty something I knew who refused to text and enjoyed phone calls, which I guess was a bonus, given her job responsibilities.

"Hi, Cal. Your morning is still open. Dr. Cohen isn't in until 11:00, so you might as well wait to come in. His first patient is at 11:30; yours is at noon."

I rubbed my forehead and tried to ignore Skye's disappointed dog look. "How's the afternoon?"

"Not bad. You have an hour break at three and no one in the last appointment. I hope you don't mind," she said. "I moved a couple of your Friday patients to tomorrow afternoon since Dr. Cohen is taking a long weekend."

"Thanks, Cammie."

"Fair warning, he asked me to print the schedule from the last couple months and the same period from last year. He's never done that before."

"Fuck," I said, then remembered I was on a work call. "Sorry, Cam."

Cammie didn't reply. I started to worry I'd upset her when she sighed and said, "Cal, you have to tell him about the reviews. It looks worse if you don't. He'll either think you don't pay close enough attention to your client feedback or that you knew there was a problem and didn't tell him. Better to get ahead of it."

Not for the first time, I questioned what Cammie was doing working a minimum wage job at a small PT practice in Peace Falls. I wasn't surprised she knew about the reviews. She took more pride in her work than anyone

I knew, which made our boss an even bigger ass for getting on her for not arriving early, on occasion.

"You're right, Cam. I'll talk to Adam as soon as he gets in. Thanks for looking out for me. By the way, those reviews have nothing to do with work."

"Of course not," she said, sounding slightly offended. "Your patients love you. They tell me all the time."

"That's good to hear."

"If you want, I can drop by Karma and get Dr. Cohen a bear claw to soften him up for the conversation. He's way less cranky after sugar."

I chuckled. "How about I get him a bear claw and bring you one of those fancy drinks you like?"

"Deal," she said. "Get me a Rowan, please. It's named after the Rowan you saw yesterday. Did you know?"

My mind flashed to the enticing redhead down the street and the coffee flavor she might inspire. Something bold and decadent. Skye gave an impatient bark.

"I didn't. I'll have to try one myself."

All through Skye's walk, when I should have practiced what to say to Adam, all I could think about was how Rowan would taste.

CHAPTER SIX

Rowan

WHEN I ENTERED KARMA, I took a deep breath and savored the smell of roasted coffee and paper. Lauren's café combined two of my favorite things: books and caffeine.

"Stop sniffing or step aside," Poppy huffed behind me. "Some of us need to get to work."

Lauren pushed through the swinging door behind the counter with a stack of coffee mugs teetering on a tray. "Rowan," she shouted with a little jump that rattled the cups. Poppy weaved through the bistro tables scattered in front of the coffee bar and around the counter to help her.

As soon as her hands were free, Lauren darted across the café and wrapped me in a gentle hug. "I've missed you so much," she said. "But I'm mad at you."

Poppy laughed and grabbed a teal apron from the back wall, tying it over her black outfit. The color suited her and brought a brightness to her features that made her look more approachable.

"I'm sorry," I said to Lauren. "Please don't take it personally. I needed time to figure things out."

"Nope. You introverted when you should have extroverted." She shook her head hard enough to swing her signature braid. When Lauren moved to Peace Falls in the middle of seventh grade, she'd worn her hair chopped in a short bob. To my knowledge, she hadn't cut it since.

"If I'd told you what happened, you would have told Poppy."

"And that's a problem because?" Poppy shouted from the counter.

A group of teenage girls flung open the front door, talking over each other and laughing. Lauren welcomed them, and they stopped their conversations long enough to tell her hello. We stepped aside to give them room, and they headed straight for the coffee bar.

"And that's a problem because?" Lauren prompted.

"Poppy would have told Chris. Chris would have told Mom. I didn't want her to see me like that. I let y'all know as soon as I was out of the hospital and had a plan."

"You never told *me* you were hurt. I heard about it from Poppy. I can keep a secret, you know."

I didn't question that. Lauren was the most open person I knew, but parts of her childhood before Peace Falls remained a mystery, even to me.

"But could you have kept away?" I asked, taking her hand and giving it three quick squeezes and one long one, the secret handshake we'd created for our club of two.

She sighed and returned our handshake. "I would have taken care of you. Cooked your meals, packed your stuff, changed your bandages. Anything."

"No doubt," I said, motioning to the cat hotel where Lauren's three-legged cat, Desdemona, slept beside her blind cat, Medusa. Lauren had a habit of adopting damaged pets, the uglier the better. Sometimes she kept them, but more often she nursed them back to health and found them loving homes. I wasn't sure what that said about her decision to adopt me as her best friend, but I was glad she did. "I'm here now. Fuss over me as much as you want."

"Ugh," she said, pulling me into a stronger hug.

My back protested the pressure, but I'd learned to pretend I didn't feel it. Otherwise, everyone would be afraid to come near me, and after everything with Brad, I needed every warm embrace as a reminder that I was still loved.

"I can't stay mad at you." She finally smiled, flashing the deep dimples that had snared more than one boy in high school before she set them free.

The teenage girls filled all the tables while Poppy fired up the milk frother. "I better go help your sister before she stabs the espresso machine. Again. You're hanging out here a while, right?"

"Yeah, I thought I'd use your Wi-Fi to look for jobs."

"Do you need a computer?"

The "career center" by the front door had two old desktop computers and a three-in-one printer/copier/fax Lauren had salvaged from a retiring lawyer. She allowed anyone to use them, whether they purchased anything or not. Unlike the library, she didn't limit the number of pages printed and supplied the paper and ink herself. At first, I worried people would take advantage of her kindness, but Lauren inspired generosity in everyone who knew her. Printer paper and ink appeared on her doorstep often, and local business owners added job listings to the cork board on the wall beside the computers regularly.

"I brought my laptop," I said, patting my large carryall bag, which was starting to hurt my shoulder and worsen the ache in my lower back.

"Great. Get settled and do some work while we handle this crowd. Then, I'm bringing you a drink, and we're having a real talk. Because texting *Brad cheated with Kelli. Getting divorced. Riding home with Poppy on Sunday* is not enough information. So, prepare to spill everything." She spun around before I could argue, not that anyone could talk Lauren out of something she wanted, which was the real reason I hadn't told her about Brad until after I'd scheduled a ride to Peace Falls with Poppy and left out the accident completely.

I adjusted the bag on my shoulder and walked deeper into the building. The café took up the front, but the back housed tall cases of books from every genre. The bookshop had been Lauren's grandfather's and was my favorite place to spend my allowance ever since I learned to read. I'd cross the street from Red Blossoms whenever I had enough for a new book and settle in a comfy chair for the day. Once Lauren moved into the apartment upstairs with her grandfather, it became my favorite place in town, whether I had spending money or not. After he died, Lauren removed the greeting cards and magazine displays to make room for the café, but much of the bookstore remained untouched. I walked to my favorite pair of worn leather chairs, dropped my bag into one, and groaned down into another.

I connected to the Wi-Fi, opened a browser, and then stared at the search bar. Pinnacle Group had hired me as a management trainee during on-campus recruiting my senior year of college. I'd worked my butt off to be promoted twice in the past four years. None of that mattered now. I sure as hell wasn't asking my old boss for a reference, which meant the best I could do was update my resume with my work experience and hope no one called Kelli to confirm it. I needed a job ASAP. My work-sponsored health insurance ended this week and COBRA cost a fortune, not to mention my student loans and lawyer fees. I'd eaten through almost all of my meager savings. I needed a job to afford rent, but I couldn't afford to rent anywhere near where I could get a job similar to the one I'd left. Let's be honest, I couldn't afford to rent a place in Peace Falls.

"Look at you being productive," Lauren said, leaning over my shoulder. "Or not?"

I closed the laptop and rubbed my forehead. Lauren set a steaming mug on the small table between us, tossed my bag on the floor, and collapsed into the chair across from me like it was the first time she'd sat in hours.

"Maybe I should think about where I want to live first."

Lauren frowned. "I hoped you might stay in Peace Falls."

"Not without changing careers." I took the mug and enjoyed a sip of the best latte on earth.

"So change careers."

I shook my head. "I'm good at what I do. Plus, it pays well. My student loan payments are insane, and I've racked up a ton of bills from the accident and divorce." I savored another gulp of my latte, which helped ease some of my panic. "You're a magician."

"No more than you when you bake."

"Oh, that reminds me. I brought you cinnamon rolls." I put down my mug and rummaged in my bag until I found the Tupperware container. Spending time kneading dough with Chris this morning had been the highlight of my month so far.

Lauren squealed. As soon as I handed her the container, she opened the lid, grabbed a roll, and shoved half in her mouth.

"This is so much better than the pastries we sell," she said, pulling apart the rest of the roll as she talked.

I looked around to check if anyone had heard her. "Perhaps not the best thing to say as the owner."

Lauren giggled. "It's true. We order all the baked goods from Bob's Bakery in Jericho, but the quality has gone downhill since Bob sold the place to his nephew."

"You could make your own."

"Let me see," Lauren said, tapping her lip and leaving a smudge of icing. "Should I do that before or after the twelve hours I work, every day, making coffee and selling books. Oh wait, I forgot about the other four hours that goes into ordering, cleaning, and managing the finances. I'm already running on six hours of sleep a night."

"Hire someone."

"Great idea," she said, clapping her hands. "You're hired. Take your pick. Finances, coffee, or baking. Or a mix of everything. Whatever you want."

I shook my head. "You know I love you, but I'm just here long enough to heal my back and find my next financial firm."

"Boo. So, you're just using me for the free Wi-Fi."

"And the coffee," I said, taking another sip. "Don't forget the coffee."

"How are you feeling?" Lauren asked, licking the icing from her lip. "I heard you started PT yesterday. Did it help?"

"Not really, but I'm told it takes time." I didn't bother asking how she knew I was in physical therapy. Chances were she'd heard about it from more than one person.

"It sucks that you're hurt, but if I ever needed PT, I wouldn't mind Cal putting his hands on me. He came in earlier, and I had to turn the thermostat down after."

We laughed and it brought me back to those high school days when we giggled about boys for hours. I hadn't stood a chance with anyone I liked, but I lived vicariously through Lauren and all the boys she agreed to go on a date with. Singular. They always asked for a second. She always turned them down. She would have flashed those dimples at Cal after he lifted his shirt and showed his insanely toned abs. And she'd be his, assuming she hadn't already gone on a date with him. I'd just sat there doing an impression of a largemouth bass. Forget the air conditioner, I needed a cold shower after I went inside.

Lauren smirked like she was somehow reading my mind. "Were you able to talk to him? Or did you stare at his hotness and go mute like usual?"

"Oh, I talked alright. But it was mortifying all the same. First, he didn't recognize me at all."

"Ouch."

"Then I told him I hurt my back when I collided with a vehicle while texting."

"Is that how it happened?"

"Sort of. I walked into the path of a tourist on a Segway and got pinned against a tree."

"Oh, my word, Rowan. I hope you weren't texting me when it happened."

"I wasn't texting. But I figured it was better than telling him I was crying so hard I couldn't see after I walked in on my boss sucking my husband's dick at her desk."

"Ew, in the middle of the day?"

I nodded.

"You're right, texting sounds better."

"I thought so. But Cal scolded me for it. He was downright frigid. It was super awkward."

Lauren nodded and all the mirth drained from her eyes, leaving them haunted. "No, I imagine that would have been hard for him to hear."

And that's when I remembered. Not when I fudged the story of how I hurt my back. Not when Cal reacted with anger. "The accident," I whispered.

I didn't need to specify. The car crash that took Logan Hendricks's life, severely injured Aiden O'Malley and Cal, and led to Theo Makris's felony conviction sent shock waves through Peace Falls. For many locals, the pain still rippled a decade later. "I thought there was alcohol involved. Was Theo texting too?"

"I don't know. Maybe Poppy does."

"Why would Poppy know?"

Lauren shrugged and licked her fingers.

"Lauren?"

"See," she said, snapping the lid on the container. "I can keep a secret."

"Lauren Arnaud. Tell me what you know right now, or I'll never bake you another treat as long as I live."

"Fine," she said, smiling. "Poppy and Theo recently became friends. She claims that's all, but I'm not convinced. The man has taken a serious liking to espressos."

"Huh. He doesn't seem like her type. She usually goes for punk guys. Tattoos. Piercings. The more the better."

"Have you seen Theo Makris recently?"

I shook my head.

"Well," she said. "Let's just say Poppy definitely has a type. Speaking of which, I better get back up front. I left her with all those girls, and you know how much Poppy hates chit chat."

I opened my laptop again and sighed.

"Hey," Lauren said, standing. "Just because the first session was awkward doesn't mean the second has to be. Good luck with your search, but don't hate me for hoping it takes you a while to find the perfect job."

"I'm pretty sure you're impossible to hate."

She smiled and headed toward the front with her cinnamon rolls.

I wanted a job that made me as happy as Lauren's made her or helped people half as much. Lauren brought joy with every coffee and book she sold. Not to mention the good she did for the community. I thought of Cammie and how grateful she sounded when she spoke of Lauren. Sure, my work lifted the company's bottom line and added a few dollars to the shareholders' accounts, but it wasn't the same. I didn't know the people who benefited from my work, and they didn't know me. I reminded myself I wasn't good with people like Lauren was. I couldn't land a job like hers, even if I knew where to look.

CHAPTER SEVEN

Cal

THE LIGHTS WERE ON inside the practice as I approached the glass door. I paused in the hallway and braced for another round with my boss. Adam only stopped yelling at me yesterday because his patient arrived. I left as soon as my last session ended while he was treating someone else. He had every right to be angry, but there's only so much I could take before I snapped back. I straightened my back and pushed through the door.

"Morning, Cal," Cammie said. She appeared to be halfway through the June invoicing, and it wasn't even seven thirty.

"Why are you here so early?" I asked leaning against the reception desk. She gave me a weak smile and went back to work.

I blew out a breath and rubbed my forehead. "I'm sorry, Cam. I shouldn't have left early. How long did he yell at you?"

Cammie waved her hand. "It doesn't matter. He's harmless."

I narrowed my eyes. "It does matter. He shouldn't yell at either of us, but you did nothing wrong."

Cammie shrugged. "I'm late sometimes. But like I said, I can handle him. Personally, I like to do the billing after the month ends. It's more efficient.

But he loves when I do it on a rolling basis. He should be in a much better mood today."

She smiled, but it looked forced.

"When he finally retires, and I buy the practice, I'm giving you the biggest raise."

Her smile looked more genuine as she reached for another invoice.

Adam burst through the glass door, glanced at Cammie and deflated a little, then saw me and puffed back up. "My office, Cal," he said as he stormed past us.

"You got this," Cammie whispered keeping her eyes on her work. "Hang your head and stare at your hands if you feel like fighting back. He'll want to flex his power. Let him. If you don't, he'll want to prove he has it—however he can."

Her voice wavered at the end, and a chill went through my body. "Cam, has he ever—"

She shook her head. "You don't want to keep him waiting. It will only make him angrier."

"Fuck Cohen. Has he hurt you? I'll go in there right now and kick his ass." It would have sounded more believable if I wasn't whispering.

Cammie's head shot up and a laugh burst from her before she slapped her hand over her mouth. Then she must have realized how serious I was. "I promise, he's never put a finger on me."

My stomach clenched. "I didn't ask if he hit you. I asked if he hurt you."

"No, never," she whispered, waving her hands at me like I was a fly circling her latte. "Now get in there before he fires you."

"We're not done with this conversation," I said walking backward toward Adam's office.

"Yes, we are," she said with a smile.

"Leave it open," Adam said when I stepped into his office and started to pull the door closed behind me. An open door was a good sign, I hoped. I did as he asked and sat in a chair facing his desk.

He leaned forward and steepled his hands. "I spent some time last night reading through your online reviews, including the comments."

Crap. If he believed Avery's were legitimate, I might as well pack my stuff. "Adam, like I said, my ex fabricated—"

He held up his palm to stop me. "Since you believe they're coming from one individual—"

"Who was never a patient," I interrupted.

"Since you believe they're all from an individual who was never a patient," he amended, "I recommend you contact an attorney who specializes in defamation and libel."

"You want me to sue my ex?"

"I want you to clean up your mess, Cal. Her actions are affecting your bookings, which is affecting my business."

I shook my head. "I can't sue Avery." I could, but part of me felt like I deserved her anger. When she'd approached me during Church's New Year's Eve Party, I'd told her I wasn't interested in a relationship. She'd assured me she was just looking to blow off steam without adding to her body count. But despite agreeing we'd only be casual, we'd fallen back into many of the same patterns we kept in high school. Dinner every Friday and Saturday night. Phone calls or texts at least once a day. In my mind, we were just having fun. She never even slept over. The moment she suggested taking a vacation together this summer, I realized she thought we'd gotten back together. I told her she wanted more than I did and ended things. I'd hurt her, and now I was paying the price.

"Why not?" Adam asked.

"She'll calm down as soon as she moves on with someone else. I'm certain I'll be able to remove the reviews. The process just takes a while."

Adam let out a disappointed sigh. "Sometimes in business you have to make hard choices. You might choose to let your ex-girlfriend hurt your reputation, but I can't. You have until the end of July to fix this, or you're fired. I won't have the practice tarnished by an associate. Am I clear?"

I nodded. For all Adam's faults as a boss, I always knew exactly where I stood with him and what he expected. This wasn't an empty threat. I was officially in deep shit. If I couldn't convince Avery to delete the reviews, I'd be out of a job by August.

Adam shifted in his chair, looking uncomfortable for the first time since the conversation started. "I'm trusting you when you say the reviews are fraudulent, but after reading them, I'm obligated as the practice owner to watch you closely. If any of your patients seem the least bit unsatisfied with your care, I have to let you go immediately. Do you understand?"

I bobbed my head again and forced down the words I wanted to say.

Adam let out a sigh. "Don't let this ruin your career, Cal," he said quietly. "You're great at what you do. I wouldn't have hired you otherwise. You can close the door on your way out."

I left his office as fast as I could, closing the door softly. It took everything in me not to punch it. Cammie hurried over from her desk and pulled me into my office. She shoved me into my chair with surprising strength and ran around the desk again to close my door.

"Fuck," I said, louder than I should. I'd heard enough of Adam's calls to know the walls between our offices were thin.

I'd spent two years building my online reputation and client list. Before Avery began her attack, I was more in-demand than Adam. He worked four days a week most of the time since, more often than not, new patients requested me. Cammie and I both hoped he'd get a taste of retirement and decide to go all in. Starting over at another practice would set my career back to the start. Worse, since I'd be working against all the negative crap Avery posted.

"Look at me, Cal," Cammie said, plopping herself on the corner of my desk and leaning in until our noses almost touched. "You're going to sit here, take some deep breaths, and calm down. Then, you're going to forget about that conversation, and focus on your patients. Got it?"

I gripped my hair but nodded.

"Good. Your first appointment is with Rowan. Try to loosen up with her. You looked super tense during your first session. She wanted to switch to Dr. Cohen, but I convinced her to stay."

"Can't say I blame her," I said rubbing my forehead.

"Bullshit. You and I both know you're the best PT in this practice. Now, get your head out of your butt and show her."

She sounded so much like my old football coach, I half expected her to order me to stand, so she could slap my ass on her way out of my office.

By the time Cammie messaged me that Rowan had arrived, my heart rate had slowed to near normal. It'd spiked a little when I read the chart notes her doctor sent. Rowan lied to me. Or misled me, which was a big problem since PT required clear communication with the patient. She'd let me assume she'd been inside a car when the accident happened. Her definition of the word "vehicle" wasn't standard. Still, given the doctor's report, she was lucky not to have fractured anything. She had to be in considerable pain, which meant I needed get my head out of my ass to help her. And to do that, I needed her to be comfortable with me.

"Rowan," I said, opening my office door.

She was in the middle of an animated conversation with Cammie, but when she looked at me, her smile fell. Damn it. Our little chat yesterday hadn't cleared the air as much as I'd hoped.

"Let's start today with the heat mat. Lie face down on the first table, and I'll grab it."

She did as I asked, and I did my best to ignore how fantastic her peach-shaped ass looked in today's leggings. She had her head turned toward me when I approached the table with the mat. Usually, I left patients to enjoy the heat and charted or started another session if the schedule was full, but today, I laid the mat over Rowan's back and took a seat on the stool beside her.

She closed her eyes and moaned, which was normal. The heat mat felt incredible, even for someone without an injury. I was used to all kinds of groans and sighs of relief, but Rowan's went straight to my dick, which had definitely missed the memo that she was off limits.

"This feels amazing. Can I bring it home?" she asked.

I shifted on the stool. It was like she'd asked to take me home, which she hadn't. She didn't like me, which was entirely my fault and something I had to fix.

"I'll build it into your treatment plan. You might try a heat pad or electric blanket at home. The mat has wet heat, which is ideal for muscle relaxation, so taking a hot shower should help too."

And now I was picturing her naked.

She opened her gorgeous green eyes. Her entire face had softened, and something tugged at my chest. "Can I just stay here the whole hour?" she asked.

I almost said yes. Which was ridiculous. My job was to push patients through their pain, not give in the moment they found a bit of comfort. I cleared my throat and looked at my tablet. "I'm afraid I'm going to work you hard after I loosen you up."

She let out a little gasp, and I realized how inappropriate that sounded. "How's Chris's training?" I asked, hoping to change the subject. I still felt guilty for refusing to help him, but I figured he might be the best way to get Rowan talking.

"I've never seen him eat so much salad," she said.

I chuckled and looked up from the tablet. She had a smile on her face, and I wanted to keep it there. "Chris is a great kid."

Her smile grew.

"He should bulk up on protein too. Lean meats like chicken or fish."

She scrunched her delicate nose.

"You don't like fish?"

"No. And if I tell him what you said the whole house will smell like a Red Lobster."

"Sashimi works too."

"I'm not telling my brother to eat raw fish. Just the thought of it. Bleh."

I found myself laughing. I tried to put my clients at ease with humor, but I rarely laughed along with them. I caught Adam staring at us across the room and dropped my eyes back to my tablet.

"So, I've reviewed your doctor's notes. I'm hoping you might clear up some inconsistencies in your chart."

Her shoulders tensed but I pressed on. "Could you give me more details about the accident?"

"Um, isn't it all in the chart notes?"

"Yes, but it doesn't match what you told me on Tuesday."

"Why do you care?" she said. "I hurt my back and you're supposed to help me fix it."

"Like I said before, knowing how you sustained the injury helps me determine how best to treat it." I should have backed off and moved to the first exercise, especially with Adam watching like a lion eyeing a kill.

"You already know, apparently. So, why ask?"

"Why wouldn't I question a discrepancy in a patient's chart?"

"Fine, I caught my husband getting a blow job from my boss and ran out of the office smack into the path of a tourist on a Segway. Happy?"

Her face went bright red. She tossed off the heat mat and climbed from the table.

"Where are you going?" I asked.

She opened her mouth to speak, then shook her head, and bent to grab her enormous bag. She winced and straightened before heading for the door.

I allowed myself two seconds to freak the fuck out before I ran after her. "Stair training," I said to Cammie, loud enough for Adam to hear.

Cammie's eyes were wide, but she said, "Great idea," in a chipper voice. "Rowan is having so much trouble with stairs."

I was too chickenshit to check if Adam was watching. Judging by Cammie's reaction he was.

Rowan moved surprisingly fast for someone with a back injury and had already pressed the button for the elevator when I stepped into the hallway. The doors opened, and she disappeared inside. I sprinted down the hall and made it into the tiny car just as the doors closed, leaving me chest-to-chest with a very upset redhead.

She swiped at her eyes and spun around to put her back to me.

"Rowan?"

The elevator jolted and started to creak toward the lobby.

"Rowan, please," I said, putting my hand on her shoulder.

She sucked in a breath and turned to face me, jabbing a finger in my chest. "Back up."

I took half a step and slammed into the elevator doors. The car wobbled, and she reached out and gripped my shirt. "Come back here, you big oaf. I'm not dying in this elevator with you."

I took a full step closer, her hands still gripping my shirt until we were pressed together, both of us breathing fast.

Chapter Eight

Rowan

My brain and my body fought for control. My brain said to turn and face the elevator wall until this ride from hell was over. My fingers wouldn't let go of Cal's shirt. My feet wouldn't move. My vagina jolted awake and sent an urgent message to my brain to hit the emergency stop button. I was so embarrassed by my own labored breathing it took a moment to realize Cal's chest was heaving beneath my hands.

I finally glanced up at his face and stopped breathing altogether.

No man had ever focused on me like that. Brad always glanced around the room, even when we were having a conversation or alone. Cal's hooded eyes bore into me with an intensity that made my knees shake. The elevator landed on the first floor with a thud, and I swayed.

Cal morphed from sex god to concerned physical therapist in an instant. The lust vanished from his face, and when he put his hand on my elbow to steady me, his touch felt gentle but clinical, much like it had when he guided me through exercises during our first session.

The doors slid open, and he backed out of the elevator, keeping his hand on me until we were both in the hallway.

"Thank you, Dr. Cardoso. I can manage from here."

I walked past him toward the lobby. His sneakers thudded behind me.

"I can't," he said, reaching around me to open the front door. He motioned for me to walk through, and I did, confused by what he'd said and the fact he'd followed me out.

I walked a few steps on the sidewalk and spun to face him. "What are you doing?"

"I'm assessing your walk to see if it's improved after the heat mat."

"Did you miss the part where I stormed out? You're not my physical therapist anymore."

"About that," he said, taking a step forward. "I know our first sessions have been tense, but I promise I'll never ask about the accident again. It's clear you're in pain, and I want to help you."

My cheeks flushed at the mention of the accident, but I straightened as much as my aching back allowed. I couldn't let embarrassment keep me from moving forward with my life. And since Cal turned me into a flustered mess every time we saw each other, I needed to find another PT. "I'm sorry, Dr. Cardoso. This isn't working."

"I'm sorry," he said, placing his hands on his chest. "Shit. I should have said that first." He gripped his thick hair and blew out a breath. "I'm really fucking this up, aren't I?"

He let his hands fall, leaving his hair an adorable mess. I hardly recognize this version of Caleb Cardoso. On Tuesday, I noticed he'd dropped the cocky strut of a high school football star, but he still moved with smooth confidence. Standing before me now, he looked rattled, almost awkward.

"Do you usually curse so much with patients?"

His eyes widened. His expression screamed "Oh shit" but he pressed his full lips together and didn't say the words.

"Goodbye, Dr. Cardoso," I said and started walking again. At first, I thought he'd gone back to his office, but before long, I heard him walking behind me again. He followed me into the park before he spoke.

"You're not as hunched as you were when you arrived."

I stopped and took a deep breath before turning around. Cal had a dangerous power over me. I didn't want him as my PT, and I had every right to go somewhere else. "Look, I'm trying to be as civil as possible here. We live on the same street for now, and Chris really looks up to you, for some reason. Please, don't make this weird. Just leave me alone."

"I can't," he said.

Ok, this was getting a little creepy. Several moms chatted nearby while their toddlers ran in and out of the playhouse that had been in the park since I was a kid. An older couple held hands as they admired a row of rose bushes. I wasn't used to ridding myself of persistent men, but this seemed as good a place as any. "Um, that's flattering, I guess, but we barely know each other. You didn't even recognize me on Tuesday. You need to go now."

Cal's eyes widened again. "I've made you uncomfortable."

"You seem surprised. I'm guessing you don't usually follow women after they tell you to leave them alone."

"I don't think a woman has ever told me that," he said.

I rolled my eyes and started walking deeper into the park.

"If you don't come back with me, I'll lose my job."

I stopped and turned to face him. That didn't make any sense. Surely one patient leaving wouldn't be a big deal. It had to happen all the time. Maybe not to Cal, but often enough his job shouldn't be in danger if I wanted a different PT. "Really?"

He nodded.

My brain and body went to battle, and yet again, my body won. Instead of walking away, I found myself walking toward him. "I don't understand. Mom made it sound like you were so busy you were doing her a favor fitting me in. Why would you get fired if I left?"

"A couple months ago, she'd have been right. And I'd have squeezed you in if she asked. Your family has done a lot for me since I moved to Sullivan Street."

"What changed?"

He took a deep breath as though giving himself time to decide where to start and how much to share. "Do you remember Avery Peterson?"

I couldn't forget Avery if I wanted. Bullies left an impression long after the daily torture ended. "Your high school girlfriend."

He nodded. "We started seeing each other again, casually, at the beginning of the year. At least, I thought it was casual. After what happened—" He shook his head as if to shake the memories from his mind. "Anyway, I realized she thought it was more than it was, so I ended things. She didn't take it well."

"Ok," I said more confused than when we started the conversation. I had zero interest in the details of Cal and Avery's relationship, past or present. "What's that got to do with me?"

"I'll show you," he said pulling his phone from his pocket and typing. After a moment he handed it to me. He'd entered his name in a search engine along with *physical therapist in Peace Falls, VA*. The site had returned several review pages. Cal had terrible cumulative ratings on all of them. I clicked on one and started reading the comments accompanying the one-star reviews.

Do not go to Dr. Cardoso. I hurt more after our session.

That didn't seem too bad. I was also in pain after my first session, but both my orthopedic surgeon and Cal had explained that was expected. Anyone familiar with the process should know not to blame the PT. The next comment was harsher.

Dr. Cardoso has terrible bedside manners. He made me cry.

Technically, Cal had made me cry too, though that'd been more from embarrassment than anything he said. It was believable he'd brought someone else to tears. The next comment, though, didn't feel right.

This man is completely incompetent. He had me do arm exercises for most of the session. I'm recovering from hip surgery.

Many of the comments didn't even explain why he'd received one star.

Just no. Run.

Cal kept silent while I read, but after a moment he said, "Now scroll down and read the comments that are older than two months."

All the reviews from April or before were positive, glowing even. Nearly all had left a five-star rating. There was also something strange about the number of recent comments. They took up a larger percentage than the prior two years combined. My analyst brain clicked on. The newest reviews had tanked his cumulative rating, and unless Cal had seen five times the patients in the past two months than in the last years, most, if not all, were bogus.

"Avery ruined your online reputation."

Cal nodded. "The bulk of my business is new clients. I do treat patients with chronic conditions, but for the most part, people come to me after surgery or an injury. I'm still getting some patients from word of mouth, but most people check online reviews before starting treatment."

"Can't you get these taken down?"

"It's not as easy as you'd think. Avery creates new accounts to post reviews faster than I can have them removed."

"But that's not your fault. Your job shouldn't be on the line."

"Dr. Cohen feels otherwise. Right before you arrived this morning, he said I had until the end of July to clean up my reviews. He also said he'd fire me if any of my current patients complained."

My stomach sank. Cal really would lose his job if I didn't continue treatment. I knew what it felt like to be at Avery's mercy, to have my life shaped by her daily decision to ignore or inflict pain. Still, I didn't want to finish PT with Cal. One: He brought out the worst in me. Two: Despite that, I still wanted to rip his scrubs off and lick his chest. And judging by his reaction in the elevator, he might not mind.

I had enough problems of my own without worrying about Cal's. Lusting after him twice a week didn't seem wise either. I handed him the phone and turned my face away, so I didn't have to look him in the eyes when I told him no.

He let out a sigh. "Claudia Nguyen works out of an office in Jericho. She's worth the ten-minute drive if you can manage it. Otherwise, I recommend Ted Savanti on Maple. If either can't see you right away, keep up with the stretches I showed you on Tuesday and try to go on a walk every day. Start small and build. Take standing breaks if you sit for a while, and if possible, elevate your feet whenever you sit to reduce the pressure on your lower back."

He started to walk away, and I blurted out the first thing that came to my mind. "Chris."

He stopped and turned as though I'd meant to call him but used the wrong name. I hadn't. Since I'd been home, I'd seen how much my little brother enjoyed spending time with Cal. Chris might be the happiest person I knew, but it couldn't be easy growing up without a father in a house full of sports-hating women, especially for a kid as athletic as Chris. He was always looking for someone to join him in a pickup game. I'd hate to see the relationship he'd built with Cal suffer because of me. "Chris needs help training for tryouts," I said.

Cal nodded, and I saw the moment he caught the hint I'd dropped. "You want me to train him in exchange for you remaining my patient."

"Would you?"

A muscle ticked in his jaw, but he nodded.

Part of me felt bad for coercing him to help my brother. But the scrap of pride I'd managed to keep after Brad and the accident felt intact. I could keep working with Cal for Chris's sake without feeling like a complete doormat.

"You can never tell Chris," I said. "He needs to believe you're helping him because you want to, not because I forced you."

"That's a given," he said with some heat.

"We better go," I said and started walking toward Main Street. "I assume your boss needs to see me with you before my session ends, and it's going to take me a while to get back."

He nodded. "I said we were doing stair training when you left. Here," he said holding out his hand. "Let me take your bag."

Usually, I wouldn't pass my purse to someone to carry but my back and shoulder were aching. I handed it over and he tested the weight of it before slinging it over his shoulder like it was the most natural thing in the world for him to carry a woman's purse. But after a minute, he frowned.

"You don't have to carry it," I said, as we passed a young woman on the sidewalk. She gave Cal a heated glance but kept walking when she saw the bag on his shoulder.

"This is too heavy."

A laugh burst from me before I could stop it. "I'm happy to carry it if it's too much for you to handle, Big Guy."

He smiled but shook his head. "I just meant you shouldn't be putting this much pressure on your back while it's healing. Not for extended periods of time."

"Yeah, I noticed that. Usually it's not so heavy, but I brought along my laptop to do some work later."

When we reached the building, he held the door for me again. I groaned as we approached the stairs.

"We can take the elevator up. At least to the third floor. It's best if you're a little out of breath when we get back, but one flight ought to do it."

I shook my head and gripped the railing. "I'm never getting in that elevator with you again."

"Yeah, probably not a good idea," he said and cleared his throat. His cheeks reddened, and I felt my own burn.

For the next ten minutes, I climbed while he stood behind me, offering words of encouragement.

Two flights up, I was such a sweaty, shaky mess, he told me to stop. "Why don't you ride the elevator the rest of the way. I'll walk up."

I nodded, too out of breath to answer. When the elevator doors slid open on the fourth floor, he was already waiting. Dr. Cohen looked up when we walked into the office together, and Cammie smiled.

"Let's cool down with some stretches," Cal said. He placed my bag carefully on the floor by the table I'd laid on earlier and guided me to the middle of the room. We talked as little as possible while he worked me through a series of stretches, but when our time ended, I smiled and thanked him, loudly.

"When should I book my next appointment?" I asked. I didn't need to raise my voice anymore since Dr. Cohen had inched closer to us as soon as his patient left.

"Let's get on a Monday and Thursday schedule, if that works for you. That will give you enough rest days in between to recuperate."

"Great. I'll see you then." I grabbed my bag and waved at Cal, and Dr. Cohen for good measure, and made my way to the reception desk.

Cammie beamed at me. "First thing in the morning again?"

"Yes. I like to catch a ride with my mom on her way to work."

"You're all set then." She glanced behind me as Dr. Cohen walked past us to his office and shut the door. "Let me walk you out," she whispered, rising from her chair.

"You don't need to," I said as she pulled the bag from my shoulder.

"Dang, woman," she said in the hall, hefting it with both hands. "You carry too much."

"Trust me, that's the least of my baggage."

For some reason, we both started laughing. Cammie pressed the elevator button. "Look," she said once the doors closed behind us. The elevator felt three times larger than when I stood inside with Cal. "I know this is entirely unprofessional, but Dr. Cardoso is like the big brother I never had. He's also an amazing practitioner."

I held up my hand to stop her. "I don't need the sales pitch. He told me about the online reviews. We have an understanding."

Her shoulders sagged with relief. "Thank goodness."

"So, Cal's like a brother to you?" I asked raising an eyebrow.

"I'm not blind," she said. "The man is hot enough to melt butter in Antarctica, but I wouldn't date him, even if I hadn't sworn off men."

"Why is that?" I asked. Not that it mattered, but Cammie and Cal seemed like a perfect match. She even had the same willowy frame and long blonde hair as Avery.

She shrugged. "Two broken people rarely make each other whole. At least not in my experience."

"Maybe," I said, softening my voice. There was something so likeable and sweet about Cammie. The thought of someone or something hurting her made me sad. "But in my experience, broken people like us make the best friends."

She smiled. "You don't seem broken to me, Rowan. Not in the way Cal and I are. I can't wait to see what happens when you realize you're not."

Chapter Nine

Cal

"How's the schedule today?" I asked Cammie.

"You have Rowan first," she said and smirked. "Then a three-hour break. Then you're booked solid until four. I put a new patient in during your usual lunch. He's trying to squeeze in sessions without missing work. I hope you don't mind."

"Not at all. I'll come in early or stay late if that helps bring people in."

"Absolutely not," Adam said, materializing at my shoulder like a damn ghost. The man could be alarmingly stealth. "You're not working alone, and I'm not paying Cammie overtime."

"Actually," Cammie said, plastering on a megawatt smile. "I don't have air conditioning at home, so I wouldn't mind staying late. I could bring my Kindle and read after clocking out."

Adam grunted, which could mean either yes or no, and went back to his office. I would never have called him a pleasant person before, but he was becoming more and more abrasive each day Avery's reviews remained online.

I'd texted her several times asking to meet, going as far as admitting that her reviews were impacting my schedule. No response. I needed to see her face-to-face to tell her my job was on the line. Otherwise, the information could inspire her to double down. Once she saw how upset I was, she'd stop.

Avery wasn't a bad person. She lashed out whenever she was hurt, but she always regretted it. In high school, she started bullying people after her dad left. She never did it in front of me, but I heard stories and called her on it.

Few people saw what I did. The guilt she carried for the things she'd done. The small ways she tried to atone. Leaving a closer parking spot open when she noticed one of her targets drive into the lot behind her. Shutting down the bullies who copied her, so the pain she caused didn't blossom and spread.

I'd hurt her, and posting trash reviews made her feel better, just like how bullying kids lower on the social ladder made her feel powerful after her dad abandoned her. I knew she'd feel guilty soon enough and want to make it right, but if she didn't talk to me soon, I was going to need a lawyer.

"Cam, you don't have to stay late for me," I said, doing my best to push aside any thoughts of Avery and my crumbling career.

"I wish I were lying about the AC. I typically go home and open the windows, then stay at Karma until closing while things cool off."

The weather had been stifling for days. Even with air conditioning, the office got so hot in the afternoons, patients complained and sweated through their sessions. Thankfully, things were cooler in the mornings. It had been difficult enough working with Rowan through her third and fourth sessions. No telling how on edge we'd both be if we were also overheated.

"Can you put in a window unit?" I asked.

"It cools off enough," she said as Rowan pushed through the front door, typing on her cell.

"It didn't dip below eighty-five last night," I said, crossing my arms over my chest. I'd noticed the dark circles swelling under Cammie's eyes all week. I didn't think she'd appreciate me pointing them out, but they were proof enough for me that the heat was making it hard for her to sleep. "There's no telling when this heat will break. You need a window unit, Cam. We can go to Walmart after work, grab one, and I'll put it in for you."

"I'm fine," she said and smiled at Rowan as she tucked her phone in her oversized bag. "Hi, Rowan. Dr. Cardoso can get you started right away."

Rowan narrowed her eyes at Cam. "You don't have any AC at home?"

Cammie blushed, and I felt like an ass for pressing her, especially in front of a patient. I didn't know where Cam lived or her financial situation. Maybe she couldn't afford the electricity to run a window unit even if I bought it for her.

"Do you rent?" Rowan asked.

Cammie nodded.

"Does the landlord allow window units?"

Cammie nodded again.

"Great. We have an old one that works fine. You're welcome to it."

"Really?" Cam said, a huge smile on her face. "I don't want to borrow something you might need."

Rowan waved her hand. "Mom installed central air a few years ago. The unit's in Poppy's way. She'll be ecstatic to have more room in her studio, and Mom will be glad someone is using it. Poppy and I can bring it over tonight if you want."

Of course Rowan would ignore her injury the moment someone needed help. It made me wonder what else she'd been doing to derail her recovery. "You can't lift an air conditioner, Rowan," I said.

"Fine, Chris and Poppy can do it."

"Chris and I will do it," I said. "Consider it part of our strength training."

Cammie paled. "Oh, shoot," she said. "I just remembered the super sent out an email saying the electric was at the limit. I don't want to be the one to overburden the system. Better get started on your session before Dr. Cohen pops out of his office."

Rowan studied Cammie a moment before following me to the table.

"She's lying," Rowan whispered.

I nodded. It stung that Cam had shot down my offer to bring the window unit to her place but had seemed ok with Rowan going there. I considered Cam a friend. Probably the closest I had apart from Aiden and Theo. Perhaps we were just work colleagues who'd bonded over our mutual dislike for our boss.

Rowan closed her eyes and let out another cock-teasing moan as I placed the heat mat on her back. "If you're like a brother to her, why wouldn't she let you help put in a window unit?" she asked.

I glanced at Cam, who looked near tears while she tapped away on her computer. "Why would you think I'm like a brother to her?"

"Because she told me," Rowan said, opening her eyes.

All the hurt I'd felt moments before evaporated. I realized I felt the same. Cammie was like the sister I never had, which made her refusal all the more confusing.

"Does that surprise you? You know, not every woman wants to sleep with you."

I wanted to ask Rowan if she was one of those women, but instead I locked eyes with her until her cheeks turned an adorable shade of red.

"Stop staring and let me enjoy the heat," she said, slightly out of breath.

"I'm just surprised she told you. Cam keeps her thoughts close." Like why she won't let me help her despite telling Rowan I was like a brother.

Rowan made a sound between a laugh and snort.

"What?"

"Aside from Lauren, that woman is the most candid person I've ever met." Rowan's eyes snapped open, and her mouth softened into an "O."

"What?"

"Nothing," she said, closing her eyes again. "Just don't press her about the window unit. I'll handle it."

"Don't lift it yourself. I'm serious, Rowan. You could set back all your progress or injure yourself more. You shouldn't be carrying anything heavier than twenty-five pounds. Less really, since you're so small."

"I'm not small," she said.

It was adorable how angry she sounded. The woman barely broke five feet and could probably shop in the children's section if she wanted. "I give the same advice to defensive linemen with a back injury. You're small."

"By comparison. Speaking of large football players, how are things going with Chris?"

I cleared my throat. "Great," I said and pretended to add something to her chart notes. "We focused on strength training last week. I got him a student summer pass to my gym, so we can lift together."

"That's really nice of you," she said and flashed a smile that sent an unwanted jolt of lust through my body. Damn this woman. No matter how much we butted heads, I still jacked off in the shower at night after every one of our sessions. I felt like a creep for fantasizing about a patient, but inevitably I'd end up with my hand wrapped around my cock, imagining all the ways I'd touch her, if only I could. And I wasn't nice. Nice would have been tossing the ball to Chris for hours, so he could practice his catches. I still hadn't picked up a football.

We sat in silence while the heat eased the tension from Rowan's face. She started stepping down her medication last week, and I worried she might be in too much pain to get through her exercises. I let her stay under the blanket a few minutes longer than usual, hoping it might make today's session less brutal.

"Chris is fun to lift with," I said when I couldn't wait any longer to move to the first exercise. "Aiden is too competitive."

"You're still friends with Aiden O'Malley?" she asked.

I nodded. "And Theo."

She groaned when I lifted the mat from her back but swung her legs to the side of the table and stepped down.

"Get started with cat and cow while I put the mat back."

Her outfit was especially form-fitting today. I swear her shirts shrank an inch with each visit. For the first time, I could make out a sliver of toned skin between the hem of her shirt and the top of her leggings. I hung up the mat, took a breath to calm my body, and joined her in the center of the room.

"Good, relax your shoulders."

She followed direction well and never complained when I added repetitions or made the exercises more difficult. It shouldn't have been erotic. With anyone else, I'd just be pleased to work with someone focused on their recovery. The fact Rowan followed my directions without question inevitably took my mind to all the things I wished I could direct her to do if she weren't my patient.

"So, Theo and Poppy," I said, hoping for a distraction from Rowan's tempting curves. "Are they together or not?"

"No idea," Rowan said, arching her back before dropping into cow pose. Staring at her ass was too much of a temptation, so I walked around to watch her from the front.

"Tighten your abs more when you're in cat," I said, even though her abs were tight.

"It's hard to do while I'm talking. Maybe you shouldn't ask me questions."

I smiled. "Why do you think I was asking?"

"Because you're an ass," she said, working through the exercise again.

"Take a quick child's pose."

"If talking while I do this will help me, ask me something else," she said, sitting onto her heels. "Poppy hasn't even told me they're friends. And that pisses me off."

Talking would not help her back heal faster, but it might cut the tension between us. "Good," I said. "Use that."

"I don't need to be angry at my sister. I'm usually pissed enough at you."

I laughed. "Ready for the resistance bands?"

She nodded. We crossed the room to the band station and moved into the first exercise in the series I'd developed for her.

"I see you're still carrying that overweight bag," I said. "Do you remote into work?"

"No," she said. "I quit my job. I'm looking for something else."

I put my hands on her hips to correct her position. She sucked in a breath, and I involuntarily gripped her. She froze. I dropped my hands and stepped back. "You can start standing row now."

She began the exercise, and I leaned against the wall to watch her. "What kind of work do you do?"

"I was an analyst for a capitol advisory group in DC."

I scratched my chin. "Must not be many of those positions around here."

"I'm not staying in Peace Falls," she said. "As soon as I find a job somewhere, I'm gone."

A flicker of pain crossed her face, and I wasn't sure if it was the exercise or the conversation. "Let's move to the treadmill," I said. "Have you been walking between our sessions?"

"Almost every day with Skye."

I stopped halfway through programming the treadmill and stared at her. "You've been walking my dog?"

"Whenever Chris does," she said, stepping onto the belt. She gave me a confused look, and I remembered I still needed to finish programming the machine.

"Do you hold the leash?" I asked, hitting the start button.

"Why?" she said, flashing a smile that made her eyes dance with mischief. "Is someone protective of his dog?"

"Yes," I said. "Skye can be hyper. She also runs after anything that moves."

"I noticed," Rowan said and chuckled. "Don't worry. Chris has leash duty. And poop duty. I'm just there for the exercise and post-walk snuggles. We stay on the porch until she's ready to go inside. I wouldn't invade your space without asking."

Avery hated dogs, mine in particular, but some of the women I'd slept with had fussed over Skye as much as Theo did. Whether a woman liked Skye or not had never made them more or less attractive to me. I assumed they wouldn't be around long enough for it to matter. But the thought of Rowan cuddled up with Skye made my chest ache.

Not my dick. My chest. Shit. This couldn't be happening. Lust was something I could handle, barely. But longing for something beyond sex? I'd avoided that my entire adult life.

Rowan's expression shifted from teasing to worried. "I'm sorry. I should have asked before I tagged along with Chris. Mom didn't want me walking alone in case my back seized up and I thought—"

"No, it's great," I said. My voice sounded off, and Rowan looked like she wanted the treadmill to take her far away from me. "This program takes about ten minutes. I'm going to get some charting done before our next set of exercises."

I turned and walked to my office, ignoring Cam's concerned look and Adam's stare. I shut the door behind me and leaned against it.

I needed to get my shit together. My sessions with Rowan had been the most awkward of my career, yet I felt this undeniable, terrifying pull toward her that had nothing to do with keeping my job. This couldn't be happening. I wouldn't let it. I grabbed my cell and typed a message into my group chat with Theo and Aiden.

> I have a problem

A reply popped up immediately.

Aiden

> You have many. Be more specific

Theo

> *Don't be a dick, A. What's up?*

> *Problem with a patient. I can't dismiss her because my boss will fire me*

Aiden

> *She trying to nail you?*

> *No*

Theo

> *How often do you dismiss patients?*

> *Never. She would be the first*

Aiden

> *What the hell did she do?*

> *Nothing*

Theo

You woke me up because a patient is doing nothing wrong, and you want to dismiss her even though you'll probably get fired if you do?

Aiden

Who's the dick now?

Is she hot?

What's that got to do with anything?

Aiden

Answer the question

I blew out a breath and rubbed my forehead.

Theo

She's a smoke show

Aiden

How do you know?

Theo

I assume it's Poppy's sister. I've seen her picture

Aiden

Wait. Rowan Stevens? Since when was she a smoke show?

She's gorgeous

Aiden

Dude. You cannot fuck a patient

I'm not

Theo

But he wants to

Did Poppy say something?

Theo

Believe it or not, your sex life or Rowan's isn't something we discuss

Aiden

What do you weirdos talk about?

Focus, A. I'm at work

Aiden

Then why are you texting? Do you want to get fired? Get back to work dickhead

Theo

He's not wrong. You can't dismiss a patient because you're attracted to her. That's had to have happened before

Not like this

Aiden

GIF of Kevin McCallister Screaming

What does that mean?

Theo

GIF of Pepe Le Pew with heart eyes

Aiden

You like her asshole

Theo

You do

You guys are no help

I put my phone on the desk and ignored the chimes of incoming texts. So what if I liked Rowan? It wouldn't change the fact she's my patient or that she's leaving Peace Falls as soon as possible. She wasn't even my usual type. My body might disagree, but I wasn't a hormonal teenager anymore. I could control myself. I was a professional, damn it.

I left the phone buzzing across my desk and returned to Rowan just as the treadmill finished. "Good job," I said. "Let's cool off with more stretches."

"Is everything ok, Caleb?" she asked.

She would stop calling me Dr. Cardoso when I needed the professional distance the most. The fact she'd called me Caleb instead of Cal felt even more intimate. Since I share a first name with my dad, I've used a nickname my whole life. Caleb sounded like a pet name, at least when Rowan said it.

"Yeah. You're doing great."

And she was. I was the problem.

"Feel free to play with Skye in the house if you walk her later. It's going to be really hot. I don't want either of you overheating."

"Ok," she said and gave me a small smile powerful enough to knock me over.

Chapter Ten

Rowan

I PULLED INTO THE grocery store parking lot and found a spot near the cart return. After two weeks at home, I'd finally weaned myself off the pain medications. Being able to drive myself felt like a gift, but I still wasn't as independent as I wanted. Brad and I had shared a Honda Civic, and rather than fight him, I'd left it in DC for the lawyers to work out. Mom had graciously offered me her station wagon, but I only drove it on the days I had physical therapy. Otherwise, Poppy or Chris had to drop whatever they were doing to fetch me since they refused to let me catch an Uber like a normal person. Chris quoted an online article he'd read about sexual predators and rideshares. Poppy just reminded me I was broke and should save money where I could. Mom had been working late into the evenings and caught a ride with her assistant manager when I had the station wagon. I felt like a burden. They were all so busy, and I wanted to scratch something off their to-do lists. With the Sullivan Street 4th of July block party in two days, the least I could do was stock up on the groceries we'd need for our contribution to the potluck.

I kept the air conditioner running and dialed Red Blossoms. Mom answered on the third ring, slightly out of breath like she'd just run across the shop.

"Hey, Mom. Sorry to bother you," I said.

"Is everything ok?"

"I'm fine. I'm at the grocery store. What are we making for the block party?"

"Oh, sweetie, don't worry about that. I have plenty of time to run to the store tomorrow. No, the Carson Wedding delivery is tomorrow. I'll have time the day after."

"On the 4th of July?"

"Shoot," Mom said rustling some papers. "That's the Silverman wedding delivery. I suppose you should grab a few things. I usually supply the dessert."

"A dessert or all the desserts?"

Mom blew out a breath into the phone and the tinny sound made my ears ache. "All."

"Why on earth did you volunteer to make dessert for sixty people at the height of wedding season?"

"You know I bake when I'm nervous. It seemed practical at the time, but I've got so many events, I'm too busy to worry. The pandemic delayed weddings, and more people than ever want summer receptions."

Mom couldn't bake that many desserts without pulling an all-nighter or two. "I'll do it. I bake when I'm nervous too."

Mom snapped into her mother hen cluck, as Poppy called it, since it was both higher pitched than Mom's usual voice and ran without interruption. "Are you nervous about your job search? Don't be. You know you can stay with us as long as you need. I love having you home. Or is it Brad? Don't waste a second worrying about that man or what people think. I'm so sorry,

Rowan. I haven't been there for you like I should. The summer is such a busy time and—"

"I need to feel useful Mom. Let me do this." And that was the truth. Oddly, I hadn't given Brad much thought apart from answering the occasional email from my lawyer. I certainly didn't miss him, and I'd been too focused on my back and my lack of a job to worry what people thought. It helped that no one had asked about Brad, but the fact I hadn't thought much about him meant we'd probably been falling out of love for a while. It didn't forgive him cheating, but it took away some of the sting. Some, not all.

Mom sucked in a breath. I braced for a lecture, but all I got was a soft "Ok."

"Did you have a dessert in mind, or can I make whatever I want?"

"You choose," Mom said and sniffed. She cleared her throat and added, "You're a better baker than me, Rowan. Whatever you make will be delicious."

"Mom?"

"There are more families with kids on Sullivan now, so make enough for at least seventy-five."

Her voice lost the wobble toward the end. I decided to pretend I hadn't made her cry on my sorry behalf, yet again. "I can do that. I finished the flour when I made cinnamon rolls, and the sugar was low. Do you have more somewhere?"

"You should assume I have nothing," Mom said and sighed. "I may have gone a little overboard in the days between when you told me about the accident and when you finally came home."

"Got it," I said. "Need anything else from the store?"

"Some more greens for Chris's salads. Oh, and whatever you'd like for dinners and lunches. Actually, I have a whole list here. I can send you a picture. Do you have money?"

"Yes, Mom. My credit cards still work."

"Ok, but save the receipt. I'm paying you back, and I don't want you rounding down."

I laughed. "Remember when you demanded receipts so we wouldn't round up?"

"You never did that."

"Poppy did."

"I know. Sometimes I even let her." Mom's voice became muffled like she'd pressed the phone to her chest to talk to someone else. "I've got to run, sweetie. Thank you."

She hung up before I could say goodbye. I tossed my phone into my purse, turned off the car, and opened the door to the soupy afternoon. If this heat wave didn't break soon, my hair would never recover. I'd given up straightening it days ago and kept it in a braid to contain the frizz. I grabbed a cart and dropped my bag in the seat. Usually, I avoided parking near the cart return, but I figured I was already pushing my back more than I should. This way, I could lean on the cart to take some weight from my spine as I walked to the store.

My shirt was already sticking to my skin when I reached the automatic doors, which opened with a rush of chilled air. Once inside, I pushed the cart away from the entrance and pulled out my phone. Mom hadn't texted me the list yet. No doubt, she was with a customer or managing a minor crisis. I decided to enjoy the air conditioning and call Lauren while I waited. My back was in no shape to wander through the aisles only to start over again once I knew what Mom wanted.

"Rowan," Lauren said. "Is everything ok?"

I hated how everyone's first instinct now when I called was to panic. "Everything's fine. I have something to ask you, and I figured it would be faster to call. But it's kind of sensitive. You can call me back if you're busy."

"Give me a sec," she said. I heard her shove through a swinging door and all the voices in the background became muffled. "What's up?"

"You know Cammie who works at the PT office?"

"Oh, yes," Lauren said with genuine affection. "I meant to ask if you'd met her."

"I did. She's really sweet."

"She is," Lauren said slowly. "What's going on in that brain of yours? You wouldn't normally call me while the café was open to tell me you thought someone was sweet."

I called instead of texting so I could hear her voice. Something was off with Cammie, and if anyone in Peace Falls knew why, it'd be Lauren, who wouldn't breathe a word about it. People trusted her for a reason. Luckily, I'd learned how to read her pauses enough to get the gist of any situation. "Cammie doesn't have AC. I offered to let her have one of our old units."

"That's a great idea, but you shouldn't be lifting it."

I gritted my teeth. "So I've been told."

"I'll stop by after we close. If you don't mind, I can give Cammie your address and meet her at your house."

"I gave her my address at the office, but feel free to give it to her again. Can the two of you manage the unit on your own?"

"Probably. If not, I'll ask Poppy."

"Why not Chris?"

Lauren went silent a moment. "Poppy is closing with me. I'll ask her as soon as I hang up."

"Cammie doesn't want men at her place, does she?"

Lauren's voice softened. "I'm not saying anything more about it."

Which meant yes.

"And I won't ask."

"Thank you," Lauren said. "Depending on the size of the unit, Cammie and I should manage just fine. She'll let Poppy help, if we need her."

"Help with what?" I heard Poppy say in the background. "The coffee grinder jammed again, so unless you want me to crush the beans by hand, I need you."

My phone buzzed with an incoming text. "Can I talk to my sister a second?"

"Here," Lauren said. "Talk to Rowan."

"What?" Poppy said. She sounded stressed, and I felt a stab of guilt for what I was about to ask.

"First, Lauren might need your help tonight moving one of the old AC units to Cammie's."

"She can have them all. I stub my toes on them all the time."

"Ok, I'm sure Mom won't care. Second, I'm making all the desserts for the block party. I was wondering if you'd like to help me decorate a cupcake tower. I think the kids would really like it."

"Um, yeah. That sounds fun."

She didn't sound sarcastic, but it was hard to tell without seeing her face.

"You sure?"

"Yeah. As long as you bake the cupcakes. Try to find some 4th of July wrappers and grab a box of food color gel and a shit ton of confectioners sugar. Oh, and a tub of Crisco. It holds up better in the heat than butter. We can talk about the shape of the tower later. I have some ideas. Get candy melts too."

"What colors?"

"Really, Rowan. I can't believe you just asked that."

"Sprinkles?"

"I mean if you want to be generic. Modeling chocolate if they have it. Red, white, and blue, obviously. See if they have gold and silver decorating dust. I could do a sparkler theme."

"What the heck is decorating dust?"

"Never mind, I doubt the grocery store has it. Just get what you can. I'll go to the craft store in Jericho tomorrow for the rest. Oh, do you think you can make different fillings for the cupcakes?"

By the time I hung up, I had ten items to add to Mom's list and spent the next hour collecting everything. Unloading it all at the checkout and loading it into the station wagon sent a throb of pain up my back. I needed to rest, but unfortunately no one would be home to help me carry everything inside. To make matters worse, a row of ominous clouds had rolled over the mountains.

The first drops of rain hit the windshield as I turned onto Sullivan Street. I opened the hatch as the dark clouds overhead opened with a crack of thunder. It was too hot to leave anything in the station wagon for more than a few minutes and no telling how long the storm would last. The milk jug was already sweating in the grocery store parking lot. I grabbed as many bags as I could with both hands and dashed to the porch despite the sharp pain shooting up my spine. I'd just made it back to the car when a speeding SUV screeched to a stop in front of the house.

"What are you doing?" Cal yelled as he ran from the SUV.

A flash of lightening shot across the sky, and I turned back to the trunk to gather more bags. Cal reached into the trunk as well and together we got everything and ran to the porch. I slipped on the top step, and Cal dropped the bags in his arms to catch me. Luckily, the eggs were in the first load.

"Perfect timing," I said, setting down my bags and bending to right the ones he'd dropped.

"Stand the fuck up, Rowan," he yelled.

I snapped to standing and winced. "Don't talk to me like that." I was so mad, I started shaking.

"You're soaked," he said taking a step toward me.

So was he. His scrubs clung to his perfect body. His hair hung in heavy clumps, dripping water onto his succulent lips. If my panties weren't already soaked, they would be. Which pissed me off. I had too much to fix in my life to be attracted to anyone, let alone a man like "casual" Cal who probably slept with half a dozen women a month.

He gripped his hair and shoved it out of his eyes. "What the hell were you thinking?"

"Excuse me?"

"I told you not to carry more than twenty-five pounds."

"In case you didn't notice," I said, motioning to the downpour. "It's raining."

He stepped closer. "All the more reason not to run with fifty pounds of groceries."

"Just because you tell me not to doesn't mean I have to listen."

"So, I'm supposed to stand by and watch you hurt yourself?"

"No, you're supposed to keep driving home like a maniac and leave me alone."

"I was not driving like a maniac."

"Really? Do you usually park in the middle of the street and leave your door open?"

He glanced at his SUV and frowned.

"Your interior is going to be a mess," I said, bending to collect a bag.

The next thing I knew, my feet flew out from under me, and the bag and I were nestled against Cal's chest.

"Put me down."

He glared at me and walked to the front door, pulling me closer to free one of his hands. My breath caught. He smelled of rain and cedar and sweet sweat. I wanted to bury my face against the curve of his neck.

He punched in the code on the electric lock and pushed the door open.

"It's kind of weird that you know that," I said.

"Don't move," he said, placing me on the couch.

I wanted to run back to the porch just to spite him, but my spine felt like it was surrounded by needles aimed to poke me if I moved. I watched him carry each bag through the front door and back to the kitchen, his breathing becoming more labored every trip, his face growing redder. Finally, he grabbed the bag off the couch beside me.

"I can get that," I said, standing with an involuntary whimper. "You better move your car."

He ignored me and carried the bag to the kitchen. I followed and found him staring out the window over the sink, gripping the counter, his shoulders hunched to his ears.

"Caleb?"

"Just give me a minute," he answered, his voice strained.

I placed my hand on his arm and felt the muscle tense at my touch. I said his name again, and he spun and pulled me close before crashing his mouth to mine. At first, I was too startled to kiss him back, but then I melted against him, savoring the feel of his fingers as they roamed my face and neck with gentle strokes. He ran his tongue along my lips, and I opened for him. The kiss deepened, each of us fighting for control. He wrapped my braid around his hand and tugged, and I moaned into his mouth. He shoved me against the counter and one of the bags fell to the floor with a thud, sending a cloud of flour into the air.

We sprang apart, both of us panting.

"Fuck," he whispered.

I took a step toward him, and he held up his hands. The man had just kissed me senseless, but the wallflower in me, the awkward girl with a hopeless crush on the hottest guy in school, was cut deep by his rejection. I shrank back against the counter.

Caleb lowered his hands and fisted them at his sides, his eyes sad. Without another word, he walked out, leaving me standing in a mess of flour and feelings, unsure if I could clean either up.

Chapter Eleven

Cal

Chris was waiting on my front steps when I returned from my run, tossing a football between his hands. "Thanks for doing this," he said. He smiled up at me with so much enthusiasm, I felt a fresh stab of guilt for delaying his training because I was too chickenshit to touch a football.

"No problem. Let me grab some water and Skye before we head out." I walked past him into the house, leaving the wooden door open but shutting the glass storm door to keep the heat out and my dog in. Skye trotted toward me with her leash in her mouth, wagging her tail. At least two out of three of us were excited.

I assumed Rowan wouldn't tell Chris about what happened yesterday, but I knew I'd shoved my tongue into his sister's mouth. And the way she'd responded to every little touch. Fuck. If that bag hadn't fallen, no telling how far it'd have gone. Judging by that kiss, sex with Rowan would be as incredible as it was impractical. I had to get myself under control before I saw her again.

Skye let out a huff when I walked past her into the kitchen. I filled a glass with water from the tap and downed it before filling it again.

I should browse a hookup app for someone to take the edge off. I hadn't gotten laid since everything with Avery went sideways. It was clearly affecting my judgment. Even if Rowan wasn't a patient, she was exactly the type I avoided: A picket-fence woman. The kind who could shred your heart to pieces. I'd bet my house she'd have stayed with her ex a lifetime if he hadn't been the world's biggest idiot. I could only offer fun, not forever. Every woman I'd slept with since the accident knew I didn't do relationships, and it had worked just fine, until Avery circled back around.

The kiss with Rowan had me on edge, but something else twisted my stomach in knots. I hadn't held a football since Logan died. Aiden, Logan, and I had continued training together long after the season ended our senior year. Aiden had a football scholarship to Tech, and I'd hoped to get a spot at JMU as a walk-on. We'd ribbed each other all summer about the prospect of playing on opposing teams. Logan had no intention of playing again since he'd joined the ROTC program at William and Mary, but he trained with us to stay in shape. Football was the reason we'd become friends and the reason we'd stuck together. Even Theo suffered through four seasons of pee-wee football before Mr. Makris finally accepted that his only son preferred art to sports. Logan, Aiden, and I played so well together, our high school coach put us on the varsity team freshman year. Honestly, only Aiden belonged, but Logan was a tank at fourteen and protected Aiden like no one else. I just ran as fast as I could and prayed I wouldn't get flattened every time I caught a pass. Theo never missed a game.

I'd never be able to hold a football and not think of Logan and everything we'd lost, so I'd avoided it. Until now.

I finished my water, left the glass on the counter, and walked back to the front door. Skye followed, bumping into my legs when I crouched to grab my gear. I hesitated. Just looking at the bag and the stack of cones made the water in my stomach swirl. I should have tossed this stuff years ago. Instead,

I'd moved it from apartment to apartment until it landed in my attic with all the other things that reminded me of Logan.

Skye dropped the leash and put her front paws on my chest with a whimper. I rubbed her soft ears and gave the top of her head a kiss. She spotted something behind me and let out an excited bark.

"Hey, girl," Chris said as he opened the storm door. She spun in a circle and picked up her leash with her mouth.

"We're taking a car ride first," I told her. She vibrated with excitement and bolted out the door. I grabbed my gear and locked up while Chris loaded Skye into the back of the SUV. He carried the conversation on the way to the park, thanking me twice for fitting in my run early, so we could train before I left for work.

"Seriously," I said, pulling to a stop in front of the park. "I don't mind."

"I would have come with you," Chris said, as he grabbed the gear. I snapped the leash onto Skye's collar while she pranced on the sidewalk. "But I didn't want to wake up Mom or Ann. They're both insanely light sleepers."

Hearing her name, even in abbreviated form, made the knot in my stomach tighten. I felt like throwing up. As we entered the deserted park, I glanced around for a discrete place to hurl, if needed, and caught sight of a tall figure walking toward us.

"Bout time y'all got here," Theo said.

Skye barked and ran for him, yanking the leash from my hand. My dog was having the best morning of her life. I was doing my best not to curl into the fetal position under Peace Falls's award-winning roses.

"You must be Chris," Theo said, holding out his hand. "I'm Theo."

"Nice to meet you," Chris said, greeting Theo like meeting a tattooed felon at the park at dawn was something he did every Tuesday.

"I'm going to keep an eye on Skye while you train," he said. Skye plopped onto his combat boots as if to agree. "You starting with a warmup, Chris? Cal looks like he's already sweated half a gallon this morning."

Chris glanced at me and frowned. "Yeah, Cal got his run in, but I'm cold. I'll jog a couple minutes to loosen up, if that's ok with you, Cal."

I nodded. Chris dropped the gear and took off at a steady pace.

Skye ran back to me and whimpered. Theo stepped closer and gripped my shoulder while Skye rubbed against my legs. "Poppy mentioned you planned to train Chris here this morning. Guess the kid was so excited to finally toss the ball, he's been talking about it nonstop. He reminds me of Aiden."

He wasn't wrong. None of us loved playing the game as much as Aiden had. Chris had that same passion. My throat tightened. I no longer felt like puking, but crying was a very real possibility. "Shit, this is hard," I said.

Theo nodded. "Just focus on Chris. You'll be ok. If that doesn't work, picture his sister naked."

"You want me to picture Poppy naked?"

He punched my shoulder, hard, and I laughed. The knot in my stomach eased.

"The sister who almost got you fired yesterday," he said.

"No thanks, I'm having a hard enough time being around Rowan without crossing the line."

Theo narrowed his eyes. "What did you do?"

"Something stupid."

Theo shook his head and a deep laugh rumbled from his chest. Theo never laughed. The sound was so unexpected and unusual, Skye's head shot up.

"Those Stevens sisters," Theo said, bending to pet Skye. "How stupid were you?"

Rowan was the last thing I wanted to think about. I needed to focus on getting through training without having a mental breakdown and traumatizing Chris with tears, vomit, or both. But Theo would keep asking, and I couldn't risk Chris overhearing.

"I yelled at her for carrying groceries."

"That's understandable. She's hurt, right?"

"Then I kissed her and ran away."

"You ran away?"

"It was that or fuck her on Rose's kitchen counter. Did Poppy mention anything? Chris seems clueless, but sisters talk."

Theo shook his head as Chris ran up.

"Ready?" Chris said, bouncing on his feet.

I nodded. Chris threw me a football so fast, I didn't have time to think. I just caught it. My fingers moved from muscle memory, twisting the ball to the laces and positioning for the throw. It felt so natural, like it had been ten hours since my last catch, not ten years.

"Let's see what we're working with. Go long," I said. Chris shot off into the park. I pulled back my arm and threw to a place in front of him. It sailed through the air in a perfect spiral, and Chris burst forward to catch it with both hands.

Theo clapped. "Nice."

I held up my hands and Chris threw the ball back. It wobbled a bit but smacked me right in the palms.

"Good," I said. "Come back here and we'll start some drills."

Chris had a real shot of making the varsity team, with or without my help. He was fast, faster than any high school player I'd ever seen and could run a decent route. With the right training, he'd make a better wide receiver than me. My stomach gave an odd dip, and it took me a moment to realize all my nerves had been replaced with something I hadn't felt in a long time: Excitement.

Theo smiled. "Does that grin mean I don't have to drag my ass out of bed at the crack of dawn again?"

"Thanks, man," I said. "It means a lot that you're here."

He nodded and dropped to the ground. Skye curled on his lap, and he buried his face in her fur. Knowing Theo, the moment had gotten to him, and he didn't want Chris or me to see.

"What do you want to do first?" Chris asked, grabbing his water bottle and taking a pull.

"Sit-up and catch."

He smiled like I'd just offered to take him shopping for his first car and dropped to the ground near Theo and Skye.

We worked another hour, while the sun rose above the mountains and the park filled with early-morning power walkers. The temperature climbed steadily. Theo moved Skye into the shade and gave her the rest of the water I'd brought along.

"Great work today, Chris. Why don't you finish with a run home. I'll pack up and drive the gear back. You can get your stuff when you walk Skye later."

"I can help," he said, gulping the rest of his water.

"Nah, it's getting hotter by the minute. If you're getting in a run today, you better go."

"Thanks again, Cal," he said. "Theo, nice meeting you."

"You too," Theo said, walking over with Skye.

Chris took off running toward Main Street, looking like he'd just started his workout instead of ending it. Theo shook his head. "Man, to be sixteen. I got tired just watching you two."

"Come on, old man," I said. "Help me get all this shit, and I'll buy you a coffee. Is your girl opening today?"

Theo grabbed the stack of cones and glared at me. "She's not my girl."

"Sorry," I said, as we walked to my SUV. "The friend you spend so much time with, you know her kid brother's training schedule."

"We don't spend that much time together. I got an espresso yesterday, and she mentioned it."

"Ok," I said, opening the trunk so he could shove the cones inside. "But hypothetically speaking, y'all seem to have a lot in common. You both love art. You both dress like extras in a Tim Burton movie. And you're both kind."

Theo cleared his throat and shoved his hands in his pockets. "Stop being sappy before I beat the shit out of you."

I shrugged. We both knew that'd never happen. Theo had his share of fights while he served time, and could no doubt drop my ass, but he'd never hurt me or anyone else. Not unless he was defending himself or someone he cared about. "So, is your friend Poppy working this morning?" I asked again, handing him Skye's leash so I could sling my bag and Chris's from my shoulders.

"She avoids mornings like I do."

I nodded. I didn't point out that was another thing they shared, but he knew me well enough to know I'd think it. After I put the rest of the gear in the SUV, we walked down Main Street toward Karma. Skye perked up when she saw the sign for the café ahead.

Theo stopped and handed me the leash. "I won't be responsible for Skye while she's hell bent on a pup cup."

"Sure," I said, taking the leash. "But I trust you to take care of her in any situation."

He let out a long breath. "You shouldn't. You of all people ought to know better."

He walked on, leaving Skye and me to follow, while one person after another moved aside, giving him extra space on the sidewalk.

CHAPTER TWELVE

Rowan

"YOU GIRLS OUTDID YOURSELVES," Mom said as she admired the dessert spread Poppy and I spent the last twenty minutes arranging.

Besides six-dozen cupcakes, I'd made cherry, coconut, and blueberry tarts, plus an assortment of cookies. The star-shaped tower held different flavors of cupcakes on each of the four tiers. The bottom two were plain chocolate and vanilla with red, white, and blue marbled frosting for the kids, but the top tiers had more exotic flavors.

My favorite was raspberry-filled chocolate with hints of hazelnut. Poppy's was a coffee-infused cupcake with salted caramel icing. She'd spent hours building the tower and shaping stars from different colored fondant. Then she piped the icing and applied decorating dust in gold and silver. She'd elevated a simple cupcake to something worthy of a Pinterest board. I found myself baking more desserts just so I could watch her work.

The few times I'd seen Poppy sculpt, she'd seemed tense, tortured even. She'd become so focused, she'd forget to eat or sleep. We were all afraid to interrupt her. She once threw a chisel at me when I asked if she wanted to take a break and go for a walk.

A completely different side of Poppy emerged when she decorated cupcakes. The work was repetitive, yet artistic. The combination made her eerily peaceful. I swear I heard her humming. During the more monotonous tasks, like piping, we chatted about the café, Chris's training, and even her current sculpture project.

"Do you think I made too much?" I asked Mom as Poppy fanned stacks of red-white-and-blue napkins.

"If there's anything left over, we'll just tell everyone to take home whatever they want."

Poppy stood back and admired the table with a huge smile on her face.

Mom glanced between Poppy and me, and her eyes widened. "You could do this professionally. You're both so talented, and your skills complement each other perfectly."

Poppy waved her hand. "Mom, you're biased. No one would pay for this."

"I would," Lauren said, walking up. She had on a billowy white-and-blue polka dot dress and a pair of red sandals. I looked down at my flour-covered t-shirt and cringed.

"You're also biased," Poppy said.

"I should change," I said, gathering the Tupperware containers we'd used to move the cupcakes outside.

"Hurry," Mom said. "We're eating at six."

The Peace Falls police had placed barricades on either end of the street at five-thirty. Up and down the block, neighbors were carrying folding tables toward our house, which sat smack in the middle of the street.

"I don't suppose you're changing for the party, Poppy?" Mom added.

Poppy looked down at her black dress. "Not unless you want me to add my skull necklace. The fancy one."

"Maybe a sun hat," Mom said. "You're still a redhead, after all."

Lauren insisted on taking the Tupperware as we followed my sister into the house and back to the kitchen.

"I'm not an invalid," I said as Lauren dumped the plasticware onto the same section of counter where Cal had pressed his hard body against mine. Despite how much I'd tried to pretend THE kiss hadn't happened, my cheeks burned. I was equally turned on and mortified by the memory. Cal couldn't leave the kitchen fast enough and hadn't spoken to me since, but it was, without question, the hottest kiss of my life.

"Are you feeling ok?" Lauren asked, putting her hand on my forehead. "You're all red."

"I'm fine," I said, forcing a smile. "We've been running around all day."

"Well cool off, or you won't be able to wear the dress I brought you. You're not wearing that star romper again."

"What's wrong with my star romper? It's festive."

"It's hideous," Poppy said.

I crossed my arms and glared at the pair of them. "Why didn't y'all say something all the other times I wore it."

Lauren shrugged. "You seemed to like wearing it."

"She means you weren't single then, so it didn't matter," Poppy said, rummaging through the hat rack in the corner. With three redheads in the house, we'd amassed an impressive collection. Poppy pulled out a large-brim black hat better suited for a high-society funeral than a 4th of July picnic.

"Do you even need a hat?" I asked. "The sun will be down in a couple hours."

"Mom's right. It completes my outfit."

"And you seriously expect me to take style advice from you."

"Fine," she said, plopping the ridiculous hat on her head. "Take it from Lauren."

Lauren smiled. "I left the dress on your bed. Oh, and take your hair down from that messy bun."

"It's eighty-nine degrees. I'm not wearing my hair down."

Lauren stuck out her bottom lip in an exaggerated pout. "Fine, but I'm doing your makeup."

"I'll guard the cupcakes," Poppy said.

Lauren sighed. "People are supposed to eat them, Poppy. Take a picture and then walk away. You'll scare the children."

"I meant from flies," my sister said, but the slight blush on her cheeks made me question if that's all she'd be swatting away.

"We better hurry," Lauren said, grabbing my hand and tugging me up the stairs to the room I shared with Poppy.

"Absolutely not," I said, when I saw the dress she'd brought.

"What's wrong with it?"

"It has spaghetti straps. I refuse to be tugging on a strapless bra all evening."

"So don't wear a bra. It's not like you're a D-cup."

True. But I wasn't one to walk around with the girls free, no matter how small they were.

"It's red, Lauren," I said, grabbing the dress.

"Which will look great with your hair." She took the dress and held it against my front. "See," she said, turning us toward the full-length mirror on the back of the door.

I shook my head. "It's too much. I'll look ridiculous."

"You'll look hot. Do you want all these people to pity you, or would you rather make them question why anyone would let you go?"

"I broke up with Brad."

"Because he cheated. And every single person out there knows it."

I sank onto my bed. "How would they know that?"

Lauren sat beside me and grabbed my hand. "I love your mom. She's one of the sweetest people I know, but sometimes her good intentions have a way of backfiring."

My stomach sank. "What did she do?"

"Try not to be mad, but she told all her friends what happened. She didn't want any of them asking you about Brad or why you were home. You can imagine how fast word spread after that."

I'd been in Peace Falls almost three weeks, and no one had asked me a single question about why I was back or why my husband wasn't with me. I should have realized something was up, but I just figured no one cared. It's not like I was the town's sweetheart. "How long have you known?"

Lauren had the decency to cringe. "I heard people talking about you at Karma the day before you arrived. I figured the harm was already done, and you've been in so much pain lately, I didn't want to make it worse."

"Great," I said, flopping back on the bed and putting my arm over my eyes. "Want to ditch the picnic and watch *Mean Girls* with me?"

Lauren pulled my arm from my face. "Then we'd have to tell your mom why. And you and I both know how much that would upset her."

"Maybe for once I don't care."

Lauren shook her head. "Come on, you have to make an appearance in this dress and make sure Poppy isn't scaring people from the dessert table. If you still feel like hiding after an hour, we can binge *Mean Girl* and *The Princess Diaries*."

"Half an hour."

"Fine."

"And no makeup."

"Mascara and lip gloss."

I nodded and she clapped her hands.

By the time Lauren finished with me, I had a high ponytail that kept my neck cool but freed my curls. The dress showed a lot of skin but somehow remained tasteful, even without a bra. I dug a pair of silver sandals from the closet and allowed Lauren exactly one minute to apply whatever makeup she wanted. I'm not sure how, but she somehow managed smokey eyes and the perfect gloss application in under sixty seconds.

"See," she said, standing behind me at the mirror. "You're stunning."

I smiled. I looked the best I had in years. As soon as I thought it, all the color drained from my face. Cal was bound to stop by the block party at some point. What if he thought I'd worn this dress to get his attention?

"Nope," Lauren said, shaking her head. "Whatever you're thinking, stop. We're going outside right now."

The party was already in full swing. Someone had set up a sound system to play an eclectic mix of songs. Thankfully, whoever selected the playlist had better taste in music than Mom. The neighbors clustered in groups to chat, others moved from one table to the next filling their paper plates. A crowd had formed around the dessert table. I was relieved to see Mom behind it, passing out treats. I spotted Poppy arranging food at the table next to ours and sucked in a breath when I saw who stood beside her.

"Aren't you glad you're not wearing that romper now," Lauren whispered in my ear.

As if he sensed me staring, Cal looked up. Our eyes locked and his jaw clenched. I dropped my gaze to my sandals and when I looked back up, he'd disappeared into the crowd.

Lauren gave me a puzzled look, and I shook my head.

"Ok," she said linking my arm with hers. "But we're discussing that later. Let's get some food before the flies find it."

The half hour I promised passed, then the hour, then another. Everyone was eager to talk to me about the desserts or my dress. Even if their compliments were inspired by pity, it felt good to spend time with the families I'd grown up with and to meet the ones who had moved to the street after I left. I spotted Cal several times, weaving through the crowd with Skye.

More than once I thought he was walking toward me, but then someone would pull one of us into a conversation. Finally, as the sun began to drop behind the mountains, I felt something lick the back of my leg and turned to find Skye staring up at me with a big doggy grin.

Cal had his back to me, talking to Principal Twillings, so I bent and scratched Skye's ears. She flopped onto her back, tugging Cal's arm enough that he turned and saw me. His eyes darkened, and I realized he could see halfway down my dress where he stood. I straightened and Skye jumped up as well, wagging her tail.

"You look," Cal started, then shook his head. "You're not making this easy, Rowan."

"Making what easy?"

He placed a gentle hand on my elbow and guided me to the edge of the crowd. His touch made my stomach flutter, and I chided myself for still being so attracted to someone who'd rejected me earlier in the week.

"First," he said, lowering his voice. "I need to apologize for how I acted the other day."

"Which part? Kissing me or running off after?" Though, I'd been pretty relieved when he left. There's only so much embarrassment I can handle before I cry, and I'd entered the danger zone.

He blew out a long breath. "Both."

Ok, so he regretted kissing me but he also regretted stopping? I wasn't sure what to make of that. "You said first. What else?"

"Only that it can't happen again. You're my patient."

"For the next three weeks," I said, then realized that sounded like I wanted to pick up where we left off as soon as I finished PT. "So, I agree, that can never happen again. With any luck, I'll find a job far from Peace Falls by the time we're done my sessions. The last thing I need is more complication in my life."

Cal smiled. "So, you're wearing that dress to torture me, not seduce me?"

"No," I huffed. "I'm wearing the dress Lauren made me wear."

Cal bit his lower lip and shook his head. "Somehow that makes it worse."

A loud boom sounded in the distance. I looked up in time to see fireworks flash weakly in the fading sky. Another screamed and exploded with a shower of sparks.

"Little early for fireworks," I said, but when I looked back, Cal and Skye were gone.

He had a real talent for running, but I was honestly glad. A man as sexy as Cal should be taken in small doses. I closed my eyes and took a few deep breaths. Any interaction with him left my heart racing. It was time to grab a cupcake, stream a couple movies, and turn off all thoughts of Cal. Once I felt more in control, I searched the crowd for Lauren and found her on her hands and knees peering under a folding table. That was odd enough, but people were peeking under lawn chairs and porches up and down Sullivan Street. Mom was knee deep in Mrs. Adams's shrubbery.

"What's going on?" I asked Lauren.

She stood and brushed off her dress. "Cal's dog ran off. We're hoping she's hiding nearby."

"Did you see which way Skye went?" Chris asked, sprinting to me.

I shook my head.

"Cal took off in that direction," Poppy said, pointing toward Broad Street. "Lauren, you're parked outside the barricade, aren't you?"

"Let me grab my keys," she said, running toward my house.

"I'm coming with you," Chris said.

"No," Poppy said. "You and I will look for Skye on foot. Lauren can drive while Rowan looks for the dog because her back is too jacked to do anything more useful."

"Um, thanks."

"Just find the damn dog, Rowan," Poppy snapped. "Skye is more than a pet. She's a support animal."

With that, Poppy and Chris took off. The rest of the neighbors were fanning out as well, many calling Skye's name. Lauren bounded down the porch steps, keys in hand.

"Did you know Cal had a support animal?" I asked as we walked to her car, which was parked on Broad Street by Cal's house.

She shook her head. "She doesn't wear a vest or anything. Plus, a service animal wouldn't bolt from her human."

"Poppy sounded certain."

"Support animal or not, we better start looking before it gets dark."

Chapter Thirteen

Cal

I reached Centennial Park as night settled like a thick blanket. The town's fireworks display would begin soon, and once it started, I had even less chance of finding Skye. I shouted her name, but my voice was so hoarse, it barely carried. I whistled and waited. Nothing.

Damn fireworks. I knew better than to have her outside during the show, but I didn't count on someone setting off bottle rockets in their backyard before dusk. My grip on the leash was too loose, my attention too focused on Rowan. At the first pop, Skye shot through the party toward our house, then past it onto Broad Street. I'd lost sight of her almost immediately, but like an idiot, had kept running in the direction she originally went. She easily could have circled back home by now. I pulled my phone from my pocket and texted Chris to check. I considered calling Theo to help me look, but I worried it might give him a panic attack. Aiden would no doubt leave his family's picnic to help. My relationship with the O'Malley clan was strained enough without ruining the big family 4th of July gathering.

My phone buzzed with a text.

Chris

I thanked him and did a quick lap around the empty park. I'd hoped she'd go somewhere she loved, but it was time to accept that Skye could be miles away. A firework exploded on the other side of Peace Falls, where most of the town had gathered in the high school stadium to watch the show. Damn it. Skye must be scared out of her mind.

I walked back to Main, thinking I should check some of the back roads that intersected the larger street. A red sedan pulled to the curb, and Rowan called my name from the passenger seat.

"Lauren and I figured we could cover more ground with a car," she said. "Any suggestion where we should look?"

I shook my head. "There's no point until after the show ends. She's hiding now. Even if she heard us calling, she won't come out. She's terrified of loud noises."

"Like thunder?" Rowan asked.

I nodded.

"Where does she usually hide during storms?" Rowan asked.

"In my house."

She let out a huff. "I meant where in the house. If she always goes to the same place, she might try to find somewhere similar."

This entire conversation felt like a waste of time, but with the colors still bursting overhead, I figured it couldn't hurt. "She hides in the half bath if we're downstairs, my closet if we're upstairs."

"Do those rooms have anything in common?"

As soon as she asked, I felt like an idiot for not making the connection before. "They don't have windows."

"So, maybe a shed or detached garage, especially one without windows?"

Here I'd been looking for Skye in open parks when her instinct would have been to go somewhere small and dark. I sent Chris another text.

Ask everyone to check their sheds and outbuildings

Chris

Already looked. Not there

"Chris says they looked."

"On our street," Rowan said, climbing from the car. "Do you bring Skye to the park often?"

"I do. I went the same route we normally walk, but I didn't check any outbuildings along the way."

"Do you go down Broad, then Church, and then onto Main?"

I nodded.

Rowan stuck her head through the passenger window and said something. She stepped closer to me on the sidewalk while Lauren did a U-turn in the deserted street and drove toward Church. Another cluster of fireworks exploded, each boom louder than the last.

I gripped my hair and pulled. This was not happening. Skye would have been terrified at home. The thought of her alone and scared in an unfamiliar place made me want to punch a wall. Or myself. This was all my fucking fault. I hoped Skye hadn't run toward the high school. Not only would she be closer to the noise, she could easily get hit by a car when everyone left after the show.

Rowan laid a gentle hand on my arm and pulled until I released the death grip on my hair. "Easy there, Big Guy."

I curled my fingers around hers and held on. Her hand was soft, warm, and fit perfectly in mine.

"Lauren is starting back at Broad Street," Rowan said, giving my hand a squeeze. "We'll look from this end of your route. We'll find her."

"We have to."

Rowan nodded. "Poppy mentioned Skye is a service animal."

If the situation weren't so serious, I'd have laughed. "Poppy must have Skye confused with another dog. Mine failed obedience school twice."

"Sorry, support animal. I'm afraid I don't know the difference."

"Ah," I said, as we started the long walk back. I waited for her to let go of my hand and was relieved when she didn't. "Are you sure you're ok to walk?"

Rowan nodded. "Honestly, walking doesn't hurt that much. Sitting is the worst. Stairs second. I'm slow though, so if you want to run ahead and check places in the middle of the route, that's fine too."

"No, slower is better. We don't want to miss anything. We should search the alley. There really isn't anywhere she could hide on Main Street."

We walked to the alley behind the store fronts and looked everywhere a dog might hide. Rowan shouted for Skye, her voice sounding hoarse like mine. She'd clearly been searching as long as I had. We walked in silence, broken only by one of us calling Skye. We looked behind every dumpster and peered into every window well. I told myself I needed to hold Rowan's hand, so she didn't fall in the dim alley and hurt herself more. The longer we walked, the more I worried we'd never find Skye. The more I worried, the tighter I held Rowan's hand.

"What Poppy said is kind of true," I said after a few blocks. "Theo gets panic attacks. If Skye is nearby, she helps calm him down."

"Let me see if I've got this right. Your dog is Theo's support animal?"

"Yeah. He should really have his own, but he refuses."

"Why if it would help him?"

I blew out a breath. "That's a whole other conversation, and honestly, not one I want to have."

"Oh," she said, in a quiet voice. "I'm sorry. Forget I asked."

She shrank into herself like she had in the kitchen after I stopped her from coming near me. When I saw her reaction, it'd taken every ounce of self-control I had not to reach for her.

"Hey," I said, stopping in the middle of the alley. "I'm the one who started this conversation, just like I'm the one who kissed you the other day. It's my fault things got awkward, not yours."

She nodded and started walking again, but her hand didn't feel as firm in mine, and her voice sounded timid the next time she called Skye. When we came to the end of the alley at the parking lot behind Church Street Brews, she stopped with a jolt. "Did you check the playhouse at the park? The one by the playground equipment. It's been there since we were kids."

I knew exactly the playhouse she meant. And though I'd called Skye's name in the park, I hadn't thought to check the playhouse.

"Go," she said, dropping my hand and shoving me.

"I'm not leaving you in an alley by yourself."

"I lived in DC years without getting mugged or murdered. Lauren is probably right around the corner. Now, go!"

I grabbed her elbow and led her to a portion of sidewalk below a streetlamp on Church Street. "Don't move until Lauren gets here," I said, taking off at a sprint. "If you fall, you'll undo all the work we've done."

I ran as fast as I could down Main Street. My high school football coach would have loved the pace I set to the park as the fireworks finale boomed overhead. Five minutes later, I skidded to a halt in front of the playhouse and stuck my head inside.

Though it was too dark to see, I could hear Skye whimpering in the corner. I shoved my six-foot two frame into the playhouse I hadn't visited since elementary school and wrapped my arms around her.

"I'm here, girl," I said. Her tense muscles started to relax. She let out another whimper, and a wave of grief crashed over me.

I should have been relieved, but all I kept thinking was one day, I would lose her. Skye was almost ten. She might act like a puppy, but she didn't have many years left. I'd lose her just like I lost Logan. She licked my hand as the tears came hot and fast from my eyes. We may have sat in the cramped playhouse all night if a dark figure hadn't shone a flashlight inside the entrance.

"Sorry," Rowan said, fumbling with her cell phone and shutting off the light. "Um, I thought you might like a ride back home."

At the sound of Rowan's voice, Skye perked up and wiggled to the exit.

"I'm so happy to see you, baby," she said, crouching to grab Skye's leash.

I used my t-shirt to dry off my face before I pulled myself out to join them.

"Let me," I said, taking the leash. "No telling when the next backyard fireworks will start."

I stood, and Rowan struggled to her feet with a groan.

"This was too much for your back," I said. I wrapped my arm around her waist. Hopefully, she'd think I was trying to steady her, not attaching myself like a leech hoping to suck the calm from her. I expected her to push me away. Instead, she turned into me and wrapped her arms around my neck. I leaned down and held her tight, resting my head on her warm shoulder. After a moment, she pulled away, but wove her arm in mine.

Lauren's red sedan idled at the curb. Rowan opened the rear passenger door and slipped across the back seat. Skye pulled on the leash until I moved forward. She clambered in beside Rowan and licked her face. I climbed in the back seat as well, my knees crammed against the front seat.

"I feel like a Lyft driver," Lauren chuckled. Skye put her head in my lap and fell asleep. When we arrived at Sullivan Street, the block party was going strong on the other side of the barricade.

"If y'all don't mind," Lauren said. "I'm going to head home."

"Thank you so much, Lauren," I said.

I nudged Skye. She let out a snort and yawned but followed me out of the car. Rowan and I waved Lauren off before walking around the barricade. I should have taken Skye straight home, but instead, I found myself moving through the party with Rowan at my side. One by one the neighbors cheered when they saw us. Skye wagged her tail, happy to be the center of attention.

We reached the Stevens's house and stopped in front of the dessert table. Only crumbs remained.

"Wow," Rowan said, smiling. "Guess everyone liked the desserts."

"I confess I sampled each of the tarts. And I'm a little pissed. I planned to take a cupcake home."

"Hm. Maybe I'll bring some to my next session." Rowan rubbed Skye's head and smiled at me. "Night, Caleb."

"I think I owe you a beer," I said before I could stop myself. I held my arm out like I was about to escort her to the homecoming court. She laughed but took it.

As soon as I opened the front door, Skye trotted to the armchair where Aiden usually sat and curled into a tight ball. Rowan flopped onto the couch with the grace of an eighty-year-old.

"You're stiff," I said.

"Just tired."

I nodded. "I'd offer you something other than beer, but that's all I have, unless you want water."

"A beer would be great," she said.

I walked to the kitchen and grabbed two IPAs. I hoped she hadn't set back her progress helping me, but, fuck, I was thankful she did.

Skye was already snoring when I returned to the living room.

"Poor thing must be exhausted," Rowan said, taking the can I offered her.

"I forgot to ask if you want a glass," I said, turning back toward the kitchen.

"Sit down, Caleb. I just walked a mile in an alley looking behind dumpsters for your dog. We're past formalities."

I settled onto the couch beside her, and we clinked cans. After a long pull, I set my can on the coffee table. "If I'm being honest, Skye is my support animal too."

She placed her can on the table next to mine and took my hand in hers.

"My mom gave me Skye when I was recovering from the accident. I didn't want to do PT or leave the house. Honestly, I barely got out of bed most days. So, Mom got the most energetic puppy she could find. Skye had these bright blue eyes then. I didn't know they'd change to green."

"The name suits her," Rowan said, giving my hand a squeeze. "She has a personality as big as the sky."

"She does," I said. Skye let out an extra loud snore as if to agree. "I can't thank you enough for helping me find her."

Rowan nodded and let go of my hand. I wanted to take it back, but she laced her fingers together and placed them on her lap. "My dad loved chocolate-covered cherries," she said softly. "Or so I thought. I gave him a box for Christmas when I was little, and he made such a big show of liking them, I bought him a box every year. Since you can only buy them at Christmas, he'd eat one a day because he said he wanted them to last. Each year I got him a bigger and bigger box."

"That's nice," I said, not following where she was going, but curious.

"Well, after he died, I missed buying those boxes. Then, during my first semester at Georgetown, my hall had a white elephant gift exchange with a five-dollar max."

"So, you bought cherries?"

"No, I bought lip gloss. But I opened a box of chocolate-covered cherries. None of my hallmates knew about my Christmas tradition with my dad. It was just an odd coincidence."

"That's incredible."

She nodded and her emerald eyes glistened. "I hadn't felt grief like that in years. By the time I sobbed through the story, all my hallmates were crying and hugging me. I took that box of cherries home, and now every Christmas I visit Dad's grave and eat a cherry."

My eyes burned. I felt on the edge of losing it all over again when Rowan's face cracked into a huge smile. "Those cherries taste awful. A couple years ago, Mom confessed that Dad hated them too. He ate one a day because that's all he could choke down."

A laugh burst out of me, pulling the ache from my chest. Rowan laughed too, but then her expression shifted. Her mouth parted and her eyes darkened. Her breathing accelerated, her perfect breasts rising and falling in that red dress.

My stomach clenched, and before I could tell myself all the reasons not to, I ran my thumb across her full bottom lip. I waited for her to pull away. When she didn't, I leaned forward and placed a gentle kiss on her mouth. Our lips moved together, soft at first, tentative. When she placed her hands on my chest, the kiss deepened, and all my commonsense evaporated.

The need to feel her roared through my body like a freight train. I kissed down her neck to the creamy skin I'd been longing to touch ever since the moment I saw her at the block party. I slid the thin straps from her shoulders and let the fabric fall from her chest. Her pink nipples pebbled beneath my fingers. She let out a gasp and threaded her hands in my hair as I bent and kissed her breast. Her grip tightened when I sucked her nipple into my mouth. I looked up. Her eyes were closed, her head thrown back, her breath coming in pants. I gave the other breast equal attention before lowering Rowan gently to the couch. She moaned as I rocked against her and the sound sent a ripple of pleasure through my body. Fuck, I was going to finish in my shorts if I kept rubbing against her.

"I have to taste you," I said.

Her eyes widened but she nodded. I ran my hands up her smooth legs, pushing the dress up as I went. I dipped my head and inhaled the scent of her, musky and sweet. She'd soaked the delicate white lace covering her sensitive skin. I ran my tongue over the thin fabric, and she arched off the sofa. Hooking my fingers in the band, I slid her panties down her legs. When I swirled my tongue on her clit, she gripped my hair again, holding me in place. I dipped a finger into her tight heat, and she shuddered. I sucked her into my mouth, and she breathed my name, arching closer. I added another finger, pumping in and out as I twirled her clit in my mouth. She tightened around my fingers as she came, her body shuddering in waves that made my dick weep.

I couldn't wait another second to feel her skin against mine. I sat up and pulled my shirt over my head. She ran her small hands down the ridges of my chest to my shorts then cupped me. I sucked in a breath. Our eyes locked, and my chest tightened. Fuck she was beautiful.

Just as I reached for her, a firework went off outside. Skye gave a startled bark and shot off the chair, straight to the downstairs bathroom.

The commotion cleared the lust hold from my mind. What was I doing? Rowan was a patient. She was coming off a nasty divorce and told me, less than a couple hours ago, that she didn't want to complicate her life. I hadn't even had my standard "I don't do relationships" talk with her.

Luckily, the fireworks and Skye seemed to have snapped Rowan back to reality as well. "Um, do you need to check on her?" she said. "I can see myself out."

"Yeah, that's probably a good idea."

She pulled the top of her dress back into place, and I held her hand as she rose from the couch.

"Thanks again for helping me tonight," I said, giving her fingers a squeeze.

"Um, thank you for," she blushed and waved her other hand toward the couch.

We smiled at each other and started laughing.

"I better go," she said, walking to the front door. "Good luck with Skye."

As soon as she closed the door behind her, I collapsed on the couch and put my head in my hands. That's when I saw the lace panties on the floor. The thought of Rowan walking through the block party bare was enough to bring me to my feet to chase after her and finish what we started. Another firework exploded and Skye let out a sharp cry inside the bathroom. I blew out a breath and prepared for a long night with the wrong type of fireworks.

Chapter Fourteen

Rowan

When I entered Karma, Poppy and Cammie were carrying the last bistro tables to the wall beneath the large picture window, leaving the padded chairs scattered in the middle of the floor. Lauren was unpacking folding chairs from a cart into rows at the rear of the café. She let out a relieved sigh when she spotted the Tupperware containers in my hands.

"Thank you so much," she said. "There's a tablecloth and trays on the counter. Would you mind setting up the cookies while we arrange the chairs?"

"Of course," I said.

"Let me get the board first," Poppy said, running into the back.

"Do you want me to help with the chairs?" I asked.

"No," Cammie and Lauren shouted together.

The swinging door bumped open, and Poppy sailed through with a massive sheet of plywood. I started toward her, but she glared at me. Cammie helped her flip it onto the bistro tables creating a large, narrow surface suitable for a buffet.

"Looks like y'all got this down to a science," I said, putting my containers on the counter and grabbing the tablecloth.

"We do these once a month," Lauren said.

Judging by the number of chairs and her frantic request for "as many cookies as you can bake by eight," she was expecting a good crowd. "What's the topic tonight?"

"Declaring Your Financial Independence," Cammie said with a smile.

Lauren shook her head. "I'd like to declare my independence from Bob's Bakery. I placed an order for tonight a month ago. When it didn't arrive with the usual morning delivery, I called right away, but they said they were short-staffed and couldn't fill it."

"That's so unprofessional," I said as I smoothed the tablecloth over the board. "You've been a customer for years. You'd think they'd try to do something."

"I agree," Lauren said, placing two large serving trays at the far edge of the table. "The coffee station goes on the side closer to the counter in case we need to refill the urns."

I snapped open a container and started arranging cookies while Lauren filled two large urns with steaming coffee. Cammie continued setting up chairs. Poppy darted back and forth with napkins, cups, pitchers of iced water, and everything else needed for a coffee service.

"Do you charge for these events?" I asked, taking in the finished table.

"Oh no," Lauren said, placing small white plates under the coffee dispensers to catch any drips.

"But all this must cost you?" I said gesturing to the table.

"That reminds me," Lauren said. "Let me get you a check for the cookies."

"Absolutely not," I said, crossing my arms.

Lauren drew her shoulders back and waved a finger at me. "Do not sell yourself short, Rowan. I was going to pay the bakery. I have no doubt what you made is way better than anything they'd have sent over. I'm paying you."

"Consider it my donation," I said with a smirk. "Good karma, and all that."

"She does have a point," Cammie said, patting Lauren on the shoulder. "Your karma bank must be overflowing."

Lauren waved her hand. "All this is free advertising."

"Minus the free part," Poppy shouted from behind the counter.

"People order things while they're here," Lauren said with her hands on her hips. "We just supply drip coffee, water, and a small treat. Besides, almost everyone comes back at some point as a paying customer."

"Do you pay for the speaker too?" I asked.

"No, they volunteer. My financial planner is giving the talk tonight."

"And what are the chances she gets a few new clients?" I asked.

Lauren huffed. "I hope she does. She's excellent at her job and could really help someone who might be too intimidated or uninformed to reach out."

Cammie raised her hand with a sheepish expression. "Me. Lauren had to drag me into the bank to open a checking account. I thought it was normal to pay a fee every time I cashed my paycheck." She blushed and straightened a chair that was already straight.

"Did you make that list of questions for tonight?" Lauren asked.

Cammie nodded.

"Good," Lauren said. "I'm counting on you to ask them. It will give people courage to ask theirs."

"That's a great idea," I said and smiled at Cammie. "I'm always too nervous in a group to ask questions. If Lauren and I were in the same class, I'd write mine down and make her ask them."

Cammie grinned. "What did you do if you weren't in the same class?"

"Get annoyed at myself and try to google the answer later."

Cammie smiled, and I felt better knowing I hadn't stuck my foot in my mouth too far.

"I'm grabbing a seat at the front," she said, taking a cookie and heading for the first row of chairs.

"I hope I didn't hurt her feelings," I whispered as Lauren and I moved a pair of flower bouquets from the counter to the table. "I know Cammie isn't taking advantage of you."

"Nah, Cammie knows you're just being an overprotective friend."

"I'm the right amount of protective," I said.

"Speaking of friends, don't think I forgot to ask what's going on between you and Cal Cardoso. I saw y'all holding hands when you walked to the car last night."

"Shut up, Lauren. Cammie works with him."

"Oh, I know," she said with a devilish smirk. "She's been telling me all about the tension between you two. We have a bet about when it'll boil over. She thought he'd behave until after your sessions ended. Judging by what I saw last night, I think she owes me five."

"I'll give you twenty bucks to never talk about this again."

My phone vibrated in my pocket, and I pulled it out to see a call from Brad. Lauren peered at the screen and frowned.

"Why is he calling you?"

"No idea," I said, sending the call to voicemail. "Anything he wants to say to me, he can tell my lawyer."

"Good," Lauren said with a nod.

My phone buzzed again. Then again. And again. After weeks with zero contact, he seemed pretty impatient to talk to me. He hadn't even bothered to send a single text to ask how I was healing from the accident. As time passed, I went from being pissed at his lack of care for my wellbeing to relieved I didn't have to deal with him. I assumed that meant he wanted a clean break, which I'd been happy to give and wanted to maintain.

Lauren narrowed her eyes. "Is he harassing you? We can go to the police station right now and file a report. Cammie and Poppy can manage the event."

"Down, girl," I said. "Who's overprotective now?" She looked so worried; I couldn't help hugging her. She let out a sigh and wrapped her arms around me.

"You'd tell me, if he was?"

"Of course," I said, patting her back.

She hugged me tighter. "I wish you'd consider staying here. I'm going to be a nervous wreck thinking about you all alone in some city."

My phone buzzed again.

"Ugh," I groaned stepping out of the hug. "Just let me deal with him. I don't want my phone going off during the event."

"Use my office," she said.

I walked to the counter, past Poppy, who shoved her own phone in her apron with a guilty expression. "What are you doing back here?" she snapped.

"Chill, I won't tell your boss you're texting at work. I'm using Lauren's office to make a phone call."

"Yeah, whatever," she said. She grabbed a bottle of Windex and started aggressively cleaning the glass countertop.

I walked through the swinging door and the small kitchen/storage area to the tiny enclosure Lauren called an office. It was about the size of an airplane bathroom, but at least it was private. I shut the door and squeezed around Lauren's cluttered desk to sit in her small chair. Brad had left a voicemail and sent three texts:

Brad

> *You owe me*

> *Don't be like this*

My phone buzzed again with a picture of his favorite loafers filled with dog poop. Picture after picture arrived: Poop on the bedsheets, poop on a stack of dishes, poop inside a cereal box, and finally, eight pictures of poop in different HVAC vents.

Poppy would have had to unscrew the covers for those, which made me laugh so hard I snorted.

I knew Poppy's prank was going to come back to bite me. I dialed Brad, and he picked up on the first ring. "Why are you sending me pictures of poop?"

"Quick," he said. "How do you run the monthly report you put together for Gwen?"

Not "How are you" or "Sorry for being a dick." He didn't give a damn about me. I wondered if he ever did. It didn't feel great to realize how little affection I'd accepted in my marriage. I couldn't do anything about the years I'd wasted or the woman I'd been with him, but I didn't have to be her now. "What?"

"The report, Rowan. The one you ran every month for her."

"Ah," I said leaning back in the chair. "You mean the one Kelli re-saved with her credentials, so it looked like she made it."

"Yes, that one."

"Sorry," I said, "I can't remember. Stop calling me and sending me pictures of poop, or I'll be forced to contact *my* lawyers."

"Those are evidence of what you did to our apartment."

"Gross, Brad. I thought you knew me better than that. Call my lawyer if you have anything else to say."

I ended the call and tossed the phone onto the desk just as Lauren opened the door and wiggled in.

"Were you listening outside?"

"Maybe," she said with a shrug. "I had to make sure you didn't let him walk all over you."

"How'd I do?"

She put two thumbs in the air and smiled. "Now, I want the dirty details about Cal. We have five minutes before everyone arrives. Spill the tea."

The truth was, I was dying to tell her. Everything happened so fast last night, I wasn't sure how I felt about it. Physically, I'd never experienced anything so satisfying. The man had a gifted tongue. I'd be lying if I said I didn't crave a repeat performance. But, I'd never had a casual physical relationship before. I wasn't sure I could enjoy sex without getting attached. Add to that my inner-sixteen-year-old doing cartwheels because Caleb Cardoso was somehow attracted to me, and I wasn't sure my heart could handle more.

"Ok," I said lowering my voice. "But you have to swear not to repeat any of this to Poppy or Cammie or really anyone."

Lauren gripped her hands together and gave an excited squeal.

"Promise."

"I told you I can keep a secret."

"He went down on me last night. I was so flustered after, I left my underwear at his house and walked home bare assed."

Lauren's eyes widened, and she fell back against the door, pushing it closed. "You did what?" she screamed.

"Lauren," I hissed.

"Sorry," she whispered. "But you can't just jump in with that. All I saw was some innocent hand holding. Given how upset he looked over his dog, it could have been friendly concern."

I nodded but didn't go into details.

Seeing Cal's distraught face in the playhouse as he held Skye had melted any lingering anger I'd had over our initial sessions and that odd kiss. I knew that pain all too well. Skye entered Cal's life during a time of immense grief. It made sense he'd be triggered by almost losing her. I told him the story about the cherries to show I could empathize without calling attention to the state he was in when I found him. I didn't know Cal well, but I sensed he hid his grief as much as possible, perhaps even from himself.

When he laughed at my story, he was the most attractive man I'd ever seen. Instead of talking through his grief like I intended, he pulled pleasure from my body and left me reeling.

"So, you went from disliking the man to feeling sorry for him to letting him put his face in your business all in the same night?"

"He kissed me earlier this week."

"And you didn't tell me," Lauren said, clutching her chest. "That hurts."

"He didn't mean to do it. I'm not even sure why it happened, really."

Lauren threw her hands in the air. "Because you're beautiful, and funny, and sweet. His lips did not accidentally land on yours. He wanted to kiss you. Clearly, since he moved the kisses south."

"Ok, fine. But before that we decided it could never happen again. I'm his patient. Plus, I'm moving soon."

"Very mature of you both. But then?" She raised her eyebrows at me and waited.

"He gave me the best orgasm of my life."

Lauren fanned her face. "I can imagine."

An unexpected stab of jealousy made me sit straighter in the chair. "Ok, you get the idea," I said, my tone a little sharp.

"So, are you seeing each other?"

"No."

"You're just hooking up?"

"Um, I don't think so."

"Rowan Eloise Stevens, if a man has his face in your lady garden you're hooking up."

"Please never call it that again."

"So, what are you doing?"

I shrugged. "I don't know, but if a firework hadn't gone off and scared Skye, I'm pretty sure we'd have slept together."

"Wow," Lauren said. "That's kind of unexpected."

"Yeah, I know."

"Brad is still the only man you've been with, right?"

I nodded.

"What did Cal say when you saw him at PT today?"

"My session is tomorrow. The schedule got shifted because of the holiday."

"Oh," Lauren said with a smirk. "So, you've been overthinking this all day, haven't you?"

"Pretty much."

"Can you have fun with Cal and not get attached?"

I twisted my hands in my lap. "I'm not even sure he'd want that. Emotions were high last night, and things got out of hand. Again, I'm his patient, and he's on thin ice at work."

Lauren nodded. "Cammie mentioned that. Avery Peterson is such a bitch."

"Wow, I don't think I've ever heard you call anyone that before."

"She's hurt a lot of people."

"That she has."

"Lauren," Poppy screamed from the other side of the door. "Get your ass out here. There are more people than I can handle."

Lauren took a deep breath and sighed. "I love your sister, and I'd never fire her, but this job isn't the best fit for Poppy."

"Whatever do you mean," I said with a laugh.

"You two really could open a custom bakery. You could bake and manage the peopling parts. Poppy could decorate and grow the business. She runs all our social media channels and comes up with the best ideas."

I shook my head. "I worked too hard for my finance degree. I can't throw it away because Poppy has a sudden passion for cake decorating, and you'd like to hire someone with a sunnier disposition."

"Of course not. You'd do it because you love baking. You always have. And I'm sure all that finance experience would help you run your own business."

"You just want me to stay in Peace Falls."

"Duh. But more importantly, I want you to be happy. You deserve that."

"I'm serious, Lauren," Poppy screamed. "Mr. Fitzwilliam took his teeth out, and I swear on my rondel chisel I would rather put my face under the frother than help him find them again when he throws them out with his napkin."

"Oh," I winced. "We better go. She cried when Mom bought her that chisel."

"Promise me you'll consider all your options."

Opening a bakery in Peace Falls seemed more like a fantasy than a valid career plan. But I nodded, and we returned to the café in time to save Mr. Fitzwilliam's teeth and Poppy's face.

Chapter Fifteen

Cal

I was screwed. Avery had worked overtime to flood the online review sites.

My skin crawled every time Dr. Cardoso touched me. Go anywhere else.

Arrogant. Doesn't listen to patients at all.

I cried after every session. Don't make the same mistake.

I kept scrolling, my stomach turning with each lie. But then, I came across three five-star reviews posted yesterday:

Dr. Cardoso is a great guy. I'll visit him anytime I need PT.

Best PT I've ever known.

You'd be stupid to go to anyone else.

I scrolled down. Several more five-star posts broke up Avery's hate rants. But even with the positive feedback, my overall rating had dipped to two-and-a-half stars. I rubbed my forehead. At this rate, Adam wouldn't give me until the end of the month to fix things. I needed to talk to Avery ASAP.

Someone knocked on my office door, and I tensed. Adam wasn't expected for another hour, but maybe he'd come in early to fire me. Then again, the knock had been gentle. Adam would have just thrown open the door and told me to get my ass out.

"Come in."

Cammie walked into my office and pulled the door closed behind her. "You saw them, huh?"

I nodded.

"Well, at least you got a few good reviews as well. Too bad it didn't help much."

"Hurt is more like it. I think the good ones pissed off Avery more."

"Yeah, but it got me thinking. Your patients love you, Cal. If I told them what was happening, I'm sure they'd all write you glowing reviews. Avery is one person. Plus, none of her reviews have a real name and photo attached to them. They're all anonymous or use letters or made-up names."

"Adam would fire you if he heard you begging my patients for reviews."

"So, I won't call from the office."

"Which means you're calling them on your own time and getting their numbers from their charts, which raises a ton of patient privacy issues."

She waved her hand. "This is Peace Falls. I see a patient whenever I go anywhere. All I have to do is tell them to spread the word, help some of the older ones set up a review account, so they can post, and I'm confident we can bring up your ratings. Dr. Cohen isn't in until nine. You could ask Rowan when she gets here. I'm sure she'd give you a glowing review."

I cleared my throat. "Um, I'll think about it. She's still in treatment."

Cammie raised her eyebrows at me. "What happened?"

"Nothing," I said shuffling a random stack of papers on my desk. "Can you scan these scripts into the system for me?"

"I would if they were scripts and not the productivity report Dr. Cohen asked me to put on your desk." She crossed her arms over her chest and glared at me. "Why wouldn't you ask Rowan for a review?"

"It wouldn't be appropriate. At least not until after we finish our sessions."

"My hairstylist asked me for a review. I don't think she meant it to be the end of our professional relationship."

"She's also my neighbor."

"All the more reason she'd write you a review, Cal. Or are you afraid she'd write something bad?"

Judging by the sounds she made when she came, I think I did alright.

Though I'd kept that last thought to myself, Cammie let out a sigh. "You owe me five bucks," she said and slunk out of my office.

I couldn't remember borrowing money from Cam, but I pulled a twenty from my wallet, walked to the reception area, and dropped the bill on her desk just as Rowan arrived.

"I said you owed me five," Cammie said and pushed the money back at me. "I wasn't about to risk a twenty on your impulse control."

Rowan's eyes widened and her face turned bright red.

"Are you ok?" I asked, reaching for her.

She took a step back and cleared her throat. "I'm fine, Dr. Cardoso. Should we get started?"

My stomach sank. Rowan looked like she wanted to disappear into the floor. I'd gone back and forth a hundred times yesterday about whether or not I should walk down the street and knock on the Stevens's door. I knew Rowan and I needed to discuss what happened, but I didn't know what to say. Usually, I set expectations before things got physical. I was down for a casual hookup, if she was, especially since we couldn't seem to keep our hands off each other, but I didn't want to hurt her feelings or make her recovery more difficult. I'd hoped to get a read on how she felt during our session, but judging by how uncomfortable she looked, we needed to clear the air right away, without Cam pretending not to eavesdrop.

"Let's warm up with stair training," I said, holding open the glass door.

Cam looked like she wanted to lean over the desk and smack me. She and I both knew stair training wasn't part of Rowan's treatment plan, and rarely something I did on the actual stairs. We had a step box that achieved the same exercise without risking a fall down a stone staircase. If Cammie suspected something was off between Rowan and me, I'd just confirmed it.

"You can leave your things here," Cammie said to Rowan with a smile.

Rowan handed over her large bag, which meant she planned to return to the office after our conversation. I smiled at her as she walked through the door, but her face remained blank. Once we were out of sight of the glass door, Rowan whirled around and shoved her finger in my chest.

"Did you also have a bet with Cammie about when you'd take your physical therapy out of the office?"

"What?"

"You know," she said, motioning her hands over my body, "*physical* therapy."

I couldn't help the laugh that escaped me. She was so adorable when she was flustered.

"I'm glad you find this amusing," she said, her eyes growing watery.

"No, Rowan." Before I could stop myself, I pulled her close. She was stiff in my arms at first but then melted against me with a shuddering breath. My chest tightened. I'd hurt her, that much was clear, but I had no idea how or why she thought I'd made a bet with Cam.

"Cammie said I owed her five bucks, so I paid her. I don't know anything about a bet. I assumed I borrowed cash from her at some point and forgot to pay her back."

"Did you tell her what happened between us?"

"No," I said. "Why would I?"

I thought that'd put her at ease, but she tensed in my arms and took a step back. "Of course," she said, wiping her eyes. "So, stairs."

"I'm sorry. I should have stopped by yesterday."

She waved her hand. "I misread the situation. Of course, you didn't tell Cammie about what happened the other night. I'm sorry I jumped to conclusions."

"About that," I said, taking a step closer. She straightened her spine, and all the warmth bled from her mossy green eyes. Everything stopped. My feet. My breath. I swear my heart stuttered. I backed away from her and pulled my tablet from my scrubs. "Let's see how you manage a flight or two before the heat mat."

She nodded and dutifully walked to the top of the stairs. On the rare occasion I did this type of exercise, I stayed beside the patient in case they needed help. This time, I remained on the top floor and watched her work down a flight, turn on the landing, and climb back up.

"Should I go again?" she asked, slightly out of breath.

"No, that's good."

She walked past me without a word, and I followed her into the office. Cammie looked between us and frowned. Rowan shuffled to the first table and laid face down. I ignored Cam's frantic hand gestures summoning me to her desk and grabbed the heat mat instead.

"Are you ok?" I asked, placing the mat on Rowan's back.

She closed her eyes. "I'm fine. Let's just forget about the other night and focus on fixing my back."

Which would be the sensible thing to do. Instead, I pulled the stool as close as I could to the table and took a seat beside her. "You know, when I was a kid, I never would have imagined I'd become a physical therapist."

She opened her eyes but didn't say anything. I figured that was enough permission to keep talking. "I switched between wanting to be a professional football player and a firefighter until I was twelve. Then, I decided I'd get a business degree and join my old man's real estate firm if pro-ball didn't work out. When I didn't get recruited for college, I knew my chances of joining the NFL were slim, so Dad and I had a long talk about the work he did, and the classes I should take." I stopped and took a deep breath. "Then, I shattered most of my right side in the accident." Her eyes softened, and I had to fist my hands on my knees to keep from reaching for her. "The doctors said it'd be unlikely I'd ever walk without a limp. I went through four surgeries, and after each, I'd go to physical therapy. At first, I didn't work very hard. Then, after I got Skye, I wanted to be able to run with her, so I did whatever the therapists asked, then I asked them for more. Little by little, I got stronger. Eventually, I could walk again. Then walk without a limp. By the time I finished PT, I could run, and I knew exactly what I wanted my life's work to be. My dad supported my decision all the way, and I've never looked back."

"Don't worry, Dr. Cardoso," she said closing her eyes again. "You keep training Chris, and I'll keep attending my sessions."

"I didn't tell you that story because I'm worried about my job," I said. "There's only one reason I ever talk about that time in my life."

I waited until she opened her eyes again to continue. "Sometimes I tell patients who are struggling, the ones who can't push through the pain to do the work they need to improve. But that's not you. From day one you've been motivated to get better."

She nodded. "So why tell me?"

"Because" I said. "I want you to know me. I want to tell you things I've never told anyone. Like how when the classes got really hard in college, I thought about Logan. He wanted to be an oncologist, and he would have been a great one. He was the smartest person I've ever known. He would have helped so many people, but he didn't have a chance. And for whatever reason, I did. So, instead of getting upset when I thought I had more work than I could do, I brewed some coffee, which I hate, by the way, and studied harder. I want you to know that. And I want to know more about your dad, and if it ever gets easier to miss someone. I want to know everything about you. I'm not sure what that means. You're still my patient. And you're only here temporarily, but I like spending time with you. I hurt you this morning, and I never want to do that again, so I guess I'm asking what I need to do to make things ok."

She smiled. "I think you just did."

"I'm glad to hear that, but you should know," I said, leaning close and lowering my voice. "I don't do relationships. Not since—" Not since my last one caused the accident. "I can't. Not that you're even looking for that, but whatever happens between us has to be casual. I should have said something before we did anything, but when I'm with you—" I stopped, feeling myself grow hard. "The things I want to do with you." I shook my head and blew out a breath, attempting to stop the rush of memories, some of which involved a certain pair of lace panties. "By the way, you're never getting your underwear back." Rowan gave me as startled look, then giggled. My dick made a valiant effort to push through my scrubs to find her.

"This blanket is stifling today," she said and fanned her reddening face.

"I'm going to roll this stool away and think about my great-aunt Martha, so I have myself under control before my boss arrives. If you have a saggy uncle, I suggest you do the same."

She laughed and the weight that had been pressing against my chest lifted, but a slight ache remained. I shoved away from the table, but instead of thinking about my elderly aunt, I pictured Rowan loading everything she owned into the back of Poppy's hearse and driving away.

CHAPTER SIXTEEN

Cal

AIDEN WAVED TO ME from a huge booth in the corner of the bar. I squeezed through the crowd and slid onto the bench across from him.

"How'd you snag this?" I asked.

Fridays at Church Street Brews were always packed, but the bar was especially crowded because amateur open mic night started in an hour. Our booth had a decent view of the stage without being in the middle of the crowd.

Aiden spread his arms wide on the bench and stretched. "I brought my crew for happy hour."

"And none of them wanted to stick around for open mic?"

"A few are still here," Aiden said, nodding his chin toward a group of men standing near the bar. "I told them to get lost just before you got here."

"That's cold man, even for you. There's plenty of room."

"For all the women we'll be inviting to join us," he said with a smirk. "Don't worry about my guys. They know the drill. Have a couple rounds on me then get lost. Besides, who'd want to hang out with their boss on a Friday night?"

"Definitely not me," I said.

A waitress stopped by the table with a full pitcher, a stack of plastic cups, and a can of Liquid Death.

"Thanks, Brandi," Aiden said with a wink and handed her a twenty. "Feel free to refill the pitcher whenever it's low and bring another can of that shit."

"You got it," she said and hurried off to a nearby table.

"I can start a tab," I said, reaching for my wallet.

Aiden shook his head. "I already have one."

"So, you just tip the waitress twenty every time she comes to the table?"

Aiden shrugged. "Her kid has a lot of medical shit. And I guarantee we'll never have to wait for drinks."

I shook my head. Typical Aiden. He liked everyone to think he's a complete dick, but he'd do anything for the guys on his crew, or anyone else who needed help. I leaned back and studied him.

Aiden poured me a beer and slid it across the table. "How's work going?"

"You wrote those reviews, didn't you?"

Aiden shrugged. "Thought it might help. I stopped when I saw how much it ticked off Avery. Sorry if I made things worse."

"Thanks, man," I said. "It was a good idea, but unless I can get her to take down the others soon, or at least stop posting, Cohen will fire me. He thinks I should sue Avery."

Aiden rolled his beer in his hands. "If she won't take them down, you might have to."

I shook my head. "She's hurt. I'm sure I can convince her to remove them, eventually."

"What happens if Cohen fires you before then? Will you get a job at another practice or start your own?"

I blew out a breath. "Honestly, I don't know. I doubt anyone else would take the risk, even if they knew the online stuff was bullshit. But with reviews like mine, I'd never be able to bring in enough patients to build a practice. At least not here. Even if I sued Avery to take them down, it would take a while, longer than I can afford to not work."

Aiden slumped back onto the bench. "Shit, you're right. You'd have to start over somewhere else."

I nodded. "Don't tell Theo."

Aiden glared at me. "How stupid do you think I am? I might swing a hammer all day, but I don't have shit for brains."

He grabbed his beer and tossed the whole cup back before crushing it against the table.

"Uh oh," Theo said sliding onto the bench beside Aiden. "Who pissed him off?"

Aiden shook his head. "Damn supplier. He said he'd have the tiles I needed by Wednesday. They still haven't arrived. Set the entire project behind."

"That sucks," Theo said, reaching for his non-alcoholic drink. "Who do I thank for this?"

Aiden held up his hand, and Theo nodded. "Thanks, man."

"You're driving my ass home later. I'm buying all night."

"You don't have to buy mine," I said.

"I said I was buying all night. Now, shut up and drink. I'm two rounds ahead of you already."

"Thanks for getting here early to grab a booth," Theo said. "I assume you wanted the extra space because you plan to get laid tonight."

Aiden nodded. "Observant as always. I have some tension to work off." He slapped Theo on the back and he winced.

"You ok?" I asked.

"Yeah," Theo said. "I got new ink today, and this dickhead found it."

Aiden smirked. "It's a gift. What'd you get?"

"Poppy," Theo said, looking across the bar.

"No shit," Aiden said. "I knew it. You and the Goth Pixie, huh? Is it her name or did you go symbolic and get the flower?"

"Shut up," Theo hissed. "I didn't get a fucking flower or her name. She just walked in."

My head snapped to the direction Theo pointed, and sure enough, Poppy was making her way toward the bar with Rowan and Lauren.

"Mind if I ask them over?" Theo asked.

"Sure," I said, relieved he'd suggested it, so I didn't have to. Aiden had been giving me shit about Rowan all week.

Aiden grunted and stared at his beer.

Theo slid from the booth and made his way to the women. Poppy smiled at him, which wasn't something she did often, and re-introduced him to Rowan. They shook hands, and I didn't miss the flash of shock that crossed her face. She pushed it down and said something that made Theo laugh. Lauren waved at Theo and headed to the bar, shooing Poppy and Rowan away.

"Hello again," Rowan said to me as she approached the booth. I stood and greeted her with a hug, the whole time fighting the urge to bury my face in her hair. She wore it down tonight in gentle waves that brushed the tops of her breasts, which peeked from a simple black tank top. Her short jean skirt showed off her toned legs, and I caught one of Aiden's guys checking her out. I motioned for her to slide into the booth first. Any asshole who tried to talk to her tonight had to lean over me. She reached across the table and offered Aiden her hand.

"Nice to see you again, Aiden," she said.

He gripped her fingers and ran his eyes up and down her body. "Very nice to see you, Rowan."

I cleared my throat and he dropped her hand with a chuckle. Theo watched the exchange and slid in beside him, creating a wall of tattooed muscle between Aiden and Poppy.

"Hey Aiden," Poppy said. "Mind passing the drink menu? I want to know what's in the fruity shit Lauren brings me."

"Sure thing," he said, grabbing the menu and shoving it down the table.

"How's Chris's training going?" Theo asked me and glanced at Aiden, who'd started shredding a napkin, something he used to do in high school whenever he was nervous about a game or asking out a girl. I hadn't seen him do it in years.

"Great. We're going to the park tomorrow at ten if you want to join us."

Theo nodded at Aiden, and I finally picked up the hint he was throwing down. "You should come, Aiden. Rowan and Poppy's little brother is trying out for wide receiver next month. I'm throwing him passes as best I can, but I was never a quarterback. He could learn a lot from you. He's really agile, and if he keeps improving his routes, I think he'll be a varsity starter."

"Really?" Rowan asked. "I mean, I think Chris is wonderful at whatever he does, but I'm biased."

"No, he's great," Theo said. "Special even. I'm surprised he didn't make varsity earlier."

Aiden narrowed his eyes. "How would you know?"

Theo chuckled and Poppy snuck a glance at him while pretending to read the drink menu. It was clear she liked him. Too bad Theo had left so much room between them he might as well be snuggling with Aiden.

"I watched y'all play for years," Theo said. "I know talent when I see it."

Aiden nodded. "Not sure what I could do for the kid. I can't throw for shit anymore."

"Have you tried?" Theo asked.

"I don't need to," Aiden snapped. "My shoulder still hurts like a bitch if I use it too much."

Theo nodded and shoved his back against the booth, shifting like he was trying to scratch an itch. To anyone else, it'd look innocent enough, but I knew better. I wanted to reach across the table and smack Aiden, and judging by the look on his face, he wished I would. Theo was hurting himself, right in front of us, rubbing his damaged skin to intensify the pain. I wasn't surprised he'd gotten another tattoo. He always marked his body in some way or another near the anniversary of the accident. Sometimes more than once. He claimed it was to honor Logan, and maybe that was part of it. But more than anything, he used the physical pain to ease his guilt.

"Stop," Aiden said, through gritted teeth.

Poppy and Rowan both stared at him, and then at Theo.

"What'd I miss?" Lauren asked, joining us with three tall pink drinks pressed together. She set them on the table and slid the first to Rowan. "Hey, Aiden," she said.

He gave her a brief nod and grabbed another napkin.

Rowan glanced between Lauren and Aiden and raised her eyebrows at her best friend. Lauren ignored her and slid into the booth beside me, passing Poppy a drink. I moved closer to Rowan to give Lauren space, and my thigh touched her leg. A bolt of lust shot through my body. Fuck, this was ridiculous. I hadn't felt so out of control since puberty.

"What is this?" Poppy said giving the glass a sniff. "I swear if it's some Carrie Bradshaw Cosmo shit, I'm throwing it at you."

"I'd never," Lauren said. "Besides, those come in a martini glass. Just try it."

Poppy brought the glass to her lips like it contained poison and sipped. "Mm," she said, and then slurped a hefty gulp. "Not bad."

"Don't tell her what it is," Rowan said, after taking a sip from her own glass. "Or she won't drink it."

"Do you know what it is?" Poppy asked, glaring at Rowan.

"Of course," Rowan said, taking another sip. "So would you if you didn't pretend to only like whiskey."

"May I?" I asked Rowan, and she slid the drink to me. It was crisp and fruity, and I couldn't taste the alcohol at all. These things could be lethal.

"Delicious," I said, handing the drink back to her. "Almost the best thing I've ever tasted."

Rowan blushed, and Theo smirked at me. Usually, Aiden would have as well but he was focused on destroying another napkin.

"Well, Cal, what the fuck is it?" Poppy snapped.

I shrugged. "I pretend to only like beer. Clearly, I've been missing out."

Poppy narrowed her eyes. "I hate all y'all."

Everyone laughed except Aiden.

"I've never been to open mic here," Rowan said, looking at the stage. "Are they any good?"

"It depends," Poppy said. At the rate she was going, she'd finish her drink before the first act. "We have some decent musicians in town, but we also have some tone-deaf ones with zero self-awareness."

"I hope Dr. Evers does his magic act tonight," Lauren said with a smile. Aiden shifted in his seat and stared at the napkin in his hands.

"I didn't know Dr. Evers was a magician," Rowan said, pushing her glass toward me. It tasted better than beer, and I enjoyed another sip before sliding it back to her.

"It's more comedy act than magic," I said. "Mrs. Evers is his assistant. She's the real comedian of the pair."

"Oh, I hope they're here tonight." Rowan scanned the room, but the bar was so crowded it was impossible to see everyone. "I haven't seen Mrs. Evers since I've been back."

"Check her Insta," Poppy said, eyeing her empty glass. "She usually posts if they're performing."

"You follow Mrs. Evers?" I asked.

"Of course," Rowan said with a smile. "She was my favorite teacher in high school."

"She hated me," I said, taking a sip of my beer.

"I doubt that," Rowan said. "I bet she just didn't worship you like all the others."

"That's an understatement," Theo said.

I shot him a look to shut the hell up. I'd just gotten back in Rowan's good graces. I didn't need Theo telling her about all the stupid shit I'd done in high school or how I almost flunked English. Luckily, he took the hint and asked Poppy about her current sculpture.

While Rowan rooted in her purse for her phone, I leaned over to Lauren and whispered, "Bring Poppy some water with the next round. She took that down pretty fast."

"I don't know," she whispered back. "Looks like someone will take care of her if she overindulges."

Poppy and Theo had started an animated conversation about some art exhibition in Charlottesville they both wanted to see, and he'd moved a couple inches closer.

"What's he drinking?" Lauren asked, looking at the can in Theo's hand. "I think they both need liquid courage, but I've never seen that before."

I shook my head. "He's straight edge," I said, pointing to the elaborate X tattoos on Theo's hands. Several lines appeared on her forehead, and I could tell she had no idea what I was talking about. "It means he doesn't drink, smoke, or do drugs."

"Never?" Rowan asked, leaning into the conversation.

I shook my head.

"What about sex?" Lauren asked.

"Let's just say I haven't seen him with a random hookup since he got those tattoos," I said.

"Damn," Lauren said, leaning back.

"Seriously, boss bitch," Poppy said to Lauren, holding up her glass. "What is this? I'll grab another round."

I laughed.

"Bet you wish you could call Dr. Cohen that," Rowan said, chuckling beside me.

"I got it," Lauren said, sliding from the booth, though she and Rowan still had half a drink each. "Can I get you anything, gentlemen?"

"We're set," Aiden said, and I realized it was the first words he'd spoken since Theo saw Poppy.

"So, are the Everses performing?" I asked Rowan, pointing at the phone in her hand.

"If they are, she didn't post anything about it." Her phone vibrated with an incoming text from *Brad*.

"Ugh," she said, dropping the phone on the table.

"Is that dickface again?" Poppy shouted.

Rowan nodded.

"Give me the fucking phone," Poppy said, holding out her hand.

"No, thank you. I only called him back because of the last thing you did to help me."

"I'm not going to talk to him. I'm going to block him since you're too chickenshit to do it."

"I'll just ignore him like I have all week."

"Is that your ex?" I asked.

Rowan nodded.

"Is he bothering you?"

Rowan said no at the same time Poppy said yes.

Poppy leaned over Theo and reached for Rowan's phone. When she still couldn't grab it, she crawled into his lap and bent over the table, her black-clad ass right in his face. Theo shut his eyes, looking pained, and Aiden laughed into his beer. Poppy swiped Rowan's phone and went back to her seat.

"Good luck opening it," Rowan said.

Poppy held the phone to her face and relaxed her features. "Ha," she said, showing Rowan the open screen. "Still got it."

"How did you do that?" Rowan asked. "And what do you mean still? How long have you been opening my phone with your face?"

I glanced between the sisters and noticed how similar they looked apart from their hairstyles and clothes. I really was the world's biggest idiot for not noticing the family resemblance when Rowan came to my office.

Lauren returned with three new drinks. Brandi followed her with a tray holding Theo's drink, a pitcher of beer, another of water, and a new stack of cups.

"Thanks, Brandi," Lauren said, "I'll see you and Max at story hour."

Brandi turned, but Aiden shouted, "Wait," and held up another twenty.

Brandi took it with a smile and left.

Lauren glared at him. "I tipped her."

"So, she got tipped twice," Aiden said. "I hope you put those on my tab."

"Why would I do that?" Lauren yelled.

Poppy stopped fiddling with Rowan's phone and stared at her. "I don't think I've ever heard you snap at someone."

"Me either," Rowan said.

"Here," Lauren said, shoving a cup of water at Poppy. "Drink this, and I'll give you another raspberry mojito."

Rowan let out a huff, but Poppy grabbed the water and chugged the entire glass in one go.

"Ok, then," Lauren said with a laugh and slid her another pink drink.

Poppy handed Lauren the phone. "Give this to my sister. I blocked dickhead."

"Good," Lauren said, handing the phone past me to Rowan.

"Please help me drink these," Rowan said, motioning to the pink glasses. "They're obviously bent on getting hammered tonight, and I'd rather not."

We finished the first drink together and moved on to the second, our fingers lingering with each pass of the glass. A microphone screeched, and we all looked to the stage where the first act, a semi-decent garage band made up of middle-aged dads, was setting up to play.

The evening unfolded with the typical mix of performers until a tall blonde took the stage for the final act. The entire bar quieted. Something about her drew everyone's attention in a way none of the other acts had. I felt a tug of recognition but couldn't place her. Her hands shook as she adjusted the microphone, but she took a deep breath and strummed a few quiet cords on her guitar.

"Is that Cammie?" Lauren said beside me. "I've never seen her in make-up or with her hair done like that."

"I think it is," Rowan said leaning into me to get a better look.

"Holy shit," I whispered as Cammie sang, her voice rich and clear.

"Did you know she could sing?" Rowan asked me when the song finished and the bar erupted in applause.

I shook my head.

"I'm going to tell her what a great job she did," Lauren said, but Cam walked straight off the stage and out the front door while the applause thundered around the bar.

"I'll try to catch her outside," Lauren said and pushed her way through the crowd toward the door.

"That was amazing," Rowan said, her eyes misty.

"It was," I said, surprised at how tight my voice sounded.

"Let's play darts," Poppy said, clapping her hands. "I always play better when I'm buzzed."

Rowan shifted beside me and winced. "Actually, I think I might walk home."

"What?" Poppy yelled. "It's not even midnight. You're not that old."

"I need to walk this kink out of my back."

"I'm sure Cal can help you with that," Aiden smirked.

I glared at him. It was clear she was in pain. I'd been so caught up in our conversations and the performances, I hadn't noticed how much time had passed. Apart from a brief trip to the restroom with her sister, she'd been sitting all night.

"I can drive you," Theo said.

"I'd rather walk," Rowan said. "It helps."

"Let's go," I said, taking her hand. "I'll come with you."

"You're seriously leaving me alone with these two?" Poppy said, motioning at Theo and Aiden. Neither seemed the least offended.

Rowan chewed her bottom lip. Poppy was more than tipsy. I knew she'd be safe with Theo, but I could understand why Rowan might not want to leave her sister with two men she didn't really know, especially when one looked like an extra on *Breaking Bad*.

"I'll make sure she and Lauren get home safe," Theo said. "And that Aiden behaves."

Rowan reached across the table and gave his hand a squeeze. "Thank you," she said and nudged me to slide out.

She had to do it a second time before I moved because I realized something that shook me. Rowan saw Theo, truly saw him for the man he'd become. And if she was perceptive enough to know him that clearly after only a few hours, what could she see in me?

CHAPTER SEVENTEEN

Rowan

CAL WAS QUIET AS we left Church, his hand rubbing gentle circles on the small of my back. It felt more comforting than therapeutic, but whatever he was doing helped relax my stiff muscles. I hadn't realized how loud and hot the bar had become until we stepped into the cool night air.

"Where are you two headed?" Lauren asked, walking toward us in the parking lot.

"My back is getting tight. We're walking home."

She nodded. "I'll make sure Poppy gets back ok."

"Theo has her," I said. "No sense in you walking all the way to Sullivan Street just to come right back here."

"He'll want to make sure you get home too," Cal added. "Let him. Or he'll worry."

"No problem," Lauren said.

"Did you catch up with Cammie?" I asked.

Lauren shook her head. "I'm texting her as soon as I get inside to tell her what a wonderful job she did. Call me tomorrow, Rowan." She beamed at us and pushed open the door to the bar, spilling loud voices and laughter into the parking lot.

"You really had no idea Cammie could sing like that?" I asked Cal, hoping he'd missed Lauren's not-so-subtle hint that she expected to hear how the night went.

Cal shook his head, his forehead scrunched.

"Hey," I said, stopping and placing my hand on his chest. "Are you ok?"

"You left your sister with Theo," he said quietly.

"Should I not have?" I asked, glancing back at Church. "She's determined to stay, and I figured he would take better care of her than anyone else there. Lauren seemed pretty clear-headed, but she's right with Poppy on the drink count."

"No, he'll make sure everyone is safe."

"Ok," I said.

Cal gripped the back of his neck. "He's a convicted felon," he said quietly. "He's done time. Real time, Rowan. Not a week in the county jail. Most people are scared of him. I saw the way you looked at him when he walked over to Poppy. He scared you too."

"No," I said, my anger rising. "He surprised me. The last time I saw Theo he didn't have any tattoos or dress the way he does now. But none of that means anything. You forget, Poppy is my sister. I know better than anyone that the people who try the hardest to push others away are often the kindest. The most vulnerable, even. I'm surprised you'd even bring it up. Isn't he one of your best friends?"

"So, you're honestly saying, you wouldn't be concerned if Theo and Poppy started dating?" Cal asked.

"Why would I be? They're both adults. They seem to have a lot in common. And it'd be clear to anyone who spent five minutes with Theo that he's incredibly caring and thoughtful."

"Most people in Peace Falls think he's dangerous," Cal said, an expression in his eyes I couldn't quite read. Sadness. Fear. Guilt.

"Well, screw those people," I said, really getting mad. "And shame on you for thinking I'm one of them."

"How did you end up with someone like Brad then?" he asked, rubbing his forehead like he was trying to solve a complex calculus problem without a calculator. "If you understand Theo so well, in so little time, how did you marry a guy who would cheat on you? Not only that, but someone who had the balls to do it at work where you could catch him? How, Rowan?"

"Because," I said, my voice shaking. "I saw what I wanted to see."

A dog barked in a nearby yard, and I realized how loud we'd been talking. No doubt, the houses around Church had heard worse, but I wasn't about to make a spectacle of myself on Saints and Sinners Street. I walked past Cal and set off toward Broad. Tears leaked from my eyes, and I swatted them away. I stumbled along the dark sidewalk past a couple houses before Cal ran up beside me.

"Please don't fall," he said quietly, taking my elbow. He gripped me, tight, and repeated it again, like he was giving himself the same warning.

We walked the rest of the way in silence, his hand steady on my arm. When we reached the corner of Sullivan and Broad, I stopped. Mom had left the porch light on for my sister and me, just like she'd done in high school. The living room lights were off, so at least she hadn't waited up like she used to when we were younger.

"Good night, Cal," I said. "I can make it from here on my own."

He let go of my arm, and I walked toward the house. He waited until I reached Mr. Twillings's yard to speak. "How did you do it?" he asked.

I turned and waited.

"How did you open up enough to fall in love after losing your dad?" he asked, walking toward me. He looked terrified, the raw fear carving his strong features into something fragile. I doubted Cal allowed many people to see him like this, and the fact he was allowing me made my chest ache.

"I guess I never thought of it that way," I answered softly. "To be fair, it wasn't an issue. At least not for a long time. My dad died before I was interested in boys. Then no one wanted to date me in high school or college. Well, maybe they did in college, but I spent most of my weekends at home. I went on a few first dates, but I was so awkward the guys moved on pretty fast. I didn't meet Brad until I started at Pinnacle Group. For whatever reason, he took an interest in me despite how much I fumbled our first conversations. To answer your question from before, I guess I was excited to finally have someone's attention, so I ignored the way he looked at other women or the lies I sometimes caught him telling."

"Brad was your first boyfriend?" he asked, stepping so close I could feel the heat rolling off his body.

"First everything really," I said with a shrug.

"Am I the second?" Cal asked.

"That depends," I said. "You can't be my second boyfriend if you don't do relationships."

"No," he said, his eyes sad, "I can't."

"But," I said, my heart racing, "You are the second man I've kissed, and the second to um, you know."

Cal threw his head back and laughed. "You can't even say it."

"Not in the street, Caleb. My house is right there."

"I love when you call me that," he said. He leaned in and placed his mouth on the shell of my ear. "Say it again."

"Caleb," I breathed, and he sucked the delicate skin on my neck. My breath caught and my knees weakened. He wrapped his powerful arms around me and pressed me close, so I could feel his hard length.

"This is all I can give you," he said, rocking into me. "But it's yours if you want it."

I moaned and he captured my mouth in a brutal kiss. Our tongues clashed for control. His hands tangled in my hair. I ran my hand down his body. His grip tightened to the point of pain and sent a throb of need between my legs. I took a step back.

He let out a slow breath, turned, and began walking toward his house.

"Don't touch me," I said, following him. "Until we're inside."

He stopped. After a moment, he started walking again, faster than he had before.

When we got to his house, he paused at the front door. "Wait here," he said. "I need to get Skye settled."

I nodded.

He pulled a key from his pocket and leaned his forehead against the door. "Promise me you won't leave," he said, his voice pained. "If I go inside now, promise me you'll be here when I get back."

"I promise," I said. Without another word, he put the key in the lock and Skye started barking inside. He slipped through the door, closing it behind him. I could hear him greet her and walk toward the back of the house.

As soon as I was alone, the reality of what I was about to do slammed into me. Was I ready to be with someone else? Someone like Cal who could be nothing more than a good time. I gripped the railing to keep from running back to my house. I knew I could change my mind if I wanted, but I couldn't leave before he returned, not after he'd made me promise. It's like he'd known I'd second guess my decision the moment he was gone. I heard some shuffling inside the house and the door opened, casting Cal in silhouette.

He held the storm door open and waited. I might regret staying, but I knew I'd think back to this moment again and again if I walked away. I let go of the railing and followed him inside. As soon as the door closed behind me, Cal lifted me up and pressed me against it. His hands roamed every inch of my heated skin, his fingers sending electric sparks straight to my core. He pressed against me, and my back hit the door at an uncomfortable angle. I stiffened.

"Shit," he said. "Are you ok?"

I nodded, but he spun and carried me to a room at the end of a long hallway. Light from the hall revealed a king-sized bed with a dark-colored comforter, the outline of a dresser, a chair. That's all I had time to see before Cal placed me carefully on the bed.

"Please don't treat me like I'm breakable," I said, grabbing his shirt and attacking the buttons. His chest heaved as I pushed the shirt from his shoulders. I explored the ridges on his stomach with my fingers, the deep V at his waist. His breath became shallower with every touch.

He closed his eyes and threw his head back when I unbuttoned his shorts and eased my hand inside to touch him. I ran my fingers along the smooth skin of his crown and his eyes shot open.

He grabbed my hand and eased it from his skin before taking a step back. My cheeks heated. I must have done something wrong, something to make him change his mind. Why would Caleb Cardoso want to sleep with me? He placed a gentle hand on my chin and lifted it until our eyes locked.

"Whatever you're thinking," he said. "Stop."

I nodded.

"I know you're not breakable, but if you keep touching me like that, I'm afraid I'll be too rough."

I let out a frustrated breath. Cal was practically naked, the tip of his impressive manhood peeking out his open shorts, while I still had every piece of clothing in place. I reached for the hem of my shirt and pulled it over my head. Cal's eyes darkened. I stood, unbuttoned my skirt, and let it drop to the floor, leaving me in nothing but my lacy black bra and matching thong.

Cal gripped my hip. "You'll tell me if I'm hurting you."

I nodded.

"Say it."

"I'll tell you if you're hurting me."

He closed his eyes and pressed his forehead to mine. "Take everything off and lay flat on the bed."

I unclasped my bra, then slid my thong off. He hummed a sound of approval but waited until I was on the bed to push his shorts and boxers completely down, freeing himself. "Holy shit," I said before I could stop myself. "Are you worried about hurting my back or something else?"

He laughed. "It's your back I'm worried about."

I nodded because anything I could think to say sounded awkward as hell, even to me. I seriously questioned how all of him could fit.

Cal walked to the edge of the bed and bent my leg, placing soft kisses on my ankle and the back of my knee. He did the same thing to my other leg, making space for him to crawl between my thighs. He'd barely touched me, but I was so turned on, I felt like I would come the moment he brushed my sensitive skin. He leaned over me and sucked my nipple into his mouth, hard. A bolt of pleasure sent me arching off the bed. Slowly, painfully so, he gave the other breast the same treatment.

I gritted my teeth and growled.

He kissed up and down my legs, avoiding the place I needed him most. When his tongue finally swirled against my clit, I let out a garbled sound, my orgasm ripping through me with embarrassing speed.

With a wicked grin, he opened the drawer of the nightstand by the bed. A rustle of foil as he ripped opened a condom, a pause while he took himself in his hand and rolled it down his hard length, and then he was easing into my slick depths.

"Fuck," he whispered, propping himself up, so we were eye to eye. He went in another inch and moaned. The sound was so erotic, I clenched around him.

"Try to relax, baby," he said. He reached between us and brushed his finger against my clit. I arched into him. He eased himself in with gentle thrusts, filling and stretching me in ways I'd never known.

"You feel so good," he murmured in my ear, pulling nearly all the way out and then rocking back into me. He started a rhythm that made me lose all sense of time. There was only him and the feeling of our bodies sliding together. I called his name as I came a second time and he jerked inside me, finding his own release with a groan.

He pulled out gently and rolled beside me, brushing a strand of hair from my face.

"How's your back?" he asked, his expression serious.

"You did not just ask me that," I said swatting his chest. He captured my hand and kissed my fingertips.

"Just making sure you're up for round two," he said with a grin that left me worried he'd leave my heart far more damaged than my back.

Chapter Eighteen

Cal

I woke to Skye's nose in my face like every other morning. Except instead of being in the bed beside me, she stood on the floor, giving me a stern look. Memories of last night came roaring back. I rolled over and found Rowan sleeping with her arm thrown over her face. Her long red curls fanned across the pillow. I resisted the urge to kiss her but couldn't stop admiring her while she slept.

Skye gave a frustrated snort, and I rolled back to rub her ears. This was not our usual routine. When I had company, I put Skye in the laundry room with her dog bed and a few extra treats and shut the door. The women I slept with never spent the night. After they left, I opened the door to the laundry room. Skye either followed me to my room or kept sleeping in her bed. She'd never opened the door herself, but then again, I'd never left her in the laundry room all night.

I grabbed my phone, checked the time, and groaned. 4:45AM was early, even for Skye, but once she was awake, she needed to go outside. Rowan stirred beside me.

"Don't get up," I said, swinging my feet to the floor. "I just have to take Skye out."

Rowan's eyes snapped opened at the sound of my voice. She sat up, looking startled, and my stomach sank. Maybe she'd had more to drink last night than I thought. Maybe she was regretting waking up with me. Skye caught sight of her and let out an excited bark before jumping onto the bed.

Rowan giggled as Skye licked her face, and the tension in my chest eased.

"What time is it?" she asked when Skye hopped off the bed and started prancing beside it. I had about two minutes to get her outside, or I'd be cleaning pee from the carpet.

"Not even five," I said, grabbing my shorts from the floor and pulling them on.

"Good," she said. "I might be able to sneak into the house before Mom wakes up."

She pulled the comforter from the bed and wrapped it around her body before searching around in the dark for her clothes, which Skye mistook for a new game. My dog grabbed Rowan's bra in her mouth and started shaking her head from side-to-side like she'd won it.

"Give me that," I said, taking the bra and handing it to Rowan. "Sorry for the dog spit."

She laughed. "I think I'll go braless this morning."

My cock liked that idea, but instead of taking my shorts off again like I wanted, I grabbed my shirt and pulled it over my head. "Let me take out Skye, then I'll walk you home."

She nodded, clutching her clothes in front of her. I'd explored every inch of her body last night, but I had a feeling she wouldn't get dressed unless I left.

I walked through the house with Skye to the laundry room, then opened the back door, so she could do her business. I stayed inside, listening for Rowan. I hoped she didn't try to sneak out the front door. Skye scampered back in record time and bolted for the bedroom.

"Incoming," I shouted, running after her.

When I reached the bedroom, Rowan was on the floor rubbing Skye's belly.

"Did she knock you over?" I asked, my heart pounding.

"No," Rowan said and laughed. "I was looking for my underwear. I'm not leaving another pair behind."

I chuckled and held out my hand, "Let me help you up, and I'll find it."

She gripped my hand. After I pulled her up, I dragged her close and wrapped my arms around her. "Good morning," I said, kissing her neck. "I had a great time last night."

She let out a little sigh and took a step back. "I did too, but I really need to get home before Mom wakes up. She'll either think I'm jumping into something too soon or get too excited because she thinks I'm moving on with you."

I nodded. "Let's find your underwear."

Rowan shoved her bra into her purse, and I tried not to notice how sexy she looked in her tank top without it. I found her thong between the bed and the nightstand and helped her into it. It took every ounce of self-restraint I had to pull my hands from under her skirt.

"Stay," I said to Skye. She jumped onto the bed and curled into a ball on the side Rowan had just left. No doubt, after waking me before dawn, my dog would be snoring before I got back.

I held Rowan's hand on the walk to her house. I loved the silence of Sullivan Street early in the morning, knowing so many families were tucked in their houses, sleeping. The ache that usually filled my chest on peaceful mornings like these didn't appear. I gave Rowan's hand a playful squeeze and she squeezed it back, the street too dark for either of us to see anything beyond the beam of light from my cell phone. I stopped when the beam landed on Theo's truck parked in front of the Stevens's house.

The porch light was on, but the house remained dark.

"Theo stayed over," I said, pointing to the black truck.

"Well, guess they aren't just friends anymore."

I shook my head, unease tightening my stomach. "I don't know. Theo has his own place. Would it have ever crossed your mind to invite me back to your house with your mom and brother home?"

"No," she said, her grip on my hand tightening. "But Poppy does have a studio in the backyard."

"And you think they'd go there instead of his apartment?"

Rowan tugged my hand as she started walking to the backyard. Light spilled onto the grass from the windows of a small building on the edge of the lot.

"Um, how should we handle this?" Rowan said. "I don't want to walk in on my sister with a guy. My eyeballs would never recover."

"I'll knock," I said, walking to the shed. Rowan stood behind me like I was her personal shield. I gave the door a light tap and Theo swung it open a moment later.

"Cal," he said. "Can you check Poppy? I've been checking her pulse every so often—"

"What's happened?" Rowan said, shoving me and then Theo aside with surprising strength. I followed her inside where Poppy laid curled on a futon with a trashcan by her head. Rowan knelt beside her and gave her sister's shoulder a shove. She didn't move.

"She threw up twice and then passed out," Theo said, his voice rough.

"How much did she have to drink after we left?" Rowan asked, brushing the short black hair from Poppy's face.

"One more of the same drink she'd had all night. Then some idiot insisted she take shots with him. I dropped off Lauren around one and then Aiden. By the time we got back here, Poppy was slurring her words. I figured she'd rather come to her studio than inside. I tried to get her to drink water, but then she got sick. I couldn't leave her."

Theo looked like he wanted to be sick himself.

"How was Lauren when you dropped her off?" Rowan asked.

"Tipsy, but judging by how much she and Aiden were bickering, she seemed fine. Shit, I didn't even think to check on her. I don't have her number. She didn't take any shots that I saw."

"I'm sure she's fine," Rowan said, but she looked worried.

"Let me check Poppy," I said, crossing the room to kneel beside Rowan. I lifted Poppy's wrist and measured her pulse. Her heart rate and breathing were steady. Her skin didn't feel clammy or appear blue. I sat her upright and snapped my fingers in her face. Poppy opened her eyes a slit, groaned, and shut them. I laid her down on her side. "She's going to feel terrible when she wakes up, but I don't think she needs to go to the hospital. Rowan, you should stay with her in case she gets sick again."

Rowan nodded.

"I'll stay," Theo said, pacing back and forth.

I had a feeling he'd done that a lot over the past few hours. Rowan put her hand on my shoulder to steady herself but stood on her own and walked to Theo.

"Thank you," she said, placing a gentle hand on his arm. "You've taken really good care of her, but I know my sister. She's going to be embarrassed when she wakes up, and if she sees you here, she'll feel so much worse. I promise to stay with her, and if you give me your number, I can text you updates, if you want."

Theo fumbled in his pockets and pulled out his cell. "Here," he said handing it to her. "Text yourself so I have your number too."

I didn't even have Rowan's number. A fact that bothered me more than it should. I lived right down the street and saw her in the office twice a week. Chris's number was one of my top contacts since he walked Skye. Hell, I even had Poppy and Rose's numbers. I could reach Rowan anytime I wanted. *While she's here.* My chest tightened.

Rowan sent herself a text from Theo's phone. It buzzed in her purse, and I fought the urge to hand her my phone as well. She gave Theo his and pulled him into a tight hug. "She'll be fine," Rowan said. He wrapped his arms around her and hugged her back. They stepped apart and he ducked his head.

"Come on, brother," I said, standing. "You can crash in my guest room for a couple hours before Chris's training. Go ahead, I'll catch up."

He nodded and left the shed without a word.

"He was pretty shaken," Rowan whispered. "Honestly, Poppy seems fine to me. I might have slept beside her with a trashcan on the floor, but I wouldn't have stayed awake all night."

I felt a small smile tug at my lips. "He's been taking care of Aiden and me for years when we've had too many. He knew exactly what to look for to know she wasn't in serious trouble. And you're right, with us he'd have just rolled us on our sides and slept nearby. He must really like her."

Rowan nodded. "The fact she let him bring her here speaks volumes. She doesn't allow any of us inside her studio. After I check on Lauren, I'm 100% snooping around. I love seeing Poppy's works in progress, but she refuses to show us anything until it's finished."

I took Rowan's face in my hands. "Well, don't let me keep you from your snooping," I said, placing a soft kiss on her mouth.

I wanted to ask when I could see her again. Monday was too far away, and I didn't want our next meeting to be at the office. Part of me wanted to make the most of the time we had before she moved on, but a larger part told me to keep my distance. She needed to understand that things between us were casual. "I'll see you," I said.

The smile slipped from her face momentarily, but she forced it back with a nod. My stomach sank as I closed the shed door behind me. When I reached the street, I found Theo standing by his truck, waiting.

"I'm going to head home," he said. "I'll be wrecked for work later if I get up and train with y'all. Tell Chris I said hi."

"You sure? We could grab Skye and take a walk first."

He chuckled and opened the door, the interior light illuminating his tired face. "Those Stevens sisters," he said. "I'm a shit substitute for Rowan."

"What the hell does that mean?" I said, walking around the front of his truck to stand beside him. "I thought you might not want to be alone after staying up all night worrying about a girl you obviously care about. I thought maybe you'd want to spend time with Skye to calm down. I did not invite you back because I needed the company. Forgive me for giving a shit."

"Admit it," he said, leaning into my face. "You like her, and that scares you to death."

"Rowan and I had sex. Big deal. I know you're not into casual hookups, but it works fine for me."

Theo nodded. "Keep telling yourself that, brother."

"Forgive me for not taking advice from a guy who feels too guilty to live his own life."

Theo rubbed his forehead. "I'm going to go before you say something you regret."

He climbed into the truck and slammed the door. As he drove away, I knew he hadn't left soon enough. I'd said plenty to regret.

CHAPTER NINETEEN

Cal

CHRIS KNOCKED ON MY door just before ten. I'd spent the last five hours doing tasks I hated around the house. I'd steamed the floors, paid bills, and scrubbed the inside of the fridge. Skye slept through most of it, padding out of the bedroom around nine to watch me rip everything from the kitchen pantry and wipe down the shelves.

"Let me grab my stuff," I said, excited to finally leave the house.

"Actually," Chris said, shifting his feet. "Can I come in, and talk to you for a minute?"

"Sure," I said opening the door wider. Skye ran to him, and he bent to pet her before walking to the living room and taking a seat on the couch.

"What's up?" I asked, sitting beside him.

"This is awkward," he said, rubbing his forehead.

Shit. I braced myself to talk about condoms or first times or any number of things a kid his age without a dad might ask. But what he said next caught me completely off guard.

"I like you."

I cleared my throat. "Um, Chris, I'm flattered but—"

Chris narrowed his eyes. "I'm not done. Why do adults always do that? Think they know where a conversation is going and interrupt before you can get the words out."

"Sorry," I said.

"I like you. As a friend, to be clear," he said, glaring at me. He let out a breath. "You're kind of like the brother I never had."

My throat tightened. "Thanks, Chris. That means a lot to me."

Chris slapped his legs and gritted his teeth. "I'm not done."

I pressed my lips together.

"As I was saying, I like you, but Ann is my favorite person in the whole world. She's been through a lot. So just don't be a dick, ok?"

"I'm not following."

He blushed bright red. "I saw you bring her home this morning."

"Ok," I said, standing. "Time out. Rowan and I are adults. Whatever happens between us is our business. Not yours."

Chris stood so fast Skye barked. I had at least twenty pounds of muscle on him, but the rage on his face made me take a step back. "I won't stand by and watch someone else hurt her." His breathing was rapid, his eyes bright, and it hit me that the kid was devastated.

"Hey," I said, gently. "I'm not her asshole ex."

Chris nodded and spun around, putting his back to me to swipe at his eyes.

"I know she's been through a lot," I said. "And I get you want to protect her, but she's a grown woman. You have to let her make her own choices."

He nodded and sniffed. "Forget I said anything. Let's go train."

He stalked past me and out the door. Skye watched him leave and gave me a reproachful look for the second time today. I grabbed my gear, and she perked up and followed me out the door. Chris was standing beside my SUV with his arms crossed, staring down the street toward his house. I glanced at the front porch, but Rowan wasn't there. I wondered if Chris had talked to her already, or if she was still in the shed taking care of Poppy. I knew better than to ask.

"Why don't you warm up with a run to the park," I said. "I'll meet you there." It was a dick move and Chris knew it, but he took off.

Skye stuck her head out the window and barked at him when we passed. I parked on Main and snapped a leash on her before grabbing all the gear. I found a bench beneath a shade tree and dropped everything in a pile while Skye settled on the ground. Pushing down the erotic replays of Rowan that kept entering my thoughts, I let the quiet of the park ease the lingering tension from my conversation with Chris. Aiden took a seat beside me just as Chris turned into the park.

"He's fast," Aiden said without so much as a hello. "I watched him sprint down Main Street."

"And dedicated. I'm glad you came."

Aiden shook his head. "Believe me, I tried not to. But I was curious. I might bust Theo's balls, but he has a great eye, especially for someone who hates sports."

Chris ran toward us. I stood and Aiden did the same, eyeing my dog with the usual apprehension.

"Chris, this is Aiden. Aiden, Chris," I said, introducing them. "Aiden played quarterback with me for years."

"Yeah, I remember," Chris said with a smile. "Ann took me to my first game when I was in kindergarten. I made her take me to every one after. Your senior year was epic."

Aiden nodded. I knew the compliment was bittersweet, and Chris, being the observant kid he was, seemed to sense it and changed the subject.

"Did Cal tell you I'm trying out to be a wide receiver on the varsity team?"

"He did," Aiden said.

"I'm pretty confident about my speed and timing," Chris continued. "My hand skills have improved a lot since I started working with Cal. I'm catching passes I would have missed last year, but I'm not consistent. Would you mind watching me catch a couple times?"

"Sure," Aiden said sinking down on the bench. Skye walked to him and flopped on the ground at his feet. Aiden glared but didn't ask me to move her.

Chris and I completed running passes back and forth until Aiden called us to the bench.

"You've got a good read on your skills," Aiden said. "But anyone can catch a ball when no one is trying to stop them. My granny could have completed all those passes."

"Don't take that too hard," I said, slapping Chris on the back. "His grandma taught him everything he knows."

Aiden shrugged. "Everything except how to take a tackle. She tried, but she doesn't weigh a hundred pounds wet. Let's see how you do under pressure. Toss me the ball."

Chris threw the ball to Aiden, and he flipped it in his hands a few times. "Ok kid," he said with a big smile. "Let's see how you do while Cal tries to get in your way. Go."

Chris and I sprinted through the park. I blocked Aiden's first pass and intercepted the next, but as we continued throwing the ball back and forth, Chris caught more and more.

"Get back over here," Aiden called. My lungs felt like they were about to burst as we made our way to him, but I couldn't erase the smile from my face.

"You're not watching the ball into your hands," Aiden said to Chris. "You're thinking ahead to what's going to happen after the catch. Focus on the moment. It doesn't matter if you avoid the tackle if you drop the ball because you're not watching it."

Chris nodded.

"I'd have you run some more routes, but Cal looks like he could use a break. See that wall over there," Aiden said, pointing to the playhouse that Skye had hid inside. "Bounce the ball against it until your arm feels like it wants to fall off or a kid gets in your way. Vary the speed and angle with each throw. Every time you miss the catch after it bounces, drop and do ten pushups."

Chris took off for the playground equipment, and I joined Aiden on the bench after chugging half my water.

"So," Aiden said a while later as Chris dropped to do a set of pushups. "How'd it go with Rowan last night?"

I rubbed my forehead. "Great. This morning, not so much. Theo and I got into it, and I said some things I shouldn't have."

"Is that why the asshole isn't here?"

I shook my head. "Poppy got sick, so he stayed up all night watching over her. He only left when I brought Rowan home at five this morning."

"Huh," Aiden said and shifted on the bench. "I didn't think she was that shitfaced. Did anyone check on Lauren? She had almost as much as Poppy."

"I think Rowan did after I left."

Aiden pressed his lips into a tight line. "You think or you know?"

"Honestly, I have no idea. Theo said she seemed ok when he dropped her off, and he doesn't think she had shots like Poppy did. I'm sure Lauren is fine. Poppy drank too much, but she wasn't in danger. Theo overreacted because he likes her."

Aiden glared at me. "Let me guess, you pushed him too hard about Poppy, and he gave you shit about messing around with Rowan."

"Pretty much. Then I thought Chris was going to take a swing at me. He saw me with his sister and insisted we have a talk. It got a little heated."

Aiden chuckled. "Can you blame him?"

"What happens between me and Rowan is none of his damn business."

Aiden shook his head. "If I ever saw you walking one of my sisters home at five in the morning, I'd be taking more than a swing at you. You'd have to call Theo to drive your ass to the hospital."

"That's different. Your sisters are all married."

"I'd beat your ass even if they weren't. You go through women like paper towels. Bet he knows that too," Aiden said, nodding his chin toward Chris.

"You're one to talk."

Aiden shook his head. "I'm an unapologetic asshole. Ain't no one falling in love with me. Women use my body, like I use theirs, and move on. But with someone like you, they're bound to want more."

"I don't play with feelings. Anyone I spend time with knows it's just fun."

Aiden nodded. "And you think Rowan is a casual fuck kind of girl?"

No. "I told her what to expect from me. Besides, she's looking for jobs anywhere but here. What's so wrong with letting off a little steam together?"

"Same reason you never should have fucked around with Avery."

"Avery and Rowan are nothing alike."

"They're more alike than you want to believe. You and Avery were serious in high school. Why would she ever believe you just wanted something casual now?"

"Because I told her. Just like I told Rowan."

Aiden shook his head. "Face it, man, you crushed Avery. And Chris is worried you'll do the same to Rowan. A chick doesn't go Kill Bill on a guy's reputation unless she has feelings for him. You loved Avery once. I'm sure she thought you were falling for her again."

"I didn't love her."

Aiden shook his head. "If that were true, would you have been so upset when she dumped you?"

We never talked about that night. Ever. Sometimes we'd mention the fallout: Mine and Aiden's recovery, Theo's trial and time in prison. We spoke of Logan often, memories that made us laugh so hard we couldn't breathe, but never how he died. The sequence of events that led to those tragic consequences wasn't something we revisited.

"Don't," I said.

"It'll be ten years next month."

"You think I've forgotten?"

"Of course not," Aiden snapped. "I just meant it's been a long time, and we still can't talk about it. Theo hurts himself every chance he can. You push away anyone who gets too close, and I want to beat the shit out of something all the time. We're all still fucked up, and I'm starting to think we always will be."

I didn't know what to say. He was right. But that didn't mean I had a clue how to change things.

Aiden blew out a long breath. "All I'm saying is, the kid had every right to get protective. He's got a good head on his shoulders, and he's got talent. Real talent."

I nodded, relieved we were changing the subject. "I have no doubt he'll make varsity."

"Fuck that, we're getting the kid scouted," Aiden said, slapping my back. "How often are you training with him?"

"We do drills two or three times a week. We run and lift the other days."

"That's why you've been ghosting me at the gym?"

"That and you're a competitive asshole who takes all the fun out of it."

Aiden threw his head back and laughed. "I'm just pushing you, dumbass. Speaking of which, I better stop the kid before he pukes. Come on back, Chris."

Chris ran up to us and bent with his hands on his knees. "How was that?"

"Good," Aiden said, "but your form falls apart when you're tired. Grab some water and stretch out your shoulders."

Chris nodded and did as he was told. Aiden tried not to smile.

"You like coaching," I whispered.

"What's not to like. I get to order someone around. Hey, Chris," he said louder. "How serious are you about football?"

"I'd play it every day if I could."

Aiden nodded. "Good, because you are. You're going to be drilling with me or Cal every day until tryouts. And keeping up with your cardio and weights."

Chris beamed at him. "Sounds great."

"And I want to know what you eat in a day. You need more muscle unless you want to get the shit knocked out of you every play."

They started talking about different ways to up Chris's protein intake, and I knelt to scratch Skye's ears. She gave my hand a lick and stared up at me with her wise eyes. My chest tightened. Aiden and Theo were right. I pushed women away. I had my parents, my friends, and my dog, and that was enough for me. But for the first time since Avery started blasting me online, I considered the possibility that I might owe *her* an apology. I pulled my phone from my bag and texted her.

> *I'm sorry, Ave. Can we meet up?*

Her response was immediate.

Avery

> *Wow. A booty text before noon. Something must be stressing you out*

> *You should know*

Avery

Sorry baby, I'm not interested in what you have to offer

A conversation, Ave. That's all I want

Avery

I don't believe you

We need to talk. Face-to-face. Please

I waited awhile, but when she didn't respond, I texted *You know where to find me.* The fact she'd texted back at all was progress. I shoved my phone in my bag and grabbed a couple resistance bands. Avery would come around eventually, like she always did. I just hoped it would be soon enough to save my job. "Let's do some arm pulls."

"Man," Aiden said shaking his head. "You're lucky, kid. You get private sessions with the best PT in the state. Did you know Cal graduated first in his program? What'd you do to get him to help you in the first place?"

Chris grinned at me, and I felt the tension between us ease. "Run faster than Skye. I'm the only other person he trusts to walk her."

Aiden looked at Skye and shook his head. "Dog people."

Chapter Twenty

Rowan

Poppy slumped into a kitchen chair and put her head on the table. "Damn Lauren, and her delicious cocktails."

I chuckled and checked the dough I had rising on the counter. "I'm sorry. In her defense, you sucked them down pretty fast."

"They didn't taste like alcohol." Poppy lifted her head and gave me a bleary-eyed stare. "I figured they were weak."

I shook my head. Poppy groaned and put her head back on the table.

"I'm making you monkey bread," I said, pulling a clump of dough from the bowl.

"With pecans?" Poppy mumbled into the table.

"Sure."

"And bacon."

"Um, that's not usually in monkey bread, but why not."

Poppy propped her head in her hands and watched me form the dough into balls and roll them in melted butter, cinnamon, and sugar. I hummed while I whisked together brown sugar, butter, and cream in a saucepan, cooking it until a rich, golden caramel formed.

"You got laid, didn't you?" Poppy said.

I'd been so focused on what I was doing, I'd almost forgotten she was there. I snapped off the gas burner and grabbed the pecans from the cabinet, ignoring her question.

"Yep," Poppy said as I started assembling the monkey bread in a Bundt pan, layering the pecans, dough, and caramel.

"Shoot, I forgot the bacon," I said. "I should have made it before the caramel."

Poppy waved her hand. "We can add it on top after the bread bakes."

I slid the monkey bread into the oven and set the timer while Poppy studied me like a specimen under a microscope. After all the exertion of last night and working in the kitchen this morning, my back was begging me to lie down and stretch. Poppy had other ideas.

"So, are you and Cal a thing now?" she asked as I tried to escape the kitchen.

I let out a sigh. Poppy wouldn't rest until she had an answer, and I worried she'd get sick if she tried to follow me upstairs. "Do you want coffee? It would help with your headache, assuming you have one."

"Of course, I have one," she said with an exaggerated sigh. "I don't see how you don't after a night of those demon drinks."

"Cal and I shared them," I said pouring her a mug. "You and Lauren drank twice as many as I did." Poppy may tell people she drank her coffee black like her soul, but I added enough sugar and milk to qualify it as a dessert.

"I hope she's just as hungover as me," Poppy said, rubbing her forehead.

I laughed and handed her a mug. "She was opening Karma when I texted her at five to make sure she was ok. She has a freakishly high tolerance for alcohol."

"That would have been good information to know before last night." Poppy took a sip of coffee and groaned. "So how did you take care of me and sleep with Cal? Please don't tell me you did the nasty in my studio."

I pulled out a chair and joined her at the table, even though sitting made the pain in my back worse. "What was the last thing you remember?"

"Watching a chick who looked like Cammie sing."

"That was Cammie."

"Really? Was she good or was that the booze?"

"She was amazing."

Poppy nodded. "Glad I remember it. But honestly, everything after that is fuzzy. What happened?"

I felt a stab of guilt. She was worse off when I left the bar than I thought. "Um, I went home with Cal after that."

Poppy's eyes widened. "You left me?"

"With Theo. He promised to make sure you got home ok. And he did. He was taking care of you when I got back this morning."

Poppy paled and wrapped her arms around her stomach.

"Do you need a bowl?"

She nodded, and I grabbed the largest mixing bowl I could find and put it on the table in front of her. I stayed beside her in case she needed me, and because I was pretty sure I wouldn't be able to hide the pain from my face if I sat again.

"Do you think he saw me puke," she asked quietly.

I didn't answer and she groaned, the sound echoing in the bowl.

"He's never going to ask me out now."

I drummed my fingers on the table, debating if I should share Cal's interpretation of Theo's X tattoos. "If he doesn't ask you, it's not because of what happened last night or anything you did. He clearly cares about you. A lot."

Poppy glanced at me over the rim of the bowl. Her hard exterior was gone. She looked so much like the little girl who refused to attend her father's funeral, my heart lurched. "But not enough," she whispered.

I took her hand and gave it a squeeze.

"Ok," she said, pulling her hand away and straightening. "I want details about you and a certain neighbor. You were a terrible sister for abandoning me last night. You owe me."

"I made you monkey bread."

Poppy shook her head. "Not good enough. You even forgot the bacon again. And now it's too late to cook it before the bread's done."

I glanced at the timer. "There's time."

"Good. Talk while you fry."

"I mean, how much detail do you want?" I asked, pulling the bacon from the fridge.

"Nothing graphic. My stomach is still queasy. Just, where things stand with y'all."

"It was just sex." I turned on the heat under Mom's favorite cast-iron skillet and laid in the bacon. I could feel Poppy's eyes boring into me while I washed my hands, but she didn't say a word.

"You had the biggest crush on him in high school," she said softly. "I remember how you used to look at him when you brought Chris and me to his football games."

I shrugged. "Everyone did."

"Fair," Poppy said. "But admit it, your inner sixteen-year-old is dying of happiness right now."

I laughed and flipped the bacon. "Maybe a little."

Poppy's chair screeched back from the table. I glanced over my shoulder to see if she was bolting for the bathroom in favor of the bowl. Instead, she wrapped her arms around me from behind, laying her head on my shoulder. "Be careful, Rowan. Brad hurt you, but a guy like Cal can break you into pieces you'll never be able to put back together."

I nodded, my eyes burning. Cal had been upfront about what sleeping together would mean, but I'd be lying if I said I had zero feelings for him. On top of his ability to tease every ounce of pleasure from my body, he had a caring side that made my heart ache to know him more. He'd make someone a wonderful partner, someday.

If Poppy hugged me any longer, I was going to break down. "Can you grab the confectioners sugar, butter, and cream cheese," I said clearing my throat. "I need to make the icing."

"Oh, we're going full guns today," Poppy said with a laugh.

She grabbed the ingredients and took over cooking the bacon while I made the glaze. We chatted while we worked, and again I was struck by how much lighter my sister was in the kitchen. When the monkey bread was ready, we filled our plates. Poppy crumbled bacon on top of hers, and I did the same.

She shot me a worried glance when I groaned into a chair, but was lost to the sugary goodness before I'd settled in my seat.

"Why haven't we ever done this before," Poppy said, moaning around another mouthful of monkey bread.

"You sound indecent."

"This bread is indecent," she said, licking the icing from one of the bread balls.

"Stop licking the balls, you perv," I said and laughed. Then a thought hit me. "Or let me take a picture of you."

"Who's the perv now?" she said raising her eyebrows.

I laughed.

"Go ahead," she said, picking up a piece of the bread with her fingers and posing with her tongue stuck out, eyes closed. I grabbed my phone, snapped the picture, and showed it to her.

"Don't show that to Mom. I look like a porn star."

She kind of did. Which was why I did my sisterly duty and forwarded the picture to Theo in reply to his last *How's she doing* text.

He typed something. Then the three dots disappeared. Then started again. Finally, he just replied *thx*.

I laughed so hard I snorted.

"What's so funny?" Poppy narrowed her eyes at me. "Did you send that picture to Lauren?"

"Nope," I said, locking my phone and putting it on the table.

She grabbed it, unlocked it, and gasped. "You bitch."

Then her face softened as she scrolled back through my text exchange with Theo. "He was really worried, huh?"

I nodded and sipped my coffee. My phone rang in Poppy's hands, and she frowned. "Wasn't Gwen your mentor at Pinnacle Group?"

"Give me that," I said, grabbing the phone. Sure enough, my former mentor was requesting a video call, which would have been strange when we worked together, let alone now.

"Good," Gwen said when I accepted the call. "You're sitting down."

She was at her desk in the office, which was also odd for a Saturday.

"All hell is breaking loose here," Gwen said, glancing toward the hallway. "I thought you'd want to see it. The head of HR just fired Kelli and Brad. Look!"

She turned the phone to the hallway, and I watched as my soon-to-be ex-husband and former boss walked down the hall, each carrying a file box.

Gwen turned the phone back to her face. "I'm assuming you knew they were sleeping together."

I nodded. "The accident happened right after I walked in on them together in her office."

Gwen blew out a breath. "Well, that explains why you quit without notice. I thought you'd had some life epiphany when that scooter hit you and decided you weren't cut out for finance. Brad never mentioned you were separating."

"It doesn't exactly paint him in a good light."

Gwen nodded, her face sad. "I wish you'd have told me. I could have moved you to a different team."

"I didn't want to see either of them again."

"Well," Gwen said. "Now you don't have to. Turns out Kelli was completely incompetent. IT did a little digging and determined you created all the reports she'd been assigned. They also looked through her emails and IMs and discovered the relationship with Brad."

"That was enough to fire him?" I asked, leaning back in my chair. "They weren't even in the same department."

Gwen shook her head. "No, but they dug into his digital history as well and discovered he was sending inappropriate messages to his new management trainee. She asked to be reassigned last week."

"Pig."

"So," Gwen said with a big smile. "There are currently two positions open in your old team, including the leadership role, which means I'm eager to hire replacements. Especially someone with experience who has proven she has the skills for the job."

Poppy had watched me through the entire exchange but dropped her eyes to her plate and began pushing the remains of her monkey bread back and forth, her fork making a horrific scraping sound.

I blew out a breath. "I'd have to think about it," I said. "You were a great mentor, and I enjoyed working at Pinnacle, but the place has some pretty dark memories for me now. Plus, I'd have to move back to DC. I'm going to need time to consider."

Gwen nodded. "That's understandable. Why don't I get together with HR and see what I can do to make this an offer you can't refuse. I'll email it over on Monday. I wish I could tell you to take as long as you need, but we're so understaffed, the best I can do is hold the position until the end of the month."

"Two weeks is fair," I said, trying to ignore the grating sound of Poppy's fork. "Thanks, Gwen."

"I'll be in touch," she said and ended the call.

"Cut that out," I said, grabbing the fork from Poppy.

"So that's it, then," Poppy said, crossing her arms. "Guess you need a ride back to DC."

"I haven't even seen the offer yet. Why are you getting worked up? You knew this was temporary. All my stuff is still in boxes in the living room."

Poppy shrugged. "I knew you'd want your own place, eventually. Mom's '80s music obsession is reason enough, but I guess I was hoping you'd stay around here."

"Poppy," I said, softly. "You know jobs like mine aren't in Peace Falls."

"Forget I said anything." She shoved her chair from the table. "I'll be in my studio. Thanks for the monkey bread."

She passed Chris on the way out. He gave her a big, sweaty hug, but instead of shoving him off like he probably expected, she wrapped her arms around him and squeezed him tight before leaving. He walked to the kitchen sink and watched her stomp across the backyard to the shed. "What's wrong with Pop?"

"She had too much to drink last night."

He turned and leaned against the sink, crossing his arms in a movement so similar to Poppy, my breath caught. "Bullshit."

"Fine," I said, throwing my hands in the air. "She's pissed I came home early from the bar. Want some monkey bread?"

He plopped into the seat Poppy had vacated and started pulling pieces from the pan.

"I can get you a plate," I said.

He shook his head. "No need. I'm going to eat the rest."

I chuckled.

"I love having you home, Ann." He looked up from the pan and flashed me a huge smile that made my heart ache. He'd grown up so much since I moved to DC. In a couple years he'd be off to college, and the little boy who once followed me everywhere would have a life full of experiences and people I'd never know.

I got up and walked around the table to give him a hug. "Oh, gross," I said, when the sweat from his t-shirt soaked mine.

"Hey, you hugged me," he said, popping the last piece of monkey bread in his mouth. "I'll go shower, but then would you help me meal plan for the rest of the week? I've got to eat better than this."

"Sounds good," I said.

I was finishing up the dishes when my phone rang again. I glanced at the unknown number and almost sent it to voicemail, but the area code was local. Thinking it could be Lauren or my mom, I answered.

"Hey," Cal said. "Hope you don't mind. Theo gave me your number."

"Well, hello," I said, leaning against the counter. "I guess this is payback for the sexy picture I sent him."

"Should I be concerned you're sending my best friend sexy pictures?"

I laughed. "Not at all." Brad was jealous any time I spoke to another man, which made sense now that I knew he cheated on me. Why would he trust that I'd take our vows seriously if he didn't? Cal's tone was teasing. But a part of me wondered if he just didn't care if I sent Theo a picture of myself. "Chris just took down half a pan of monkey bread, so I'm guessing your training went well this morning."

"It did. Aiden joined us. He's going to work with Chris on the days I can't."

"That's really nice of him."

Cal started laughing, the deep, rich sound sending ripples of some emotion through my body. Lust. Longing. The feeling strong and indescribable. "Oh, yeah. Theo hates you right now."

I felt a smile tug at my lips. Cal might pretend not to care, but he'd been texting Theo while we talked.

"I should have come inside with Chris. I clearly missed out on that monkey bread."

"I'll make it for you anytime."

"How about tomorrow?"

I laughed. "I could probably fit that into my schedule."

"Could you fit a picnic in as well? Eating one. Not making it."

"Caleb Cardoso, are you asking me out?"

He paused a moment and my cheeks heated. Maybe he had a work event he needed to attend and thought it'd be smart to bring a patient who hadn't bashed him online. Or a church picnic. He didn't strike me as particularly devout, but maybe he was one of those evangelical types that was encouraged to bring a friend to Sunday service. Then again, those people typically didn't have hot, no-strings sex.

"I am," he said, so quietly I almost didn't hear him.

"Oh, ok," I said, suddenly nervous. "Well, in that case, I might make something else. Monkey bread is really sticky. Too sticky for a picnic. It would draw in ants, and we don't want that."

Cal chuckled. "No, we do not. I'm sure whatever you bring will be delicious."

His voice had dropped to a sexy timbre as he spoke, and my stomach flipped.

"How's eleven, tomorrow?" he asked, returning to his normal tone.

"Sounds good," I said, suddenly very warm. I needed to stop panting before my brother came back. "Bye."

I ended the call before he had a chance to say anything else.

"Did you tell him you're leaving?"

I glanced over my shoulder and found Chris standing in the kitchen doorway, his hair still damp from the shower. "I texted Pop to make sure she was ok, and she filled me in. So, does Cal know? It's pretty shitty either way. Either you told him before you told me, or you're going out with him when you know it can't last more than a couple weeks."

"Chris—"

"And don't tell me it's none of my business, Ann. You're my family. Both you and Cal. I don't want to see either of you get hurt." He stopped and shook his head.

I opened my arms. He crossed the kitchen and wrapped me in a tight hug. "I didn't tell him or you about the job offer because I haven't seen it yet. I honestly don't know if I want to take it. Cal knows I plan to move from Peace Falls as soon as I find a job. I promise, I'd never do anything to jeopardize your friendship with him."

Chris pulled away. "DC sucks. There's nothing but traffic and politics and assholes like Brad. Plus, if you stay in Peace Falls, you can come to all my games this fall."

"Noted," I said, giving his back a pat. "But you have to make the team first. Let's plan some meals. But not here. If I have to sit in those wooden chairs, I might cry."

He grabbed a notepad and a pen as I settled on the couch. For the next hour we looked up recipes and made a grocery list. The whole time, I couldn't stop thinking about how much I'd enjoyed being with my family and Lauren since I'd been back, and how much I'd miss them if I left. I did my best not to think about Cal. It was too soon to tell if he'd be something to keep me here or the push I might need to leave.

Chapter Twenty-One

Cal

Rowan answered the door in a little blue sundress that hugged her curves in all the right places. Her hair was down in long waves again, framing her beautiful face.

"Wow," I said, leaning in to kiss her soft cheek. "You look amazing, but I screwed up."

Her smile fell. "Oh, do you need to cancel?"

"No, I just should have said to wear clothes you can hike in. I thought we could go over to Sawtooth Ridge and do the trail. If you're up for it." I rubbed my neck while she considered the idea. I should have asked if she liked hiking. Her mobility had improved so much over the past weeks, I thought it'd be a good trail to push her. "It was a bad idea. We can go to Centennial Park."

"No way," she said with a huge smile. "I was just trying to remember where I packed my hiking boots. Give me five minutes."

I waited on the porch, and a few minutes later she returned in a crop top and a pair of spandex shorts that made my mouth go dry. She'd put her hair into a ponytail and threaded it through a Karma baseball cap, which shouldn't have been sexy but was.

"Where's Skye?" she asked, sitting on the steps to lace up her well-worn hiking boots. Her small backpack and reusable water bottle looked equally used.

"Theo has her. I wanted to have my hands free for you."

She blushed an adorable shade of pink, and my pulse quickened. I cleared my throat. "In case you need my help on the trail."

"I used to hike it all the time with my dad. I think I'll be ok, but you're right, I'm in no shape to run after Skye if she spots a squirrel." She grabbed onto the railing beside the steps and pulled herself up.

The front door opened, and Rose leaned out. "Did you remember sunscreen and bug spray?"

"Yes, Mom," Rowan said, blushing again.

"What about you, Cal? I'm sure you don't burn like a redhead, but the mosquitos will eat y'all alive this time of year."

"I have some in the car."

"Ok, kids. Have fun," she said and smiled again before closing the door.

"Sorry about that," Rowan said as she climbed into the passenger seat after we'd stowed her pack in the back with mine. "She forgets I'm a grown woman sometimes."

"That's nothing. My mom would have doused us with bug spray without asking. She has a serious fear of ticks."

Rowan scrunched her delicate nose. "I don't blame her."

I couldn't stop myself from leaning into the SUV and giving her a quick kiss. She smelled like sunscreen and citronella and a hint of chocolate. When I pulled away, she bit her bottom lip and smiled up at me. I considered skipping the entire hiking trip and driving her down the street to my house. Instead, I closed her door and walked around to the driver's side. Rose stood in the picture window waving, and I congratulated myself on not mauling Rowan the second I thought we were alone.

Rowan waved to her mother, a huge smile on her face. "I'm so excited," she said. "I haven't been hiking since I came back to Peace Falls. My family is too scared I'll hurt myself, and I'm concerned enough I won't hike alone."

I felt a sudden rush of worry and glanced at her. "Do you ever hike alone?"

Rowan shrugged. "Sometimes. If my back weren't messed up, I'd have done the Triple Crown by now."

"Alone?" I said, turning onto Broad Street.

"It's more fun with a friend. But yeah, I've had a lot of time on my hands. So, I might have tackled one or two hikes by myself."

"Those trails can be dangerous."

"Sure, if you don't know what you're doing. My dad took Poppy and me hiking almost every weekend before he got sick. I know those trails like the back of my hand. And I always bring a Garmin with gps and satellite messaging, plus my phone, of course."

"Still, you don't know who else is out there."

"Caleb Cardoso," she said with a smirk. "Are you usually this overprotective?"

I shook my head. "I'm protective. Nothing *over* about it. You're a beautiful woman and the world is full of creeps."

She threw her head back and laughed. "You're serious, aren't you?"

"Yep."

"Is it wrong that I kind of like that about you?" she said, drumming her fingers on her leg.

I reached across the car and took her hand in mine. We traveled several miles in comfortable silence, Rowan admiring the view as we drove to the trail head. I let go of her hand when I turned into the parking lot. It was filled with cars for the popular McAffee Knob trail, which ran eight miles and, along with Dragon's Tooth and Tinkers Cliffs, made up the Triple Crown. I was beginning to think we wouldn't find a parking spot when a family emerged from the trailhead of the two-mile out-and-back hike I'd planned to make with Rowan. I pulled into the space they left behind at the edge of the lot.

Rowan was already out of her seat and at the back of the SUV before I'd finished placing the sunshade across the windshield.

I chuckled as I joined her and pulled out my pack. She practically climbed into the trunk for hers. "Let me help you. I want to lighten your pack as much as possible."

Some of the excitement dimmed from her face. "Yeah, that's probably a good idea."

"Hey," I said, laying my hands gently on her shoulders. "I wouldn't have suggested this if I didn't think you were strong enough. But there's no sense carrying extra weight. I have plenty of room in my pack."

She unzipped her pack and handed me a massive plastic bag of brownies. "I thought they'd be easier to eat on a picnic than cupcakes or monkey bread."

"These look amazing." I opened my pack and put the bag on top of the lunch I'd made, then held out my hand for more. She sighed and handed me her large aluminum water bottle. "Anything else?"

She shook her head. I frowned and lifted her pack but found it surprisingly light.

"Satisfied, doctor?"

"Never." I gave her a wolfish grin and she laughed.

"Come on," she said, gripping my arm. "The sun's only getting hotter."

It was much cooler than last week, but still, I was thankful for the shade cover as we started out. Sawtooth Ridge was a sliver of the Appalachian trail that ran from Maine to Georgia. This portion of the trail hugged the ridgeline and mountain edge, with only a 417-foot rise in elevation. Still, it offered fantastic views of the valley below. We stopped after a quarter mile to drink from our water bottles and admire the view. I'd watched Rowan carefully for any signs of discomfort, but the smile never left her face.

"I missed this so much," she said, twisting the cap back on her bottle and handing it to me. I'd thought we'd share my water, but with the heat, I was glad to have my own.

"Do you hike often?" she asked.

I nodded. "Theo, Aiden, and I got into it during the pandemic."

"I have to get Poppy and Chris back out here with me," she said. "They haven't even let me make the short hike to see the waterfall by town. They'll be easier to convince if you wrote a note. Preferably on letterhead."

I laughed as she swung her pack onto her back. When the trail narrowed, I walked behind her and studied her gait again. She moved slower than someone of her age and fitness level, but her steps were much more fluid than they'd been in our first session. Before long I stopped focusing on her footfalls and found myself staring at her perfect ass. If Adam weren't on my case, I'd probably suggest Rowan switch to another PT since I clearly couldn't tamp down my attraction when I observed her.

The trail opened to a large rock scramble, which Rowan eyed with interest. I could picture her hopping from boulder to boulder as she worked her way to the top.

"Don't even think about it," I said, guiding her to a flat rock with views of Brushy Mountain. I opened my pack and took out the water bottles. We both drank deeply before she helped me spread out the blanket I'd brought on the boulder.

Once we were sitting, I pulled out the soft cooler from inside my pack and laid out the sandwich wraps and fruit salad I'd made as well as the brownies. "I realized this morning I should have asked what you liked, so there's a turkey, a ham, and a veggie wrap. Take whichever you want. There's hummus on the veggie wrap, mustard on the ham, and mayo on the turkey. Now that I think about it, there's a good chance you don't like any of those combinations. I should have left them plain."

She smiled. "You don't do this often do you?"

"Picnics?"

She shook her head. "Dates."

"Is it that obvious?"

She laughed. "No, not if I didn't know you. It's just you always seem so confident and in control. It's like you've thought everything out five steps ahead, but you forgot to include another person in your plans."

"Guilty," I said, taking the ham sandwich after she grabbed the turkey. "You're right. I don't date. I just—."

She raised her eyebrows. "Keep things casual."

"Exactly," I said, taking a bite of my sandwich.

But this was a date. I'd said so yesterday, yet the knot in my stomach that usually formed whenever the word snuck into a conversation with a woman never came. I might have eaten a few meals with Avery, but I never planned something just to spend time talking with her. I'd tried not to give her the wrong idea about our arrangement—and utterly failed. Rowan was different. Our end was built into our beginning. She'd be leaving Peace Falls and me soon enough, and I planned to enjoy whatever time I had with her.

I finished my sandwich and polished off the veggie wrap as well. Then we shared the fruit and opened the brownies, the rich chocolate finally filling my stomach.

"Have you ever considered hiking the full trail?" she asked, looking past the end of Sawtooth Ridge where the Appalachian trail continued south.

"I enjoy day hikes more than camping. What about you?"

"My dad and I used to talk about doing the thru-hike. I thought I could take a gap year between high school and college or right after I got my degree, but then he got sick again."

"Again?"

Rowan nodded. "He was diagnosed the first time when Poppy and I were in elementary school. He went through chemo and all the terrible side effects. The doctors thought they'd gotten everything. Chris was a complete oops," she said laughing. "Mom and Dad didn't think they needed birth control after all his treatments. Chris was a year old when the cancer came back, worse than before. After Dad died, I let go of the thru-hike. When I graduated high school, Chris was still so young. Mom needed my help, which was why I drove down on the weekends when I was in college. And now I have a ton of student loans."

"But you still hike."

She nodded.

"Does it ever make you sad? Hiking?"

"No," she said, giving me a curious look. "I love it."

I nodded. "This summer was the first time I've held a football since the accident."

She paled and reached for my hand.

"Logan and I had been teammates since we were little. I couldn't even watch a football game that first year while I was going through PT. Eventually, Aiden visited me at JMU and dragged me to a game, then another. I enjoyed watching again, but I never played. Not once."

"Until I made you," she whispered. "I'm so sorry, Caleb."

I shook my head. "Don't be. Training Chris has been the second-best thing to happen to me this summer."

She blushed. "And the first?"

"Finding Skye, obviously."

"Yeah, I'm really glad we found her," Rowan said, looking at the mountains. I felt like the world's biggest asshole. Most of the women I hung around would have recognized the humor and given me a playful slap on the chest, but Rowan was different. She didn't see herself the way the world did, and I wanted to punch every idiot who'd made her feel less about herself, myself included.

"Hey," I said, squeezing her hand. "That was a dumb joke. I'm glad we found Skye. Very. But I wouldn't have if you hadn't walked into my practice. And I wouldn't be here with you now."

I rubbed my thumb across her cheek with my other hand and she leaned into my touch. I lowered my head and kissed her, sweet at first, then deeper, hungrier. She moaned and I went as hard as the rock we were sitting on.

She climbed into my lap, rolling her hips over me in waves that made my dick ache. "We better stop," I said breaking the kiss. "Unless you want me to fuck you in the middle of the trail for anyone to see."

She jerked as though realizing where we were and looked around, her eyes wild.

I chuckled. "No one can see us right now. But we won't be alone long."

"Your back windows are tinted," she said. "And you put that sunshade in the front."

I've never packed up so fast in my life. We managed the return hike in less than twenty minutes and were both out of breath and sweating by the time we reached the parking lot. It was only a fifteen-minute drive to my house, but after starting the air conditioner and shoving our packs in the rear, we both squeezed into the back seat, tearing at each other's clothes. I grabbed a condom from my wallet but before I could put it on, she took it, tore it opened, and rolled it down my heated skin.

I threw my head back and knocked it against the window. Our eyes locked. My heart ached in my chest. "Come here," I said.

She climbed up my body, our faces pressed together. Her eyes never left mine as she reached between us, positioned me at her entrance, and sank down. We both moaned when I rocked up into her. We moved together, gentle at first, then frantic, each desperate for release. She called my name as she came, sending me over the edge, pleasure ripping through my body with a force that left me dizzy.

She smiled, and I begged the world to stop, to hold the moment a bit longer, but a horn sounded in the parking lot, breaking it into a million pieces. She giggled. I wanted to wrap my arms around her and stay locked with her body for as long as she'd let me. Instead, I eased out of her, hoping she wouldn't notice how much it pained me to leave.

Chapter Twenty-Two

Rowan

I'D AVOIDED KARMA AND Lauren all week, but late Thursday morning, I pushed through the door of the café and found my best friend behind the counter, frowning at a tray of pastries.

"Taste this," she said by way of a greeting, thrusting an odd-shaped biscuit in my face.

I took a bite and almost choked on the dried-out clump of awful. She handed me a napkin to spit it in and a cup of water. "Why would you tell me to taste that?" I asked, coughing into the napkin. "That's terrible."

"Because I wanted your honest opinion. Plus, that's payback for ghosting me after you went home with Cal last week."

"I have not ghosted you."

Lauren pulled her phone from her apron pocket and showed me our text exchange for the week, which consisted of my one-word replies and her increasingly agitated texts. The last one was just a GIF of a kitten breathing fire.

"I had a lot to think about. But that's no reason to poison me. What was that?"

"A basil-lemon scone."

"It tasted like a dish detergent tablet. Not that I've ever eaten one, but the consistency is so bad and the lemon is way too strong. I didn't taste any basil, but I'm not taking another bite to confirm."

Lauren nodded. "Agreed. I can't serve these. I'm going to have to taste test everything in the display case. Mr. Wilson pointed out this disaster. Poor thing. I felt so bad, I gave him free coffee all next week."

"For once, I don't think you're being too generous."

Lauren sighed and dumped the entire tray of pastries into the trash.

"You should have saved one to give to the bakery when you ask for a refund."

Lauren shook her head. "I called and told them, thinking they'd want to pull the product before selling it to anyone else. They said my customer had an unrefined palette. I told them the scones tasted off to me too, and they said that maybe my coffee was distorting the taste."

I let out a snort of laughter before I could stop myself. "I'm sorry. I shouldn't laugh, but that's so ridiculous it's funny."

"No, I'd be laughing too if I didn't have to find a new baker ASAP. This is it for me. I won't subject my customers to sub-par food. Are you sure you won't consider baking for Karma?"

I blew out a breath. "I've been considering a lot lately."

Lauren put her hands on her hips. "Ok, I've been patient. But you need to tell me what's going on before I force feed you another scone, straight from the trash."

I cringed but then my face warmed, thinking about what I was about to tell her. "I've been sleeping with Cal since Friday."

Lauren clapped her hands and did a little dance, hopping like she had a trampoline behind the counter. "I tried to get confirmation from Poppy, but she just gave me a death glare and told me to ask you."

"Well, you know we went home together after Church."

Lauren nodded. When I didn't say anything else, she yanked a scone from the trash. "Details, woman. I've been dying over here."

"It was amazing. But before it happened, he clarified that he didn't want a relationship. It'd just be sex."

"Oh," Lauren said, her smile falling as she tossed the scone back in the garbage where it belonged. "Well, at least he was up front about it, right? You're coming off a really bad breakup, so hot sex with no feelings might be just what you need."

I nodded. "But then he took me hiking on Sunday, and it felt like a real date, like the start of something."

"Oh, I like the sound of this," Lauren said. "Both the date part and the fact your back must be doing better if Cal took you on a hike. He seemed really worried about you on Friday."

"Yeah, he's stopped being so careful with me." I glanced around to make sure the café was still empty and someone hadn't wandered up from the book shelves in the back. "We had sex in the trailhead parking lot in the back seat of his SUV like a couple of horny teenagers."

Lauren threw her head back and laughed. "You did not. Which trail?"

"Sawtooth."

Lauren laughed so hard, she bent over and clutched her stomach. "That parking lot is crazy. I had no idea you were such a freak."

"I'm not," I said, blushing. "We just got caught up in the moment. And it's been like that all week. After my PT session on Monday, we had a quickie in the building's elevator. He's invited me over for dinner twice, and I stayed the whole night both times. I've had more orgasms this week than the last year of my marriage."

Lauren fanned her face. "Damn. I'm jealous. I'm so busy here, I haven't had a man-induced orgasm in months."

"Not going to lie, the sex is amazing. But that's not the only reason I've been avoiding you."

"Uh oh," Lauren said, walking around the counter. "I know that look. Sit." She pulled out a chair at one of the bistro tables and pushed me into it before taking a seat across from me. My back protested the sudden movement, but I did my best to keep my face neutral.

"What's going on?" Lauren asked. "You got pale. Well, paler than usual. Did Brad do something?"

I shook my head. I hadn't realized how much blood had rushed from my head to my stomach until Lauren forced me into the chair. "He and Kelli got fired."

"What! When?"

"On Saturday. Which now that I think about it, is pretty unusual. HR must have been really pissed if they couldn't wait until after the weekend. Apparently, Brad was creeping on his intern in addition to sleeping with my boss."

Lauren slapped my arm, hard. "I don't care how magical Cal's dick is, you do not keep info like that from your best friend."

"Well, it's more than that. Remember my mentor, Gwen?"

Lauren nodded.

"She offered me a job. Not my old job. Kelli's. I got the official letter on Monday. The pay jump is enough I could afford rent in Dupont Circle or even buy a townhouse in Arlington. I'd get to hire a new member for the team and choose them myself. It's a huge opportunity."

"Sounds like it," Lauren said, softly.

"I have until the end of next week to accept. I'm not sure what I want to do. The job would be a giant leap for my career."

"What does Cal think?"

"I haven't told him."

Lauren pushed back from the table and blew out a breath. "Damn, Rowan. That feels a little cold. You've been riding him all week, and it never crossed your mind to mention you might leave soon?"

"He knows I'm job hunting, and that I'll probably move as soon as I find one."

Lauren nodded. "Which fits with the whole casual hook up, I guess."

"It's just, it doesn't feel casual," I whispered. "At least not to me."

Lauren's face softened. "You're falling for him, aren't you?"

I nodded and swiped at my eyes. "He says he doesn't do relationships, but he's so caring and thoughtful. And when we're together, we have conversations about things that are so personal, like losing my dad or his recovery from the accident."

"Did he say why he wants to keep things casual? I bet it's because of Avery. Cammie showed me Cal's online reviews. We're trying to get his patients to leave good ones, but Avery is a piece of work. She buries anything positive with terrible comments."

I shook my head. "She's an awful person, but he told her the same thing he told me. I bet she's angry because it felt like a real relationship to her. He hurt her. That's the only reason she'd go to so much trouble to ruin him. I never thought I'd have so much in common with Avery Peterson."

"You aren't Avery. Who knows what she thought or how he felt. Honestly, it doesn't matter. But understanding why he's so against committing to someone would."

I let out a huge sigh. The problem was I think I did know. Cal clearly hadn't worked through his grief from the accident enough to let anyone get close, yet what we had didn't feel casual. "I don't know what to do. This job would be amazing for me, career wise. It should be an easy yes. But I've really enjoyed being home, spending time with Cal and my family and you, of course."

"When you're not avoiding me," Lauren said with a laugh.

I cringed and nodded.

"I almost don't want to ask this, because you know I'm biased and want you to stay here, but did you like the work you did with Pinnacle?"

I chewed my bottom lip as I considered her question. "I didn't dislike it. Finance pays well, especially with the promotion. I worked really hard to get to this point in my career, and people respect the work I do."

Lauren nodded. "But you don't love it."

"No," I said, shaking my head. "But most people don't love their jobs."

"I do," Lauren said. "It's stressful and exhausting sometimes, but every day I'm glad I get to put on this Karma apron and bring a little joy to people's lives. I'm sure your mom feels the same."

I nodded. "But I saw how much she struggled to open her own business after Dad died. The hours she worked. The stress. Things were really tight for us, financially. We always made do, but I could see how much it weighed on her."

"Fair," Lauren said. "But you're not a widow with three kids to feed. If you were ever going to take a risk, now's the time. Either way, you need to tell Cal. About the job and your feelings."

I shook my head. "He was adamant. He doesn't want a relationship." I wasn't sure he was ready for one even if he did. I decided to keep that part to myself. If Lauren knew, she'd tell me to enjoy the sex then run, whether or not I moved to DC.

Lauren shrugged. "People change their minds. But, no matter how he takes it, promise me you'll make the best decision for you. Whatever you decide, you know I have your back."

"I know you do," I said grabbing her hand and giving it a squeeze. "Which is why I'm going home right now and baking something for that display case. Even if I'm only here another week, I can fill the gap until you find a new baker."

She squealed and jumped out of her chair to hug me. "Thank you! Thank you! I don't care what you make as long as it doesn't taste like lemons. It's too soon."

I laughed. "Ok, I'll have something ready for Poppy to bring in for her afternoon shift."

Lauren pulled back. "Promise me you won't ghost me again. Whatever happens, I want to know. You're my best friend, and I feel like you've been keeping so much from me lately. First Brad and the accident and now this."

My stomach dropped. I was still keeping things from her, but Cal's grief wasn't something I felt comfortable sharing with anyone. "I'm sorry. My life isn't usually this dramatic. I'm overwhelmed."

She smiled. "I know. You were exactly like this when I met you, hiding in your shell like a turtle. It took you forever to warm up to me."

"Everyone wanted to be your friend. I still don't understand why you insisted on being mine."

"Because," she said, wrapping her arm around my shoulder, "the people with the hardest shells have the softest insides." She gave me a squeeze, then stood. "I'm getting you a Rowan to go. I need a fully caffeinated baking machine."

As I watched her make my drink, I couldn't help imagining what it would be like to settle in Peace Falls. Coffee and chats with my best friend whenever I wanted. Never missing one of Chris's games or Poppy's art shows. Early-morning dance parties with Mom. That one wasn't always a positive, but on certain mornings, it made my entire day feel lighter. And Cal. Lauren was right. I needed to tell him, but I was scared. Brad had tossed me away like I was one of those terrible scones. Even if I was the one who ended it, he'd left the relationship long before I realized. I was just starting to feel like myself again, and Cal was a big reason why. He'd helped heal more than my back. Even though we'd only been together a short time, I worried he already had a hold on my heart. My stomach twisted as I realized Poppy might be right. Cal could break me into pieces that would never fit together again.

Chapter Twenty-Three

Cal

"Did you see?" Cammie shouted as I opened the door. "You're back up to three stars, and that witch hasn't posted a review in two days."

I heard a grunt from Adam's office. He'd started leaving his door ajar, and Cammie and I both knew he listened to every word we said. He had to be monitoring my reviews online, but oddly we hadn't discussed my ratings since he threatened to fire me. Other than being grumpier than usual and watching me like a hawk waiting for a field mouse to move into an exposed position, it was as if the conversation never happened. I couldn't decide if his silence was a positive or negative indication of my future employment.

"That's great. Did anyone pushed back when you asked for a review?"

"Of course not," she yelled. "Like I've been saying, they all love you. Now let me work, I have patient bills to send."

She winked at me, and I pushed down a laugh.

"Thanks, Cam," I said and placed a large cinnamon toast latte on her desk.

She'd been arriving earlier and earlier to beat Adam into the office, which always seemed to put him in a better mood. Even if she grabbed her own coffee, I knew she'd be ready for another.

"Between you and Rowan, I'm going to gain fifteen pounds," she said and tipped back the cup.

"The latte or the person?" I asked.

"Well, honestly, both. Rowan filled the pastry case at Karma, and I had to try a few things. Your girl has skills."

I cleared my throat. Rowan wasn't mine, and I didn't need Adam watching us any closer. Monday's session had been torture. After an hour of watching Rowan bend, stretch, and move, I announced we'd be ending with stair exercises and took her in the elevator instead.

"Your patient," Cammie amended. "She's first up today."

"Speaking of skills," I said, lowering my voice. "Are we ever going to talk about your performance at Church?"

"I have no idea what you're talking about," she said and sipped her coffee.

I shook my head. "I'll be in my office."

I walked past Adam's door and said hello. He gave me a curt nod and went back to typing. I closed my office door and woke up my desktop to check the most recent reviews. Pride filled my chest as I read the heartfelt words from my patients. Some had given me similar praise in real life, but others, like Mr. Carmichael, came to their sessions, did the exercises, and left without so much as a thank you. Carmichael's comment made my eyes burn.

Good man. Knows how to get the work done. I don't like chit chat and most of my doctors talk my ear off. Dr. Cardoso is a friendly fella. He'd joke around with the other patients, but he understood I was there to get better, not cluck like a chicken. My hip don't hurt at all now. I hope I never need PT again, but if I do, he's the only physical therapist I'd see.

My overall ranking had improved since Avery had stopped posting as well. Instead of relief, the pause made me nervous. Our brief text exchange hadn't settled anything. She'd dumped several more negative reviews online after it, then gone oddly quiet.

Cammie sent me a message saying Rowan had arrived. My stomach did an odd flip. I needed to get myself under control around her. At least for the next hour. We had an entire weekend ahead of us, but just thinking about the possibilities of what we could do in that time made me hard. I ran through a couple JMU vs. Tech final scores to cool down and headed to the front.

Thankfully, Rowan had swapped the crop top and leggings combo she wore on Monday for a baggy t-shirt and athletic shorts. Even without the skin show, her warm smile hit me straight in the chest. My whole body tightened with anticipation as I erased the distance between us.

"Good morning," I said. It took an absurd effort to stop several feet from her. I hadn't seen her since yesterday morning when I'd greeted her with my head between her legs. She'd delayed her Thursday session a day to accommodate a rare new patient request I received, and I'd been looking forward to thanking her again when we were alone.

"Morning, Dr. Cardoso," she said.

Cammie looked between us and smirked before turning back to her computer screen.

"How's your back feeling today?" I asked as I led her to the table for heat therapy. She was walking slower than usual.

"A little tight," she said. "I may have overdone it yesterday. I baked for several hours."

My stomach sank. She hadn't progressed as much as I'd hoped by this point in our sessions, but her gait had improved. I'd noticed her pain ebbed and flowed depending on her exertion level. I hoped the peaks would level out before our sessions ended. "Cammie mentioned you're helping Lauren."

"Standing is usually better than sitting for me," she said, lying face down on the table. "But I'm definitely feeling it today."

"Were you standing on a rubber mat?"

"Mostly the tile. There's a mat like that by the sink."

"An anti-fatigue mat at your workspace would help. Also, shoes with proper support."

She nodded. "That makes sense."

I grabbed the heat blanket and checked that Adam was still at his desk on the opposite side of the office. When I got back to the table, I ran my hands across Rowan's lower back before putting the blanket over her. She sighed, and I grabbed the stool and scooted as close to her as I dared.

"Maybe I've been too rough with you," I whispered, lowering my voice.

She opened her eyes and smiled at me. "No rougher than I've been on you."

"You can't hurt me."

Something flickered across her eyes before she pushed it down and smiled. "I'm fine, really. Your suggestion about the shoes and mat should help. I admit, I wore flip flops yesterday while I worked."

I cringed and a small laugh escaped her.

"After work, I'm taking you shopping for a mat and orthotic inserts."

"Just tell me what inserts to get. I'm not wasting a Friday night with you at Walmart."

"Did you have something else in mind?" I knew what I wanted to do with her, but I could spare a half hour to get her things that could help her back.

"Well, you've made me dinner twice. I thought I could bring groceries to your place and cook for you. There's something I want to talk about as well."

My stomach sank. Planning a talk was never a good sign. Still, I nodded and pretended to add notes to her chart. The front door opened, and

I glanced up, expecting to see Adam's first patient. Avery stood in the doorway instead, wearing a sports bra as a top and a pair of leggings with more cutouts than fabric.

"What the hell," I breathed.

Rowan twisted her head to the other side and her shoulders tensed.

"Can I help you?" Cammie asked in a sharp tone I'd never heard her use before.

"I'm here to see Cal," Avery said, waving her fingers at me.

"He's with a patient," Cammie said. "I'm happy to schedule you an appointment."

"Oh no," Avery said, loudly. "This is personal. I'm certain he won't mind the interruption."

Adam's door opened all the way, and he hurried across the room to stand at the end of Rowan's table.

"This is entirely unprofessional," he said loud enough for Cammie and Avery to hear.

Rowan sat up and glared at him. "I agree. You're interrupting my session."

Adam blanched but quickly recovered. "Dr. Cardoso, kindly escort that young lady out," he said, pointing to Avery. "I'll take over here."

Rowan didn't look too pleased but flopped back on the table with a huff. I hurried to the reception area where Cammie was already holding open the glass door.

Avery smiled but didn't move until I walked out ahead of her.

"What the hell, Ave," I said as soon as we were beyond sight of the glass door. "When I said you knew where to find me, I meant my house. Not here."

Avery shrugged and tucked her elbows into her sides, which pushed her breasts up more. "I wasn't sure we could control ourselves somewhere private."

I decided telling her I'd rather take a cheese grater to my dick than sleep with her again wouldn't help the situation. "I would have met you at Church or Karma. Anywhere but here."

She stuck out her full bottom lip. "I thought you'd be happy to see me. You spend so much time working with saggy old people, I thought you'd like the change in scenery."

"You being here is unprofessional. I'm already on thin ice with my boss, Ave."

"Was that Rowan Stevens in there?" Avery asked. "I heard she was back in town after her husband left her. How embarrassing."

"That's enough, Avery," I snapped.

She pressed her lips in a grim line. "So, it's true." She shook her head. "When someone told me they saw the two of you together at Church, I laughed."

"Leave Rowan out of this," I hissed. I knew I was making it worse by continuing to protect her, but I couldn't help myself.

Moisture pooled in Avery's eyes and her shoulders slumped. "I didn't think you'd move on so quickly," she said with a shaky voice.

Fuck. She was still hurt. As angry as I was at Avery, I couldn't help but feel sorry for her and the pain I'd caused. "Let's grab a drink at Church, tonight," I said, softly. "Talk things through."

A slow smile spread across her face. "Sure, baby."

I shook my head. "Talk, Ave. About why you're ruining my career."

She gripped my arm and leaned in to whisper in my ear. "I'll see you at Church at seven. Don't be late." She placed a kiss on my cheek and walked away, swinging her hips.

Before, my eyes would have been glued to the hypnotic swish. Now, her little show just looked overly dramatic, like everything with Avery. But beneath all the flash, I knew there was a person so deeply insecure, she needed everyone's eyes on her to feel good about herself.

Cammie glared at me when I returned to the office, which set off alarm bells. I hurried to the center of the room where Adam had Rowan alternating knee-to-chest stretches with lower back rotational stretches.

"Thank you, Dr. Cohen. I can take it from here."

Adam kept his eyes focused on Rowan, watching her movements. "You've made a lot of progress with her," he said, then frowned when Rowan grimaced.

I knew Adam was testing her range of motion but seeing Rowan in pain grated my already frayed nerves. "That's enough," I said, my voice stern.

Rowan laid flat on her back, breathing hard.

"How many more sessions does she have prescribed?" Adam asked.

"Two," Rowan and I answered together.

Adam looked at me and shook his head. As much as I disliked the man, he'd been a PT decades longer than me, and he'd just confirmed what I'd suspected. The exercises had helped Rowan, but they hadn't diminished her pain as much as I'd hoped. The issue was likely her discs. She'd need an MRI and possibly surgery at some point. With continued exercise, she could postpone it, but she'd always have pain.

Rowan looked up at me, worry etched on her beautiful face.

"Great work, young lady," Adam said. "You too, Dr. Cardoso," he added before heading back to his office.

"He seemed upset," Rowan said, standing. "So do you."

"Let's do some work with the resistance bands," I said, placing a hand on the small of her back and rubbing gentle circles.

"Caleb?" she asked looking up at me.

I blew out a breath. "You should request an MRI after our last session."

She nodded. "I know," she said in a quiet voice. "My back feels a lot better than when we started, but it still hurts every day."

I wanted to pull her into a hug. Instead, I set up the bands and guided her into the next exercise. She followed my directions but was otherwise quiet.

I assumed she was focused on the work or in too much pain to speak, but at the end of our session she lowered her voice and asked how things went with Avery.

"Fine," I said, shocked at how the conversation with my ex had completely left my mind. "I almost forgot," I added, as we started toward Cam's desk. "I have to take a rain check on dinner. I told Avery I'd meet her for drinks tonight. The sooner I talk to her about the reviews the better."

"Oh," Rowan said.

"I'm free tomorrow though," I said. "I don't want to stress your back any more than necessary. Let's order takeout."

"Sure," she said and smiled, but it didn't reach her eyes.

"Six?"

"Sounds great," she said.

"Make sure you get that mat. I'll text you a picture of the inserts later."

"I will. Bye, Cammie," she said and hurried to the hallway before I could offer to walk her out.

Cammie shook her head at me.

"What?" I asked.

She stood and grabbed my arm, dragging me into my office and shutting the door. Adam was busy with a patient, but he'd undoubtedly noticed.

"What's wrong with you?" she snapped.

"Um, right now, the fact you're yelling at me for some reason."

"Oh," she said, crossing her arms over her chest. "I have reason. Why on earth would you cancel plans with Rowan to spend the evening with that rattlesnake?"

"You heard me. I'm going to convince Avery to take down her reviews. If I make her wait too long to meet, she might change her mind."

Cammie poked me hard in the chest. "Do not sleep with her."

"I didn't plan to," I snapped. Then my stomach sank. "You don't think Rowan assumed that, do you?"

Cammie shrugged. "Maybe. It was pretty clear what Avery wanted, dressed like that. Then you have a private chat in the hall and come back in here and tell Rowan you can't see her tonight because you're seeing Avery."

"But I told Rowan why we're meeting. You heard me."

Cammie let out a sigh and put her hand on her forehead. "You might be the dumbest smart person I know."

Avery had been flirting pretty hard. I'd just wanted to get her out of the office without pissing her off more, but I could see how the amount of time we spent in the hallway might have given the wrong impression. "So, you think I should text Rowan and tell her I'm not interested in Avery?"

Cammie threw her hands up in the air. "No, Cal. You should text Avery and say you're happy to meet her at Karma for coffee tomorrow morning. Drinks on a Friday night sends a signal you don't want to send. Then you're going to call Rowan and say you messed up and ask her to dinner. Somewhere with candles and tablecloths."

"Right," I said grabbing my phone. "Candles and tablecloths."

"Antonia's is nice and walking distance from Sullivan Street. You can both have a drink and laugh about this."

I put my phone down. "Or Uber," I said, remembering how much pain Rowan had been in during her session. "I don't want her to walk too far after she worked so hard here."

Cammie's eyes softened. "She needs to build strength, Cal. Even if it hurts."

I nodded. But the thought of seeing Rowan in pain again twisted my stomach into knots. What was wrong with me? I saw patients hurting every day. Hell, I'd seen Rowan wince more times than I could count.

"Thanks, Cam," I said, rubbing my forehead.

She recognized the dismissal and left, but not without shooting me a worried look.

I'm not sure when it happened, but I could no longer deny I felt something for Rowan. Instead of calling her or texting Avery, I stared at my closed office door, contemplating how best to get myself out of the mess I'd made.

Chapter Twenty-Four

Rowan

My heart pounded as I checked my reflection in the mirror.

"You look fantastic," Lauren said behind me.

I'd borrowed another of her flirty dresses, this one a soft pink with a skirt that swirled when I moved. Lauren dug around in her closet and handed me a rose gold clutch that matched the dangly earrings she'd lent me as well.

"You have the best date wardrobe," I said, peering into her closet. Lauren wore black leggings, a plain t-shirt, and an apron to work. The abundance of dresses seemed odd.

She shrugged. "I go on a lot of dates."

"But how many see you in more than one outfit?"

"Plenty. Plus, you have to dress for the occasion. You can't wear the same thing to a rodeo you'd wear to a five-star restaurant."

I clutched the soft skirt while she went through her impressive belt collection. I wanted to ask why she'd never had a boyfriend. She had friends with benefits, one-night stands, and the occasional guy she dated once or twice before cutting him loose. The relationship habits of my best friend and the man who'd burrowed into my heart were shockingly similar.

"Why are you afraid to fall in love?" I asked.

She dropped the belt she was holding, then fumbled to pick it up. When she turned to face me, she'd plastered a smile on her face. "I'm not afraid. I'm too busy. Here, I think this turquoise belt will add just the right pop of color."

"Lauren?"

She shook her head and held out the belt. I knew, from years of abbreviated conversations, the subject was closed. I sighed and adjusted the belt on my waist.

"Perfect," Lauren said, clapping her hands.

Poppy burst through Lauren's front door as we walked into the living room. "The hearse is leaving, and no one is behind the counter," she said. "Let's go. I have ten minutes to get home and load my sculpture, or I'll be late for critique group."

Poppy looked me up and down and nodded. "Nice."

"You're welcome to borrow my clothes too," Lauren said.

Poppy flipped her off and headed for the stairs that exited to either the café's back room or the doorway to the alley.

"Just wait," Lauren said. "I'll get her wearing colors any day now."

"Don't hold your breath," I said, giving her a tight hug. "Thanks again for this."

Lauren squeezed me back, holding the embrace longer than usual. "Good luck tonight. Call me after, ok? Unless you're having wild sex. Then just text me a picture of a monkey, and I'll know the date went well."

Despite the nerves in my stomach, I laughed. "Got it."

She pulled the door to her apartment closed and ran down the narrow staircase to the café. I took my time, gripping the railing for the steep descent. Despite how much I'd improved, I knew my back ached more than it should. Hearing Dr. Cohen and Cal confirm my fears had been upsetting, but not as much as seeing Avery with Cal. When he canceled our dinner plans after talking to her, my heart cracked, and I knew I had to tell him about the job offer and how I felt. I'd been so relieved when Cal called to apologize and asked me to dinner, I'd almost forgotten that this date could be our last. It was time to end things or move forward with the understanding it wasn't casual, at least not for me.

Poppy stuck her head through the alley door. "You ok there, Granny?"

"Yes," I said, picking up the pace a little. "I don't want to fall and hurt myself more."

Poppy nodded, and despite her rush, waited patiently for me to join her at the bottom of the stairs.

"I could have met Cal at the restaurant," I said as I followed her to the hearse and climbed into the passenger seat.

"Admit it, when you were in high school, you fantasized about Cal Cardoso ringing your doorbell with flowers to take you on a date."

We drove down Main Street, right past Antonia's. "We're not in high school, and I doubt he'd bring me flowers. He knows I live with a florist. We have flowers all the time."

"But you had that fantasy, didn't you? And it didn't involve waiting alone at a restaurant, worried he won't show up."

Poppy turned onto Church Street where the corner bar hummed with loud music. I was glad Cal wasn't meeting Avery there tonight, but my stomach continued to tighten. "You think he won't show up?"

"Of course, he will. But I know you. You'd arrive early and start thinking the worst. Relax."

I nodded and she drove the rest of the way in silence. She turned off the ignition but instead of bolting from the hearse like I expected, she grabbed my hand.

"You have to tell him about the job offer. Tonight."

"I know."

Poppy blew out a breath. "I've really liked having you back."

I smiled at her. "Maybe I don't have to leave."

Her eyes widened. "You think they'd let you work from home?"

I shook my head. "No, but I'm not sure I want to accept the offer. To be honest, I don't love finance."

Poppy narrowed her eyes at me. "Who are you and what have you done with my sister?"

"I've had a lot of time to think since the accident. As bad as it was, it could have been so much worse. And I would have spent the last years of my life working my ass off at a job I only tolerated, with a social life that began and ended with Brad."

Poppy nodded. "So, you're having a quarter-life crisis. Are you planning to live in a van and travel around making crappy videos about getting lost to find yourself?"

"Um, no. I was thinking of starting my own business."

"I guess that could work. Though, I doubt there'd be many big accounts around here for a financial firm."

"No, a bakery. Mom and Lauren keep suggesting the idea. And it doesn't sound as crazy as I first thought."

Poppy sat back in the driver's seat as though I'd just announced I was pregnant with quadruplets. "Don't fuck with me," she said in a small voice. "I know I give off badass chick vibes, but my little black heart can still break. Don't mention something like that again unless you're certain."

"Ok," I said, giving her hand a squeeze. "I won't."

She blew out a breath and dropped my hand. "Now, get out of my car, bitch. I'm already late."

I walked inside but watched at the window as Poppy rolled a dolly to the back of the hearse and lifted a blanket-wrapped blob inside. She slid the dolly in after it, then climbed into the back to secure the piece with Bungie cords for the ride to wherever she was going. I'd peaked under the blanket last week and seen the work in progress, two girls made of clay, one larger than the other, their hands entwined. A pair of hearts, one large, one small, lay on a stretch of grass in front of them. I'd cried as soon as I pulled away the blanket, recognizing the moment I'd finally convinced Poppy to visit our father's grave. I hoped her critique group had the same response, and she moved to the next step of casting it in plaster or metal. Until then, I had to pretend I hadn't seen it.

Cal walked up as Poppy backed out of the driveway. He waved at her and started toward the house carrying a paper bag. He looked amazing in a pair of dark slacks and a blue button-down shirt open at the collar. He'd rolled up the sleeves, showing off his sculpted forearms. I took a few breaths, trying to calm down. I hadn't been this nervous since I sat for my professional exams.

The doorbell rang, and I opened it so fast Cal probably knew I'd been watching for him. His eyes darkened as they traveled down my body. "Wow," he said, biting his bottom lip. He shook his head and chuckled, then held out the bag.

"What's so funny?" I asked, taking the bag with Wilson's Pharmacy stamped on the front.

"I just realized I should have brought you flowers instead of those."

I peered into the bag and laughed at the package of orthotic inserts. "I kept waiting for you to text me which ones to get."

He gripped the back of his neck. "I wasn't sure either, so I went to the pharmacy to check out the options. Since I was already there, I figured I should get the ones that looked best. I wanted you to have them as soon as possible. The receipt's inside if you need a different size."

"Thank you," I said, clutching the bag to my chest. "That's really thoughtful."

He smiled and my stomach flipped.

"Ready?" he asked holding out his arm. I put the inserts on the hall table and grabbed the clutch, linking my arm with his.

"Are you ok to walk in those shoes?" he asked, frowning down at my sandals.

"Yes," I said. "They have great arch support." At least I think they did. They were definitely a step up from my flip flops. If Cal had his way, I'd be in old lady shoes, hiking boots, or sneakers.

"Ok," he said, his brow still furrowed. "If the walk gets to be too much, I'll run back and get the car."

"I'm fine," I said, giving his arm a squeeze. "It's a beautiful night. Let's enjoy it."

We started off, our pace agonizingly slow.

"I'm not decrepit," I said with a soft laugh. "Honestly, walking feels good. It's only an issue after I've been sitting too long."

Cal nodded. "That makes sense with a disc bulge or excision."

"Hey," I said, stopping in the middle of the street. "I appreciate the concern, Dr. Cardoso, but I'd rather enjoy a walk with Caleb."

He laughed. "Sorry. I meant to thank you, by the way. Adam seemed pleased with your progress, all things considered. He hasn't complimented me since everything with Avery went down. It gives me hope I'll be able to hang onto my job."

I had more important things to discuss than Avery Peterson, but I couldn't shake her perfect face from my mind. "Do you think you can convince her to take down her reviews?"

Cal blew out a breath. "I hope so. Honestly, I'd rather not talk about her, especially with you."

"Oh," I said, my stomach sinking. "Sure."

Cal glanced at me and frowned. "I said the wrong thing again, didn't I?"

I waved my hand. "No, it's fine."

We turned onto Broad Street, and he stepped closer to wrap his arm around my waist. I relaxed into his touch.

"As long as Avery stops writing new reviews, I might be ok. Cam has gotten a ton of my former patients to write glowing reviews to help counteract the negative ones."

"That's fantastic," I said, looking up at him. "I'll write one when I get home."

"You're still my patient," he said, placing a gentle kiss on my forehead.

I stopped walking, and he looked at me with concern. "What else am I?"

"What do you mean?"

"To you, Caleb. What am I?"

"Someone I enjoy spending time with."

I nodded. "Same."

He smiled and started to walk again, but I kept my feet firmly on the sidewalk. After a few steps, he turned to face me.

"My old company offered me a job," I said. "A promotion really. They fired my ex and my boss, then offered me her job."

Several emotions flashed across his face before he settled on a huge smile. "That's great."

"Is it?"

"Well, it means you can stop job hunting, right?"

"It also means I'd be moving back to DC."

"Yeah," he said, staring down at his shoes. "I figured that."

"I'm not sure if it's what I want. The job or living in DC. I'm curious what you think about it."

He looked at me, his expression suddenly blank. "Why would you care what I think?"

I felt the words like a punch to the chest, but still I drew myself up as tall as I could and said, "Because I care about you."

He shook his head and stared past my shoulder down Broad Street toward Sullivan, as though he wanted to rewind the conversation to a point in the walk before it began and steer it, and us, in a different direction.

"Rowan," he said, and in my name I heard everything he was about to say. He didn't feel the same. He didn't want a relationship, at least not with me. We would never be anything more.

I held up my hands to stop him. "It's ok. You were very clear. If you don't mind, though, I think I'll head back. If I'm moving to DC in a week, I have a lot to do. I'll finish my last two PT sessions up there. Thank you," I said as though we were wrapping up an unsuccessful job interview. "You really helped my back. I know whatever pain I still have isn't something you can fix. I'll be sure to write a glowing review. Good luck with Avery."

I turned and started back toward Sullivan Street. He called my name twice, each time a hint of something painful growing, but didn't follow. Before I turned the corner, I looked back to the stretch of sidewalk where I'd left him. He was already gone.

CHAPTER TWENTY-FIVE

Rowan

AT THREE AM, I gave up falling asleep and went down to the kitchen. Luckily, everyone was out when I returned home last night, so I grabbed a box of tissues and shut myself in the room I shared with Poppy. After a couple hours, I sent Lauren an image of a monkey because, despite her belief that I introverted when I should extrovert, I wanted to be alone. I turned off all the lights around nine, before Mom and Chris came home. When Mom cracked open the door and peeked into the room, I pretended to sleep. Poppy didn't sneak in until after one. I know because I'd been staring at the ceiling for hours before I heard her hearse pull into the driveway. I rolled over to face the wall, and I listened for her breaths to even before I returned to my back to stare at the ceiling again, silent tears dripping from my eyes into my ears.

It shouldn't hurt this much. Five weeks shouldn't be enough for anyone to break my heart, especially someone who told me he could never love me. Sometime in the night, I decided there must be something seriously wrong with me for falling in love with men who were incapable of loving me back. Sure, Brad said he loved me. Early in our relationship he said it first and kept right on saying it, including the day I caught him with Kelli.

The words were empty, and a part of me wondered if I meant them either. I had nothing to compare how I felt about Brad until Cal.

The way Cal treated me sometimes, like I was the most precious person in the world, had whittled through the walls I'd built around my heart. In the short time we were together, I'd never felt so interesting or beautiful. As much as it hurt, I wasn't even mad at him. He'd flat-out told me not to get attached. Every tear I'd cried was my own fault.

It'd taken me five minutes to drag myself out of bed and downstairs. I went slow so I wouldn't make noise and wake Mom, but it didn't help that my feet felt like twenty-pound weights and my legs wobbled like overcooked spaghetti. Once I finally reached the kitchen, I pulled the flour and sugar from the pantry and got to work, grateful Lauren needed me to bake, so I had something to do other than wallow in self-pity. I'd knocked out three dozen cookies and was sliding a pan of jumbo blueberry muffins into the oven when Mom shuffled into the kitchen.

"I guess you're on baker's hours now," she said, pouring herself a mug of coffee from the pot I'd brewed.

"I'm sorry. Did I wake you?"

Mom shook her head. "No, I was up there debating whether I should talk to you or let you work through whatever is wrong while you baked."

"I'm not angst baking, Mom. I'm helping Lauren. She fired her baker."

Mom nodded. "So I heard. I was talking about the fact you were in your room with the lights out when I got home instead of spending the night at Cal's."

"I was tired," I said, dumping a measuring cup of batter into a fresh muffin pan.

"And I heard you crying."

I spun around, flinging batter onto the floor. "You did not."

"Maybe not with my ears," Mom said with a sad smile. "But a mother's heart is a powerful thing. Plus, your eyes are all swollen, and your nose is red."

I shook my head. "I'm fine. You should stop drinking that coffee and go back to bed. I know you have a wedding later today."

Mom yawned. "I do. I have to deliver the arrangements to a resort in Meadows of Dan. I hope I can keep my eyes open for the drive."

I let out a sigh. "What time do they need to be there?"

"Noon. The trip takes an hour and a half."

I nodded and glanced at the cookies cooling on racks and the waiting batter. "I should have enough done by then to ride along with you."

"Great," Mom said with way too much energy for someone who claimed she wouldn't be able to keep her eyes open moments before. "The arrangements are finished. Mind if I help you? I do love a good baking sprint."

"Fine. But no music."

Mom nodded and went to the sink to wash her hands. "I was thinking," she said as I kneaded the dough I had rising on the counter. "Why don't we stay over. It might be nice to get away for a bit."

I narrowed my eyes. "And you just happen to know they have a room available?"

"I checked before I came downstairs. The night clerk offered the room at a great price for Saturday and Sunday night. I've always wanted to stay over."

"You can leave Red Blossoms that long?"

"I usually take Sundays off. And we'd be back Monday before ten."

"I don't know, Mom. Lauren is relying on me."

"Between the two of us, we can bake enough to supply Karma until Monday afternoon. Come on, Rowan. The resort has a spa and a fire pit and the best hiking trails. Plus, there's an observatory where you can look at the stars. I've been so busy, I feel like I've barely seen you, and if you accept that job offer, you'll be leaving soon."

I blew out a breath. "You know about the job."

"Of course," Mom said, pulling the finished tin of muffins from the oven and sliding in a new one. "A mother's heart hears everything."

By ten thirty, we'd delivered enough baked goods to keep Lauren stocked until Monday, and Chris had loaded the Red Blossoms delivery van with all the flowers for the wedding.

"Want me to follow you in my car and help unload?" Chris asked as Mom and I climbed into the van.

Mom shook her head. "No, sweetie. You have training with Cal later. I can handle these on my own."

My heart ached when I heard his name, but I busied myself arranging the snacks Mom had insisted we bring. I felt like a kid again, going on a delivery run with my mother. She'd even bought a box of Sour Patch Kids, a bag of Doritos, and two large fountain Pibbs, our standard snack selections on the rare occasions we made deliveries together once Poppy was old enough to watch Chris.

"I know you like your quiet in the mornings," Mom said, buckling her seatbelt as I waved goodbye to Chris. "But I need my music to drive."

I smiled, despite how exhausted and broken I felt. "It wouldn't be a road trip without Cyndi."

"This is a Tina Turner kind of day," Mom said, blasting her favorite play list.

We sang along, badly, sharing snacks the entire drive, and pulled into the resort just before noon. Mom drove the van to the back entrance of an enormous structure that looked like a grain silo. At first, it seemed out of place with the overall elegance of the resort, but then I noticed all the windows in the tower.

"Is this the observatory?"

Mom nodded. "The roof opens at the top. The wedding is taking place in the Galaxy Room."

"That's so romantic," I said, looking up at the tall tower.

Mom nodded. "I've always hoped one of you kids would get married here."

Brad and I had eloped to Las Vegas, which wasn't something I'd ever thought I'd do, but he convinced me he couldn't wait another day to marry me. I told myself it was easier, but a part of me regretted not having a moment to shine. Now I think he just assumed we'd have to pay for the event ourselves and decided he'd rather not.

"There's still time," Mom said with a smile.

My eyes stung. "Let's get these flowers inside before they wilt."

Mom shook her head. "No, way. You're sitting here until I've unloaded everything, and then we can check in."

I shifted in my seat. "I'm going to take a walk to stretch my back."

My phone rang as I admired the stunning mountain views from the resort's lawn. I blew out a breath when I saw Lauren's name.

"You lied," she said.

"Technically, I texted you a monkey."

"Which, we'd established meant you were having wild sex, not crying your eyes out because Cal's an idiot. He was just in here with Avery, and that combined with how you looked this morning when you made the delivery makes me wonder if I should have spat in his Chai."

"He's just asking her to take down the negative reviews she posted."

"Yeah, I gathered that while I made their drinks, which is the only reason I kept my spit to myself. But he avoided eye contact the whole time. Admit it, you sent me a lying monkey. I need info."

"Please, Lauren," I said, my throat tightening. "It hurts too much to talk about it." Someone grabbed the phone from my hand. Mom had abandoned her flowers on a cart behind the van. "Lauren, sweetheart," she said, after putting the call on speaker. "Rowan and I are staying at a resort in Meadows of Dan until Monday morning. If I haven't gotten the information out of her by then, you can have a crack at her when we get back."

"Ok, Mrs. Stevens," Lauren said and ended the call.

"That should buy you some time." Mom returned my phone, then gripped my shoulders. "I brought you here because I want you to think about your next step. You need to decide what you want. Not what I want or Poppy or Lauren wants, but what would make you happy. Which is why I'm driving home after I set up these arrangements and check you into your room."

"You're seriously leaving me here alone?" I said, looking around the picture-perfect grounds where couples and families drifted toward the golf course, trails, and tennis courts.

Mom nodded. "There's an amazing spa where you can get a massage, or you can just order room service and watch TV."

"This place had to cost a fortune," I said. "You could have rented me a room at the Holiday Inn off 81 if you wanted me to sit alone and think."

"No," Mom said with an edge to her voice. "You deserve the best in life, Rowan. I wasn't able to give you that when you were younger. You spent too much of your childhood taking care of Poppy, Chris, even me, on occasion. I know you gave and gave in your marriage, and it kills me that all that love and care was wasted on a man like Brad. But, baby, it's time to stop putting everyone else first. You refused to let me help you after the accident because you wanted to protect me. Well, I refuse to let you drift into the next chapter of your life without being absolutely certain it's what you want. Peace Falls is your home and always will be. But if it's too small for the life you dream of, then go. If you want that big job in DC, take it, and I will help you pack with a smile on my face. But don't do it because you think you have to prove yourself to anyone. Or because you're running away from a man who's too damaged to recognize love when it smacks him in his ridiculously chiseled face."

"Mom," I said, my voice breaking.

"I mean it, Rowan. Do not let a man stop you from being where you want to be. Whether that's DC, Peace Falls, or anywhere else in this big world."

She pulled me into a hug, and I sobbed on her shoulder long enough to worry about the flowers.

"You can't ruin someone's wedding because I'm having a breakdown," I sniffed.

Mom handed me a rumpled tissue from her pocket and turned us to face the van, where someone had already removed the cart. "A friend of mine works here and insists on helping me bring in the arrangements."

She blushed and cleared her throat when a silver fox of a guy pushed the cart outside and folded it into the van. He gave us both a wave before he went back inside the building.

I raised my eyebrows at Mom, but she just swatted my arm. "Let's go. I'll get you checked in and come back to place everything."

After a stop at the front desk, Mom carried my bag to a gorgeous room overlooking the mountains and placed it on one of the two queen-sized beds. There were rich hardwood floors throughout and a separate sitting area by the windows with a plush couch. It was without question the nicest room I'd ever stayed in.

"This is huge," I said. "Are you sure you don't want to stay with me?"

Mom shook her head but let out a sigh when she peeked in the bathroom. "Promise me you'll soak in the tub."

I leaned into the bathroom and took in the deep soaking tub surrounded by beautiful glass tiles. It looked like something out of a luxury travel blog.

"Order whatever you want to eat," she said, giving my shoulder a squeeze. "Do whatever you want to do. I'll know if you don't charge anything to the room or put something on your own card."

"Can you afford all this?" I asked, motioning to the room.

"Honestly, yes," she said. "I know things were tight when you were younger, and you had to take out loans for school. If you let me, I'd like to pay them back now, or help you somehow. I never could have built Red Blossoms without you taking on what you did at home. Staying here a couple nights is small by comparison. Just promise me you'll enjoy it. Have a good cry if you need to, but then hike or swim. Eat all the desserts."

I pulled Mom into one more hug before she left me alone to figure out what I wanted to do with the rest of my life.

Chapter Twenty-Six

Cal

As soon as I paid for our drinks, I led Avery to a table on the sidewalk outside Karma. Skye devoured her pup cup then tucked herself under the table, laying her head on my feet.

Avery settled into a chair with a smile, angling her body toward the street, either to avoid touching Skye or so everyone could see her face as they traveled down Main. Half the town would assume we'd rekindled our relationship before she finished her cappuccino.

My stomach protested the first sip of iced Chai. I'd had nothing but beer since lunch yesterday. I wanted to be hungover in the comfort of my home, but the sooner I got through this conversation the better.

"You look terrible, baby," Avery said, eyeing me over the lid of her to-go cup. "Normally, I'd be annoyed you hadn't dressed up for our date, but I'll let it slide this time since you're clearly so upset over us."

"This isn't a date," I said. "It's a conversation."

"Still, you could have worn something better than old gym clothes."

I rubbed my forehead. This was a mistake. Avery would never take down her reviews, and this little chat could end up doubling her efforts to ruin my career.

"Hey," Avery said, reaching across the table to take my hand.

I pulled my fingers away like she'd burned me, and she leaned back with a hurt expression on her face.

"You're really mad at me," she said in a soft voice.

"Why the fuck wouldn't I be mad? I'm about to get fired because of the crap you posted online."

Her eyes filled with tears but she blinked them back and sat taller. "I just wanted you to understand how much you'd hurt me."

I blew out a breath. "I told you from the beginning, we were just messing around."

"Did you honestly think I wouldn't still have feelings for you?" she said, slapping her manicured hand on the metal table. Skye whimpered and buried her nose between my feet. "You were my first everything, Cal."

"And you were mine. But a whole lot happened between high school and now, including you dumping me."

"Admit it. If it'd just been sex, we wouldn't have talked so much on the phone or gone out to dinner as often as we did. This was all payback, wasn't it?"

"You honestly believe I'm so petty that I'd plan to hurt your feelings over a decade after you hurt mine? I'll admit I slipped back into the habits we had in high school, but I figured you were still just having fun like I was."

She shook her head; the tears she fought earlier returned. This time, she allowed them to stream down her face. "Breaking up with you is the biggest regret of my life. I still cared about you then. The truth is, I've never stopped caring. I was afraid you'd go off to college and meet someone else. I just couldn't take being left again. My dad really messed me up, but I shouldn't have taken it out on you."

"You're better off without him, Ave," I said, taking her hand.

"I know," she said, giving my fingers a squeeze. "But I guess I've never really gotten over it or losing you. When you joined Dr. Cohen's practice,

I was excited you were back in town, but more than that, I was relieved. Despite everything that happened, you were doing so well. I mean, who would have thought the guy who almost failed freshman biology would earn a doctorate in physical therapy?"

She chuckled and the knot in my throat relaxed enough for me to speak. "It was English. I got an A in biology freshman year."

Avery nodded, a soft smile on her face. "That's right, Mrs. Evers made you memorize and perform that entire Hamlet speech in front of the class. That's when I knew I wanted to be your girlfriend."

I nodded. "I was so nervous. I didn't think I'd get through it. Logan memorized the whole thing with me and mouthed the words from the front row."

She let out a shuddery breath. "He was a good guy."

"The best," I said, giving her hand a squeeze before letting it go. We looked at each other and smiled. "I hope you believe that I never meant to hurt you. I was being honest when I said I don't do relationships."

She pressed her lips together and nodded. "I know that now. I just figured you'd want more after we were together, and the way we were always talking and hanging out, I assumed we were more than casual. I'm sorry about the reviews. I knew I'd taken it too far when people started glaring at me around town. Even Mr. Wilson was cold to me. If the sweetest man on the planet hates you, there's a good chance everyone does. I know what I did wasn't right, but I was hurt and trying to get your attention. I didn't think it through. I never meant to put your job in danger."

"An apology isn't enough, Ave. I need you to undo some of the damage you've caused. If you take down all your reviews, I should be ok."

"I'll start as soon as I get home," she said, wiping the tears from her cheeks.

I let out a long breath and sagged back into my chair. "Thank you. And I'll be sure to let people know you did."

She pushed back from the table and stood. "I get now that you and I will never work. There's too much history, good and bad. You bring out the worst in me, and I don't bring out the best in you." She paused and gripped my shoulder. "For what it's worth, you're ready for more than casual. And I think you want it too. Otherwise, it wouldn't have been so easy for me to assume we were in a relationship. You'll make someone a great partner. Goodbye, Cal."

"Bye, Ave," I said. "See you around."

In a town this size, it would be impossible not to, but whether those moments were awkward or not was up to her. As long as she took down her reviews, I could pass her on the street with a smile, and I hoped she'd be able to do the same. I watched her climb into her car before I tossed my full cup in a trash bin and headed for the park with Skye. Chris and Aiden were already there when I arrived, passing a ball back and forth.

"Looking good," I said, walking toward them.

Chris's eyes hardened and he threw the ball at me so hard it knocked the air from my lungs.

"I see you've packed some heat on your throw," I said with a laugh.

"Fuck you, Cal," Chris said, lunging at me.

Aiden stepped between us, placing a firm hand on Chris's chest. Skye barked but seemed unsure who to protect, her eyes flicking from Chris to me.

"If you punch him, you might get hurt," Aiden said. "You don't want an injury this close to tryouts."

"What the hell?" I asked, throwing the ball to the ground.

"Seriously," Chris said, trying to duck around Aiden.

"Would you feel better if I punched him?" Aiden asked.

Chris nodded. Aiden turned, and I had half a second to dodge his fist. Skye growled at Aiden and he took a step back.

"What the fuck, man," I said.

"Sorry, kid," Aiden said. "He's agile."

"I bet I could hit him." Chris lunged again and Aiden pinned his arms.

"Suicide sprints. Now," Aiden shouted. "Run out the anger. Got it? I'll deal with him."

Chris nodded and took off with a stack of cones, which he set up as far away from us as he could without leaving the park. Aiden waited until Chris started running intervals before he shook his head and said, "You know I gave you time to dodge."

"Yeah," I said, eyeing him cautiously as I bent to pet Skye. "I still don't understand why you wanted to hit me. Or why Chris does, for that matter."

"Because, dumbass, you broke up with his sister last night, and he saw you getting cozy with Avery this morning. Believe me, I wanted to punch you. Rowan seems like a sweetheart, and the kid adores her. But I figured I should hear your side first. Plus, I don't trust your dog not to bite me."

"I didn't break up with Rowan," I said rubbing the sudden ache in my chest. "We were never together. We had some fun, but she got offered a job in DC. She's moving, so that's it."

"So, now you're fucking Avery again?"

"Of course not," I yelled, standing. Skye let out a huff and laid on the ground. "We talked out our shit. She's taking down the reviews and moving on with her life. Just like I am."

He nodded and yelled to Chris, "He's just an idiot, not a douchebag. There's nothing going on with him and Avery. Get over here."

Chris ran to us, his face red from rage, exertion, or both. "I thought you wanted me to run out the anger."

"Nah," Aiden said, patting Chris's shoulder. "You need some of that for the training exercises I have planned. I just wanted more info before I decided if Cal deserved to be punched."

"Nice," I said. "What have you decided?"

Aiden shook his head. "There's no point," he said to Chris. "He's hurt himself more than either of us could. He still thinks he doesn't want a relationship with anyone."

Chris nodded. "Yeah, he's an idiot."

"Hey," I said, stepping toward them. "Like I said before, what happens between Rowan and me is our business."

"And what about what doesn't happen?" Chris said, raising his eyebrow.

"You don't know what you're talking about," I said.

Chris laughed, but it sounded hollow. "Why? Because I'm still in high school? I might be younger than you, but I've lived with three women my whole life. I have a pretty good understanding of them, overall, and my sisters, especially. And unlike you, I'm not a jaded prick."

"Watch it," I said through gritted teeth.

Chris shook his head. "Thanks for all the time you've given me this summer, but I'd rather train with Aiden from now on. Assuming you don't mind?" he added, glancing at Aiden.

"Happy to help," Aiden said, tossing a football in his hands. "You heard the kid, Cal. Go home. Take a nap. You look like shit."

"You're serious?" I asked.

Chris nodded. "Don't worry. I'll still walk Skye. It's not her fault you're an idiot."

With that, he grabbed the ball from Aiden and took off. Aiden raced after him, leaving me alone with Skye, who snuggled up to me with a whimper. After watching them work together a few minutes, it became clear they had no intention of including me, so Skye and I walked back to where I'd parked my car near Karma.

As I loaded Skye into the SUV, Lauren threw open the café door and ran toward me. I held up my hands to protect my face, but instead of hitting me, she wrapped her arms around my waist and pulled me into a strong hug. Lauren made great hot chocolate, and we usually exchanged a few words when I came into Karma, but we weren't on hugging terms, or so I thought.

I dropped my hands from their defensive position and patted her back awkwardly.

"Sorry I almost spit in your Chai," she said, taking a step back.

"No worries," I said. "I'm not dating Avery. I don't do relationships." I had no idea why I was spilling my guts on the sidewalk to the woman whose role in my life could best be described as my favorite barista.

She nodded. "I get it. Better than anyone."

I realized then that I'd often seen Lauren around town on dates, but never with the same guy. I couldn't name anyone she'd been with longer than a week, though several men I knew had taken her out and asked for another date only to be turned down. Gently, of course. But turned down all the same.

"You don't do relationships either?" I asked, even though I already knew the answer.

She shook her head. "Nope. I've never met anyone worth the risk."

I nodded, and her eyes hardened.

"But you have." She slapped my chest and then pulled me in for another hug. "No matter what you're afraid of, I promise, she's worth it." Before I could say anything, Lauren let me go and went back into Karma.

I stood on the sidewalk as the truth of her words sank in. I knew I'd hurt Rowan last night. I saw the pain on her face. I kept seeing it, despite every beer I drank at Church, until I passed out on my living room couch. I felt guilty. Plain and simple. Or so I thought. Pain shot through my chest, the ache so powerful and sudden, I wondered if I was having some kind of medical event. It was the type of hurt that had its own mass, the sheer weight of it enough to crush the breath from your lungs. I'd felt it before, waking up in the hospital to a broken body, my parents holding my hands as they delivered the news that shattered my entire life. I lived with that weight until I pushed it down. I focused on healing my body, then earning my degree, building a career, and deciding what color to paint my fucking house. I'd kept moving forward, one step beyond this terrible pain that wanted to eat me alive.

I stumbled to the driver's side, but when I saw how badly my keys shook in my hands, I dropped them on the street and pulled my phone from my pocket.

"I can't drive," I said, each word pushed out with a burst of air that tightened the ache in my chest.

There was a pause as I fumbled on the ground for my keys.

"The app says you're near Karma," Theo said. "Is that right?"

I nodded. Then made a noise that I hoped sounded like a confirmation.

"I'm on my way, brother."

I ended the call, started the engine, and crawled into the back seat with Skye, praying I could hold it together long enough for Theo to drive me home.

CHAPTER TWENTY-SEVEN

Rowan

I'D JUST SHOWERED AFTER a long swim on Sunday afternoon when someone beat on my hotel door. Tightening the fluffy robe around my waist, I peered through the peep hole.

"I can hear you breathing," Poppy yelled.

"No, you can't," Lauren said, shoving her aside to lean closer to the door.

I opened it, and they flashed matching grins.

"Surprise!" Lauren said, giving me a hug. "We're here for a sleepover."

"If you're both here, who's at the café?" I asked as my sister walked past me without saying hello.

"Dibs," Poppy said, throwing her bag onto the queen bed I hadn't slept in.

"Cammie is closing," Lauren said. "It occurred to me she spent so much time at Karma, she'd make a great part-time employee, and I thought she could use the money. She knows all the drink combinations and most of the regulars. Plus, the girl learns faster than anything I've ever seen."

"You left your business with a new hire to drive over an hour and a half for a sleepover with me?"

"I left my friend in charge, so I could take advantage of an amazing resort I would otherwise never be able to afford, and because you've introverted enough."

"I'm here for the observatory," Poppy said, shaking the box of Sour Patch Kids leftover from my drive with Mom and popping a piece in her mouth. "And because Lauren made me," she added around a mouthful of candy.

Lauren rolled her eyes. "She's joking. We're both concerned about you and wanted to check in."

"I can't believe Mom paid for two nights here," Poppy said, walking to the sitting area and admiring the view. "That woman still wears the same sweatshirts she had when we were in elementary school."

"She wanted me to have time alone to think about my next steps," I said.

Lauren peered into the trashcan and frowned. "How many boxes of tissues have you gone through?"

"Wrong question," Poppy said. "How many desserts have you eaten?"

I cleared my throat. "A couple. Of both."

Lauren flopped onto my unmade bed and stretched out like a cat. "Wow, this bed is amazing." She closed her eyes, and I noticed the dark circles under them had deepened. "If it makes you feel better, Cal looked terrible yesterday."

"It'd make me feel better if we didn't talk about him." I'd done as Mom asked, alternating my crying sessions with short hikes, room service, and a swim. After a full day of thinking and letting myself feel whatever I wanted, I was emotionally exhausted and no closer to deciding about the job offer. But I'd come to one conclusion: I had to stop thinking about Caleb Cardoso and focus on the decisions I could control.

"You really are Mom's favorite," Poppy said, walking into the bathroom. "I figured it might be Chris since he's the baby and all, but damn."

"As great as this room is," Lauren said, "I want to see everything else. Have you been to the spa?"

"Just the pool," I said.

"What's wrong with you?" Poppy said, glaring at me. "Let's go. Do you have a couple more of those robes?"

It took a few minutes to convince Poppy that I should change into real clothes for the walk down to the spa instead of all of us parading through the lobby in matching terrycloth robes. After we'd checked in at the spa and were given the exact same robes to wear for our massage, Poppy shook her head.

"That's your problem, Rowan. You complicate your life because you do what people expect you to do. So what if you wore a robe in the lobby? You don't know anyone here but us, and we'd already seen you in it."

Lauren laughed as she tightened the sash on her own robe. "I agree with Poppy, in theory, but no way would I have walked through the lobby half naked."

"Y'all are no fun," Poppy said as an employee led us to the massage room.

The tables reminded me of the ones in Cal's office, and my chest tightened. The masseur directed me to lie face down, but I stood beside the massage table, my fingers gripping the edge.

"Um, can you give us five minutes before we start," Lauren said, lifting her head up from the table where she was already face down.

"No," I said, hopping onto my table and stretching out. "I'm fine."

"No, you're not," Poppy mumbled. "Crap on a cracker," she groaned as her masseur worked her shoulders, "why haven't I done this before?"

"Because it's $225 an hour," I said as my masseur got to work on the tight muscles in my neck.

"Mom's favorite, for sure," Poppy said and moaned.

"I know your mom told us to get massages," Lauren said, "but I'll be sending her a very large gift card to Karma."

I lifted my head. "Mom knows you're here? I thought y'all just hijacked my hotel stay."

"Yes," Lauren said. "She asked us to spend the night and drive you home in the morning. Sorry, it's going to be early. Cammie is opening, but she has to be at Dr. Cohen's by eight."

Poppy groaned but I wasn't sure if it was in response to the massage or Lauren's announcement we'd be leaving before the sun rose.

Thinking of Cammie made me think of Cal, which made the corners of my eyes burn. I took a deep breath and pushed his handsome face from my mind. "If we're missing breakfast," I said, "let's have dinner in the restaurant. I haven't been yet."

Poppy lifted her head. "Mom said you only ordered peanut butter pie, baklava, and a pot of coffee to the room since you've been here."

"Healthy," Lauren said with a laugh.

"I guess I wasn't that hungry," I said, laying my head back down. The masseur placed hot stones down my back, and I let out a groan to rival Poppy's.

"If we don't feed you a real dinner, Mom will never let me hear the end of it," Poppy said.

"I brought dresses," Lauren said in a small voice. "We can do our hair and—"

Poppy and I both lifted our heads and looked at Lauren. Her eyes were shut, her lips parted.

"Did Lauren seriously just fall asleep mid-sentence?" I asked.

"Yeah," Poppy said, lowering her head. "She insisted on driving, so I made her talk the whole time to keep her awake. Lauren has a lot of words."

I chuckled. "Yes, she does."

As if to prove how few words Poppy and I had, we went the rest of the massage without talking. I tried to clear my mind and enjoy the luxury around me, but I couldn't stop wondering if Cal was upset about me or his conversation with Avery.

"Lauren needs another full-time employee," Poppy said after the masseurs had left us. "She's at Karma eighty plus hours a week."

I looked at my best friend passed out on the table and nodded. "She's working herself to death."

"Cammie would be perfect, but she needs full time. I doubt there's anyone else Lauren would trust to run the place while she wasn't there."

"Can't you pick up more hours?" I asked.

"Don't tell Lauren this, but I hate working at Karma. I know she teases you for being introverted, but at least you can talk to people without wanting to strangle them. I'm not cut out to be a barista. I need a job where I can work with minimal interaction."

I nodded. "Like decorating cakes. You're really talented."

"So are you," she said, propping herself up on her elbows. "We could do it. Start our own custom bakery. Even if it doesn't make a ton of money at first, so what? It's not like we have mortgages or families to support. Mom loves having us all in the house, and I know for a fact she wants to take over your student loan payments. As much as I want my own place, I wouldn't mind living at home longer while I built my own business. You could handle all the baking and the customer interactions. I could do all the decorating and marketing, honestly, anything that didn't involve people. If you taught me how to handle the finances, I'd even do that."

"But that would mean I'd have to stay in Peace Falls."

Poppy nodded. "We could open a bakery anywhere, but Peace Falls makes the most sense. Not only do we have a free place to live and work, but Mom knows a ton of people in the special event industry. We could even cross promote each other's businesses."

"I'm not sure I can live in a place as small as Peace Falls after living in DC for so long."

"Of course, you can," Poppy said, gently. "It's whether or not you want to."

Lauren let out a loud snore, and Poppy and I burst out laughing. "What," she stammered, lifting her head. "Did I fall asleep?"

"That has to be the most expensive nap in the history of naps," Poppy laughed.

Lauren waved her hand. "Nah, any surgery where you go under would cost more."

"Yeah, about that," I said.

Poppy and Lauren both snapped their attention to me with matching frowns.

"I might need back surgery. Which is why starting my own business without health insurance wouldn't be a good idea."

"So, you COBRA your old policy until you can enroll in an open market plan in November," Lauren said. "Besides, if you need a job, I'm happy to hire you."

"No," Poppy said. "You can buy her baked goods and hire Cammie full time. Assuming Rowan decides she's woman enough to live in Peace Falls."

Lauren and Poppy both looked at me with hopeful expressions. I blew out a breath. "I'm considering it," I said. "I've enjoyed being in the mountains again and spending time with y'all."

Lauren squealed and Poppy smiled. I hadn't realized how few friends I had in DC until I had the chance to see Lauren and Poppy whenever I wanted. Though we'd just met, Cammie could easily become someone I could count on to grab dinner or a coffee. But living in Peace Falls meant seeing Cal. Even if I moved off Sullivan Street, we'd still cross paths. Poppy seemed smitten with Theo, which would put Cal and me together from time to time. Heck, I couldn't go to the grocery store without the risk of running into him. It was inevitable. As much as I didn't want to think about Cal, I needed to know what to expect the next time I saw him.

"Do you think Cal was upset because of me?" I asked Lauren.

She nodded. "I think he might be afraid to get close to people after what happened to Logan."

"Bullshit," Poppy said, swinging her feet to the floor, flashing us both. "He's gotten close to plenty of people since then. Cammie makes it sound like he's her brother, and Chris says the same. Cal's capable of loving people. He just hasn't let that extend beyond friendships."

Lauren stared up at the ceiling while Poppy wiggled into her robe. "I agree. But it's different being friends with someone and allowing yourself to be vulnerable enough to fall in love."

"Speaking from experience there?" I asked.

Lauren shrugged. "Are you decent, Poppy?"

"Never," Poppy said, tying the sash of her robe in a knot.

"At least she's honest," I said, with a laugh, covering myself with a sheet as I slipped into my own robe. I let out a breath and put my head in my hands. "I forgot to tell Cammie to cancel my PT session tomorrow."

"No problem," Lauren said, tightening her robe. "I'll text her after we eat. I'd already planned to check in with her later. Let's stop on the way upstairs and make a reservation for dinner."

"Tell Cammie to move Rowan's appointment to Tuesday," Poppy said. She walked to my table and gripped my shoulders. "You're not letting your back get worse because Cal can't pull his head from his ass. Besides, any longer than that, and you'll work yourself up too much. Better to get it over with."

I nodded.

"You could just switch your appointment to Dr. Cohen," Lauren said.

"No," I said. "Caleb is not losing his job because of me. We're adults. I only have two sessions left. I might as well finish them this week, whether I decide to move or stay."

"Great," Poppy said, helping me from the table. "Let's make that reservation. I could hear Rowan's stomach rumbling across the room."

"Oh," Lauren said, standing. "I have the perfect dress for you, Poppy. It's floral."

Poppy made a gagging sound, and a huge laugh burst through the ache in my chest.

They both stared at me. I laughed harder, bending at the waist and gripping my knees.

"Is she losing it?" Poppy asked.

"Maybe," Lauren said.

I stood up, wiping the tears that had suddenly sprung from my eyes. "Poppy wearing floral is about as likely as Caleb Cardoso falling for me. Men like him do not end up with women like me, even if they hadn't sworn off relationships. I'm so stupid. I couldn't keep a guy like Brad faithful. Why in a million years would I think a man like Cal would want more from me than a casual fuck? It's embarrassing how much this hurts. Honestly, he's the only reason I'm still considering that job in DC. When we were in school, would either of you have imagined I'd have to worry about dodging Cal Cardoso at Church because he's seen me naked? We might as well be different species."

"Lauren," Poppy gritted out. "I'm going to rock the shit out of that floral dress."

As we made our way into the restaurant later that night, I had to admit, she did.

Chapter Twenty-Eight

Cal

Skye didn't move her head from my knee when the doorbell rang. Other than when I went to work today, she hadn't left my side in days. I patted her head and stood. The short distance to the front door felt like miles. I must have walked too slowly since Theo pushed the door open before I could. Skye burst past me, no doubt relieved someone else had come to take care of my sorry ass. Theo put his key to my house in his pocket before crouching to rub Skye's belly.

Aiden paused in the doorway behind Theo and scanned me like a crack in a foundation he'd been hired to fix. "Let's go," he said.

Theo stopped petting Skye and gave him a confused look. "Where are we going?"

"My house. Bring the dog. We might need her."

I shook my head. "The game's about to start."

"None of us give a shit about that game," Aiden said. "There's something I need to show y'all."

"You're finally letting us in your house?" Theo asked.

"Nope," Aiden said, rubbing his forehead like it ached. "What I have to show you is on the property. Grab a leash for the mutt. I don't feel like chasing her through a cornfield."

At the word leash, Skye took off and grabbed hers, then pranced beside the door. I clipped it to her collar and stepped onto the porch in time to see Poppy drive by in her hearse. She slowed, rolled down the window, and flipped me off.

Theo raised his hand and waved. She waved her single-finger salute at him as well. The bastard smiled but cleared his throat and adapted his signature scowl when he caught me watching him.

"Shotgun," Aiden called.

I folded myself into the backseat of Theo's extended cab with Skye. The drive to Aiden's was long and quiet. Theo took back roads to avoid the stretch of Route 33 that had changed all our lives.

When we pulled in front of Aiden's old farmhouse, Theo turned off the truck and looked at him. "Well?"

Instead of answering, Aiden climbed out and tromped into the field behind his house. Theo, Skye, and I followed through the overgrown grass. A grasshopper jumped out of our path, and I wondered what other creatures lurked in the tall blades. I'd have to do a tick check on Skye and myself for sure.

"Where are we going?" Theo asked, jogging to catch up with Aiden.

Aiden pointed ahead but didn't say anything. I followed behind them with Skye, the knot in my stomach tightening. It wasn't like Aiden to be quiet. He shouted his thoughts as soon as he had them. Whatever he was about to show us wasn't something he wanted to talk about, and that scared the hell out of me. At the edge of the field, Aiden stopped and leaned against an old split-rail fence. He stood several minutes, staring across the road at a neighboring field.

"What are we looking at?" Theo asked.

Aiden pointed to the far right and my heart stopped.

"Fuck," I said, leaning against the fence.

Theo looked between us, confusion on his face.

Far across the field, through a slight break in a stand of trees, stood a dilapidated barn. The entire structure listed to the right, the faded red paint chipped in places to bare wood. The tree break framed the barn on either side, a gouge of fresh earth marking where more had been.

"Through the trees," Aiden said.

Theo looked again and tensed, then sank to the ground. Skye whimpered and tugged on her leash. I walked closer, so she could curl into Theo's lap. He buried his face in her fur, his shoulders heaving as he struggled to breathe.

"What's wrong with you?" I asked Aiden, shoving him hard in the chest. The man was such a tank, his feet didn't budge.

"The same thing that's wrong with you and Theo," he said.

"You're a sick fuck," I said.

Aiden nodded. "I know. That barn is why I bought this place."

"Why would you want to see that?" I asked. "And from your own backyard, no less."

Aiden turned from me and stared off at the barn again.

Theo lifted his head, his face pale. "Why?" He forced out between labored breaths.

"Because," Aiden said, his voice so quiet, I had to lean in to hear. "I wanted to be close to Logan."

Logan was buried in the Baptist cemetery in Peace Falls, but he'd spent his last night in the barn on Old Man Crawford's farm. While her grandparents visited friends in Richmond, Crawford's granddaughter had hosted a final party before everyone scattered to their post-high-school lives.

Aiden kicked the fence post by his foot. "I moved here to be close. Earlier this year, I bought Crawford's place too."

"You bought the barn?" I asked.

Aiden nodded.

"So you could knock it down?" Theo asked. Some of the color had returned to his face. Skye licked his hand, and he rubbed her ears.

"No," Aiden said. "Maybe. I don't know. I just wanted it. At the rate Peace Falls is growing, it's only a matter of time before a developer builds subdivisions out here. I figured I ought to snatch it up while I could. Plus, Old Man Crawford needed money. We made a deal that lets him stay in the house as long as he wants."

"So, you're going to build a subdivision?" I asked, still confused.

"No," Aiden snapped. "Hell, no. I like it out here. It's peaceful. I bought it so no one else would."

"Because you feel close to Logan here," Theo said.

Aiden nodded. "I know it seems dumb. It's not like it's the football field where we practiced together or any other place in town with so many memories I want to choke. The barn is special. It was the last place our lives made sense."

Theo nodded. "Still, it's triggering as hell. I wouldn't want to look at it every day."

"Yeah," Aiden said. "Hurts every time I do."

"Then why do you?" I snapped. "You give Theo shit for his tattoos and cutting, but what you're doing is worst. Not to mention, you thought it'd be a good idea to drag us here to suffer with you."

"Just you," Aiden said, slapping my shoulder. "Sorry, Theo. I took one look at Cal and knew it was time, but I should have given you a head's up."

"I get it, man," Theo said, standing. He pulled Aiden into a crushing hug, thumping his back.

"Well, I still don't," I said, crossing my arms.

"Do you want to tell him?" Aiden asked. "Or should I?"

"I'll do it," Theo said. "If he takes a swing at me, hold him back."

Aiden nodded.

Theo took a deep breath and said, "You can't run from it anymore."

"Run from what?" I asked, bending to check Skye's ears for ticks. I should be home watching a game I hated, not standing in a bug-infested field talking riddles.

"The grief," Aiden said.

"He's getting waves of it already," Theo said. "I saw it on Saturday. Bad burrito my ass. Admit it. You were shaking so bad you couldn't drive because something made you think of Logan, more specifically losing him."

"Ah," Aiden said, nodding. "The kid's sister."

"Yeah," Theo said, "That's my guess too. Did you break up or something?"

"She got a job offer in DC," Aiden said. "And like an idiot, he told her good luck."

"I didn't tell her good luck." Skye whimpered and I patted her head.

"But you didn't ask her to stay. Or suggest you keep dating long distance," Aiden said.

"I don't do relationships," I said.

Theo and Aiden both started laughing.

"I don't," I said, standing.

Aiden knocked my shoulder. "You're the king of relationships, Cal. You've practically adopted the kid and that hot little piece at your office."

My blood boiled. I shoved Aiden hard enough this time to knock him into the fence. "Do not call Cammie that."

"Spoken like a true brother," Aiden said, laughing. "Thanks for proving my point."

"I meant romantic relationships," I said. "I don't date. I don't have girlfriends. I fuck when I need to and move on."

"Charming," Theo said, shaking his head.

"I should have let the kid clock him," Aiden said.

"Answer me this," Theo said. "Do you think you're honoring Logan with the work you do?"

My chest tightened and a lump formed in my throat. I did, but I'd never said that to either of my friends. Logan wanted to be a physician. He was so ridiculously smart; he would have been an amazing one. Hell, he might have cured cancer. Bare minimum, he would have given the best care he could to every patient he treated. I nodded. "I try to."

"You are," Aiden said, gripping my shoulder. "You should see the love fest for you online now."

He pulled his phone from his pocket, scrolled a bit, and held it out. Sure enough, my rating was now a 4.9. Avery must have followed through and taken down her reviews. I started to hand the phone back, but Aiden shook his head.

"Scroll down."

I did as he said, and the first comment sent a searing pain through my chest.

Dr. Cardoso is a dedicated physical therapist. He does everything he can to help his patients heal from their injuries. It's no exaggeration to say he changed my life. I was so broken at our first session, I could barely walk. He helped me gain the strength I needed to climb whatever mountains life puts in my way. I'm certain he will help many more people find the strength they need to live the lives they want. He's five stars as both a PT and a person. I wish him all the best.

"Rowan," I said. She left the review despite canceling her appointment today. Cammie assured me Rowan had just moved her session to tomorrow, but I thought for sure I'd never see her in the office again.

"You're falling for her, idiot," Theo said. "And you're pushing her away either because it scares the shit out of you or because you think you don't deserve to be happy. Which is it?"

"Scared shitless," Aiden said.

I swallowed and nodded.

"I'm scared of that damn dog," Aiden said pointing at Skye, who perked up at the attention. "All dogs, really. But you two love her, so I grew a pair and put up with her."

"Sort of," Theo said and chuckled.

"Look, Cal," Aiden said, "all I know is you've smiled more since you started spending time with Rowan than you have in years."

"And he made a picnic and took her hiking," Theo added.

"How did you know that?" I asked.

"Poppy told me. Admit it, you're crushed she's moving," Theo said.

"I'm fine," I said automatically.

Theo and Aiden shook their heads.

"You've done a great job living your best life, professionally," Theo said. "You went from goofing around and planning to take the easy route with your dad's business to working your ass off in school and after. All of that kept you busy enough you never considered why you didn't want a girlfriend, but you owe it to yourself, and to Logan, to consider it now. To want more in your life than work."

"It's been ten years," Aiden said lifting his chin toward the barn. "I don't know about y'all, but I'm tired. Tired of pretending like I'm ok when I'm not. Tired of seeing you hurt yourself, Theo, or you living half the life you could be, Cal. Of the three of us, you've got your shit together the most, and you're about to let an amazing woman walk out of your life without a fight. It's time. I don't know what that means yet, for any of us. But for me, it starts there," he said pointing to the barn.

"What do you have in mind?" I asked.

Aiden shrugged. "Hell if I know."

"We go to the barn," Theo said. "On the anniversary. I can't go back to where the accident happened." Theo looked between Aiden and me, his eyes pleading. "I can't. I remember every detail of every moment, anyway."

Aiden nodded, but the two of us shared a look. We'd both been knocked out cold, but Theo had lived the entire event, including finding Logan's body. Like Theo, I avoided that same stretch of Route 33. Maybe it was time I faced it. But not with him.

"No, the barn makes sense," I said. Theo sagged with relief.

"I like it," Aiden said. "What about the Stevens sisters? Should we ask them to join us, so they understand what a fucked-up mess they're getting themselves into with the pair of you?"

"Rowan," Theo said.

"The Stevens sisters," Aiden repeated.

Theo shook his head. "Poppy is just a friend."

Aiden let out a sigh and rubbed his forehead again. "We'll focus on Cal. Poppy isn't moving anywhere."

Adrenaline flooded my system, and my skin instantly went clammy. Rowan was days from leaving Peace Falls and taking my heart with her.

"I have to tell her how I feel," I said.

"Try not to look like you want to puke when you do," Aiden said and laughed.

Theo put his hand on my shoulder. "You've got this, brother. Now, let's go pretend to watch some baseball, and you can practice sharing your feelings with us."

"Hell, no," Aiden said. "I'm glad he has them, but I'm not role playing. Our friendship is weird enough."

"I love you too, man," Theo said pulling him into a hug. Aiden thumped his back before shoving him off and stomping back to the truck.

CHAPTER TWENTY-NINE

Rowan

"ARE YOU SURE ABOUT this?" Poppy asked. Her short black hair stuck out in every direction. Usually, my sister slept through me getting ready in the mornings, but today, she'd popped off her pillow the second I started to change out of my pajamas.

"Yes. I'm going to call Gwen after PT and decline the offer. I want to give her time to get to her desk and get settled for the day."

"Duh," she said. "I meant PT with Cal."

I shrugged. "I'm not getting him fired over two sessions. He's a professional. I'm sure it'll be fine."

"For Cal," Poppy said punching her pillow.

"Hey," I said, taking a seat on her bed. "Are you doubting me?"

Poppy's shoulders sagged. "You're right. I'm worried you'll see him and decide you can't live in Peace Falls anymore, and I would have gotten my hopes up for nothing."

"I'm not calling Gwen before I see Cal because she's wrangling her kids to daycare right now. I owe her a real conversation. That's all. I promise, Poppy, Red Blossoms Bakery is happening, and it will be amazing."

She surprised me by leaning forward and pulling me into a tight hug. When she sat back, her eyes were wet. "Ok, get out of here," she said, swatting my arm. "I need to sleep at least two more hours to be human."

"Love you," I said as she rolled onto her stomach.

"Same," she said into her pillow.

After I finished getting ready, I headed downstairs where Mom and Chris were voguing in the kitchen.

"Don't let me interrupt," I said, grabbing the keys to the station wagon.

Chris tugged my arm and spun me around. "Come on, Ann. You know this is how Mom celebrates. If I have to do it, so do you. It's your fault, anyway."

"Don't pretend like you're not thrilled I'm staying," I said and struck a ridiculous pose. Mom danced around the kitchen with a huge smile on her face. Chris performed a kneeling spin move that looked more breakdance than voguing. The song finished, and I hugged them both.

"Now that I'm warmed up, I better get going. I'm stopping at Karma on the way to PT to check how many scones I need to bake later."

Chris frowned. "I can take you and wait while you finish your session."

Mom shook her head. "Nope, you're helping me bring a load of Rowan's boxes to the storage unit. I want my living room back, and your sister can handle herself just fine."

"Thanks, Mom," I said, giving her hand a squeeze. "You too, Chris. I marked all the boxes that can go with an S."

"You're welcome, sweetie," Mom said and restarted the song. Chris let out a sigh but struck a pose. I grabbed my purse and opened the front door but came to a stop when I found Cal and Skye on the porch.

All the air whooshed out of my lungs. He looked handsome as usual, despite the dark circles under his eyes. Part of me wanted to retreat inside, another wanted to run down the steps and wrap my arms around him. But all of me wanted to know why he'd come to see me outside his office.

"Um, hi," I said, pulling the door closed behind me and muffling the '80s music inside.

Cal swallowed hard. "I thought we could start today's session with a walk," he said. "Assuming that's where you're headed."

At the word walk, Skye spun in a full circle.

"Ok," I said.

He handed me Skye's leash and then stepped close to take the bag from my shoulder. My body came alive when he neared, my heart racing, my breath shallow. Skye bumped into me, tail wagging. I knelt to pet her, relieved to put some distance between me and Cal.

Skye licked my face and I laughed. "I missed you too, girl."

"We should get going," Cal said, walking down the stairs with his shoulders bunched to his ears.

"Sure," I said, standing.

Skye and I followed him to the street. He walked on the asphalt, giving us the full sidewalk. We walked past a few houses without talking, our pace painfully slow. I was beginning to think he planned to walk all the way to Main Street without speaking when he cleared his throat.

"Thank you," he said softly. "For your review."

"No problem. I saw Avery removed hers."

He nodded. Well, if that was all the conversation he had, this was going to be a very uncomfortable walk.

"I'm happy for you, Cal," I said. "I meant what I wrote. You really are great at your job."

"You could have canceled your sessions," he said, stopping and staring ahead toward Broad Street. "Once Adam sees the review sites, my job won't be in danger."

"Did you want me to cancel?" I asked.

He shook his head and took a deep breath. Skye whimpered and dragged me into the street to Cal.

"Hey," I said, putting my hand on his arm. "Talk to me."

He turned to face me, his eyes searching mine. "I'm not ready for this to be over."

My heart pounded in my chest. "This" was everything to me, but I still didn't know what it meant for Cal. "Me either," I said, and all the tension seemed to leave his body at once.

"I know DC is a drive, but we could meet halfway some weekends," he said. "Maybe take turns driving the whole trip."

I shook my head. Our time apart had taught me I couldn't do casual, at least not with Cal. Even if I was staying in Peace Falls, I couldn't fall back in his bed unless he wanted more than my body.

"Ok," he said, pacing back and forth. "I could join a practice in Northern Virginia. It might take a while, but I'm sure I could find one."

"You'd move for me?" I asked, my chest filling with warmth.

He stopped and grabbed my hands. "If that's the only way I could have you, yeah."

"Sounds like a lot of effort for a casual hookup," I said, taking a step back from him.

His face fell. "I'm messing this up. When I said I don't want this to end, I meant I want more, not more of the same. You said you cared for me. I hope that's still true because I'm in love with you."

I was so startled I dropped Skye's leash and fumbled to grab it. "I'm sorry," I said, blowing out a breath. "It's kind of hard for me to believe you. Words are just words."

Cal nodded. "You're right. Which is why I'm asking for the opportunity to prove to you they're true."

"By moving to Northern Virginia?"

"If that's what it takes," he said.

"You'd leave your job, your family, and your friends for someone you just started seeing?"

"Not someone," he said, putting his hand on my face. "You. The most beautiful, kind, funny woman I've ever met. The person I want to hold every night, and the one I think about all day long. You're it for me, Rowan. I feel it. I understand you may need more time, and that's ok. That's all I want. A chance to prove that what I'm feeling is real."

"You're Caleb Cardoso."

"And you're Rowan Stevens," he said, raising an eyebrow at me. "Sorry, I refuse to call you by the asshole's last name. I hope you plan to change it back."

I nodded.

"So, Rowan Stevens," he said, stepping close. "When do we leave?"

"Um, never," I said.

He stepped back. "I'm sorry," he said, his eyes sad. "I shouldn't have put you in this position, especially when you were kind enough to keep seeing me professionally. Forget I said anything."

"No, Cal," I said, rising on my toes to wrap my arms around his neck. "I just meant I'm not moving to DC. I'm staying in Peace Falls. Poppy and I are going to open a bakery together."

He rested his head on my shoulder and pulled me close. "Thank God. I hate NoVa. The traffic is a nightmare."

I giggled. "Yeah, that alone makes me believe you a little."

"Both of you have rooms nearby," Principal Twillings shouted. "Stop canoodling in the street."

"Lay off them, Twill," Mrs. Adams yelled from her own porch. "Just because you're a dried-up old fart doesn't mean the rest of us don't appreciate a good show."

I glanced around. The neighbors had gathered to watch us, including my entire family, who were standing on the sidewalk in front of our house for a better view.

"Kiss her already," Poppy shouted, wearing nothing but the over-sized shirt she'd slept in. "I have shit to do."

"Language, Ms. Stevens," Principal Twillings shouted.

"Bite me, Twill. Come on, Cal."

Cal smiled and leaned down to place a gentle kiss on my lips.

"Boo," Mrs. Adams shouted. "You call that a kiss?"

I laughed and Cal used the opportunity to slide his tongue into my mouth, deepening the kiss until my knees threatened to give out. He pulled back but leaned his forehead on mine as the neighbors cheered. I laughed. Only in Peace Falls. Sure, a crowd might have clapped for us in DC, but here I knew each and every person was cheering because they wanted to see us together long after this moment. They didn't think it was unbelievable that a man like Cal would want a woman like me, which meant the fear was mine alone. Skye ran circles around our feet, wrapping our legs in the leash like she was trying to keep us together. Cal placed a soft kiss on my forehead and bent to catch her.

"Come here," he said, grabbing Skye's collar and unhooking it from the leash. He looked up at me and smiled. "We don't want Rowan to fall, unless it's for us."

I wanted to tell him I already had. But part of me still didn't trust his words. I knew, without a doubt, that if I gave my whole heart to Caleb, I'd never get it back.

He untangled the leash from around our feet before snapping it back to Skye's collar and standing. "What do you think about skipping the walk and taking Twill's advice?"

I looked at everyone watching us. "I think the entire street would tease me for months."

He smiled and leaned in to whisper in my ear. "Not if we go to Maple and cut through my backyard."

I nodded, and he gripped my hand. We set off toward Broad Street at a much faster pace. Someone booed behind us, and I stifled a laugh. By the time we circled around to Cal's back yard, the only person to see us sneak inside was Principal Twillings. He had the decency not to shout anything, but he laughed behind the paper he pretended to read.

Skye huffed when she realized her walk had been cut short.

"Sorry, girl," Cal said, unclipping Skye's leash in the mud room and tossing treats on the floor as he pulled me toward the kitchen.

As soon as the mudroom door shut behind us, his mouth crashed to mine. Then he jumped back, his eyes dark, chest heaving. "Walk to the bedroom, Rowan," he gritted out with his hands balled at his sides. "If I touch you again, I'm going to fuck you right here."

"What's wrong with that?" I kicked off my sneakers, ripped off my shirt, and shimmied out of my leggings.

Cal closed his eyes and banged his head against the wall. "I promise to take you against any surface you want later, but right now I'd like to make love to you."

"Oh," I said.

He opened his eyes, and I caught a glimpse of something fragile. I reached for him, and he took my hand, bringing it to his lips before he laced his fingers with mine and lead me to his bedroom. When we reached the edge of the bed, he started by trailing a line of kisses down my neck to my breasts.

"Caleb," I breathed, while he unhooked my bra. "I'm practically naked and you're fully dressed."

He stepped back and pulled his scrub top off in one swift motion. I ran my hands across his broad shoulders and down the sculpted muscles of his chest before sliding his pants and boxers down his legs. I followed them to the floor.

His thick cock bobbed free, and I wet my lips.

"Don't even think about it," he said, tugging me to my feet past his impressive erection.

"You want me to file that for later with the kitchen sex," I said, smirking.

That's when he snapped. He gripped my face and kissed me so hard my knees gave out. He lifted me, and I wrapped my legs around his waist, desperate to feel every inch of his skin against mine. He tossed me on the bed and climbed up my body, sinking into me in one thrust. I closed my eyes and moaned, but he stilled.

"Look at me," he softly.

I opened my eyes and found his warm brown ones staring down at me. He wove our fingers together, and with a small smile, pulled away before rocking into me slowly, his eyes never leaving mine. The way he looked at me with such intense sweetness made me tighten around him. I arched closer, my body begging for more friction. He groaned and began to piston his hips, the rhythm brutal as we raced toward release. My orgasm ripped through me, powerful and fast. I cried out, riding wave after wave of pleasure, as he shouted my name and came.

He kissed me gently on the forehead and groaned. "That wasn't what I had in mind."

"No," I said, running my hands along his muscular arms. "It was better."

He smiled. "I've never done that before."

I laughed. "You and I both know that's not true."

He shook his head and ran his fingers down my face. "I've never had sex without a condom. And never with someone I loved."

"Oh, I got tested while I was in the hospital, and I'm on the pill."

His eyes bore into me.

"All that is probably in my medical charts, huh?"

He nodded.

He wanted me to tell him how I felt. My mouth went dry. Tears burned my eyes, and my stomach sank.

"Come here," he said, pulling my head to his chest and running his fingers through my hair. "I'll be here when you're ready. Until then, I'm going to spend every day showing you how much I love you."

I nodded, embarrassed that I'd ruined the moment with tears. His heart thudded fast against my ear.

Chapter Thirty

Cal

THIS HAD TO BE the longest workday of my career. At least, it felt like it. Rowan and I were only fifteen minutes late to her session. A fact I'm not proud of. Which, on top of our reunion sex ending with her in tears, left me uneasy. I relaxed as we worked through her exercises, my confidence building every time she smiled, the warmth in her eyes impossible to hide.

I meant every word I'd said. I'd been crushed when Avery dumped me after high school, but even then, I knew it had more to do with my ego than my heart. What I felt for Rowan scared the shit out of me and made everything brighter at the same time. I swear the damn birds were singing during our session like some scene in a Disney movie. I couldn't wipe the stupid smile from my face.

After she left, I counted the hours until I could see her again. I needed to prove what she meant to me, and I intended to start the moment my last patient left. Unfortunately, Adam had other ideas.

"Dr. Cardoso," he said as I headed for the door. "A word."

Cammie gave me an encouraging double thumbs up as I followed him into his office. I took a seat in the chair in front of his desk and waited while he woke his computer.

"Cammie tells me you've sorted your online mess," Adam said, clicking around.

"I have."

He nodded, scanning the screen. "I hate these sites. Word of mouth is great. People recommend you to someone they know because they've experienced your abilities. But this," he said, waving his hand at the screen, "There's no accountability. People make decisions for their care based on recommendations in anonymous posts. Many of which, as you've had the misfortune to learn, are lies. I'm getting too old for this. And if I'm being honest, too old for the work itself. Which is why, if you're ready, I'm willing to discuss selling the practice to you."

"Really?" I said, leaning forward. Weeks ago, he'd been ready to fire me, and now he trusted me to take over the practice he'd built from the ground up. Before the Avery debacle, I wouldn't have been surprised. I'd joined Adam because I knew he was nearing retirement age and would be looking for someone to buy him out. I'd assumed Review-gate would delay his transition plans, not accelerate them. "Are you sure?"

Adam nodded. "It's bad enough I have to deal with all the electronic charts and tablets. Now Cammie says she's been offered a full-time job at that coffee place she loves. I do not have it in me to hire and train a new front desk person. It's time. Find a lawyer for your end, and we can get together next week to discuss the valuation and transition plan. We'll omit the numbers from this past quarter to come to a fair price."

I stood. "Thank you," I said, shaking his hand.

He waved me off. "Let me know when you have representation, and we'll schedule a meeting."

I nodded and closed the door to his office as I left. Cammie was bouncing on her feet by the reception desk, silently cheering. I motioned with my head to the glass door, and she grabbed her bag and followed me into the hallway.

"Congrats," she said, pulling me into a hug.

"You're quitting?" I asked, holding her at arm's length.

She shook her head. "Let him think that until the paperwork is signed. Honestly, I didn't enjoy working for him, and Lauren really did offer me a full-time job at Karma, but if you're in charge, I'll just keep my part-time hours there."

"Until you decide to become a famous singer."

"We do not speak of that. What happens in Church—"

"Stays in Church," I finished. "Thanks, Cam. The thought of replacing you was the last straw for Adam."

She giggled. "If I'd known, I'd have threatened to quit months ago. Now come on, you've been checking the clock all day."

"Was it that obvious?" I asked as we headed down the steps together.

She nodded. "I'm glad to see you worked things out with Rowan."

I paused on the landing between the third and second floors. "Do you think I have? I told her I loved her, and she didn't say it back."

Cammie's eyes widened. "You told her you love her?"

"Um, should I not have?"

"Well, do you?"

"Yes," I said, simply.

"Oh, thank goodness," she said, patting my arm. "If you'd rambled about how she was the best sex of your life or that you told her you loved her because you didn't want her to move, I might have had to kick you in the balls and take that job at Karma."

I cleared my throat. "Well, she is the best sex of my life, and I don't want her to move. But I also love her."

"Obviously," Cammie said starting down the stairs again. "Passion is part of love, and no one wants to be far from the person who holds their heart. But knowing how you felt should be a simple yes or no. Because at the end of the day, love is simple. Or at least it should be."

"So, she doesn't love me?"

Cammie rolled her eyes. "I said it should be simple. Not that it was. She's been burned, Cal. Big time. For all your rough edges, and your unfortunate experience with that she-devil, a lover has never broken your heart. Right?"

I shook my head.

"I'm sure Rowan is head over heels for you. She just needs to admit it to herself first. Give her time. Just don't do something stupid like getting your ego hurt because she can't say it back. It's not about you."

I nodded, but my chest still ached.

"Snap out of it, Cal. This is the best day of your life. You told a woman you love her, and she didn't tell you to get lost. She's staying in Peace Falls with you. She's probably waiting at your house right now, as eager to see you as you are to see her. On top of that, Dr. Cohen is finally retiring. Smile, damn it."

"You're right," I said, giving her a quick hug and running down the rest of the stairs. The last thing I heard as I pushed through the door was Cammie's laughter echoing in the staircase.

Either Cammie was psychic, or texted Rowan, because she was waiting on my porch steps with Skye when I arrived home.

"Hey," I said, bending to kiss her, eager to show her how much I'd missed her in the hours we were apart.

When I stood, Rowan seemed a little breathless. "I thought we could take Skye on a walk. She seemed so disappointed this morning."

Skye flashed me a doggie smile, and I knew there was no use fighting it. My dog and I were completely in love with this woman, whether she felt the same or not.

"I have a better idea. How about we take her on a sunset hike?"

Rowan's eyes lit up. "Give me five minutes to change and throw together some sandwiches."

With that she took off down Sullivan Street, her steps more labored than they should be, but improved from when we met. Skye whimpered, and I rubbed her head. "Don't worry, girl. She isn't leaving us. We're just getting started."

Chapter Thirty-One

Rowan

Two Weeks Later

My stomach danced with nerves as I placed the last snickerdoodle onto a cooling rack.

"Want to talk about it now?" Poppy asked, not looking up from the delicate design she was icing onto a sugar cookie I'd baked earlier.

I blew out a breath and flopped into the chair across from my sister. "I think I'm in love with Cal."

"No shit," Poppy said, reaching for another cookie.

"I'm serious, Poppy. I haven't been separated from Brad long enough to file for divorce. I can't be in love with someone else."

Poppy put down the cookie and glared at me. "You did not just lump Cal together with that dickface you had the misfortune to marry."

"But we've only been together a little over a month. Plus, we broke up, so I don't think you can count the full time."

"So what," Poppy said, picking up the cookie again like the conversation bored her. "When you know, you know."

I watched her finish the design before I said, "It's not that simple."

"He told you he loves you, right?" Poppy said, placing the cookie carefully on the sheet of parchment paper where half a dozen more were drying.

"Yes," I said, rubbing my forehead. "Every day since we got back together."

"Then it is that simple," she said, staring me down. "Tell him today."

I shook my head. "Today is—"

"The anniversary of the worst day of his life. I know. And he asked you to be with him. If that doesn't prove how much he loves you, I don't know what the poor man has to do." Poppy let out a sigh and reached for another cookie. "What time is he coming to get you?"

"Six," I said, glancing at the clock on the stove. I wasn't sure my nerves could handle another half hour of waiting, but I wanted to give Cal whatever space he needed today.

"Any idea what you're doing?" Poppy asked like she didn't know exactly where Cal was taking me or why.

I reached across the table and put my hand on her arm. "Want to talk about it?"

She shook her head and grabbed another icing bag to add detail in a different color. I watched her work, fascinated by her talent and speed.

Fifteen minutes later, someone knocked on the door, and I ran to get it. Instead of Cal, Aiden stood on the porch with his hands shoved in the pockets of his cargo shorts.

"Is everything ok?" I asked, my mind jumping from one scenario to another. None that put Aiden on my porch instead of Cal seemed good.

"Everything is fine," Aiden said. "I'm actually here to see your sister."

"Oh," I said, opening the door wider. "Come on in."

"I'll wait out here, if you don't mind."

"Um, sure," I said and went to the kitchen.

"Aiden O'Malley is on the porch. He said he wants to speak with you."

Poppy looked as confused as I felt, but she set her icing bag on the table. I followed her to the porch, curious what was going on.

"Pixie," he said, looking her up and down and frowning at her Grinch slippers.

"I'm sure most women fall apart at a good O'Malley once over, but I have dozens of cookies to ice," she said. "What do you want?"

"I think you should be there today," he said. "For Theo."

"I think Theo would have asked me if he wanted me there."

"What Theo wants and what he allows himself are two very different things."

She took a step closer and poked him in the chest. "Maybe you should respect that what he's telling you is what he wants."

"Nope," Aiden said, pulling his right hand from his pocket. A handcuff with red feathers was clamped around his wrist. He snapped the other end onto Poppy's left arm.

"What the fuck?" she said, tugging at the cuff.

"Careful, Pixie, don't want to mark you up. Unless you're into that."

"Rowan," Poppy shouted. "A little help."

Aiden chuckled. "The pair of you weigh as much as my biceps."

Poppy drew in a large breath and screamed for Chris. He ran to the porch and skidded to a halt when he saw Aiden and Poppy handcuffed together.

"Hey, kid," Aiden said as he somehow swung Poppy onto his shoulder. "Congrats on making the starting lineup."

"Thanks," Chris said. "I couldn't have done it without you."

"Don't thank him, idiot," Poppy howled. "Stop him."

"Quiet there, Hell Cat," Aiden said, smacking Poppy's butt with his left hand. "I know Principal Twillings lives on your street, and that man has no problem calling the cops on me."

"Good," Poppy huffed. "Glad someone would."

"Um, you're not going to hurt her, are you?" Chris asked, taking a step toward them.

"I swear on my nieces and nephews, she'll be fine."

Chris nodded. "Well, ok then. Coach said he'd love for you to drop by practice sometime."

"Yeah," Aiden said, smiling. "I just might."

"Seriously?" Poppy squealed.

"He loves those kids, Pop. You'll be fine."

With that Chris turned and went back inside the house.

"Aiden," I shouted when he started toward his truck. "Is this really necessary?"

"It is," he said. He'd left the driver's side door wide open and pushed Poppy inside. "The cuff keys are at my house. Hop over the gear shift, Pixie. Don't think Theo would appreciate me reaching between your legs to change gears."

"You're a pig," she shouted.

"Word of advice," he said as he climbed in after her. "Don't tell Theo unless you want to go ninety the whole way to my place."

"Noted. Also, I might be small, but hurt my sister, and I will hit you so hard you'll pee blood for a week."

"I'd expect nothing less," he said and slammed the door. He drove off, and I stood frozen in the yard until Theo pulled up. Cal jumped out of the passenger seat, but the smile slid from his face when he saw me.

"What happened?" he asked.

"Aiden just kidnapped my sister," I whispered, "But don't tell Theo."

Cal chuckled. "We better go before she murders him." He opened the rear passenger door of the extended cab, and I took a seat in the back beside Skye.

"Hi Theo," I said. He nodded, his hands gripping the steering wheel. I expected Cal to climb into the front, but instead he walked around the truck and slid in behind Theo.

"Go sit with Theo," he said, and Skye slithered through the opening to the front. She put her head in Theo's lap and stretched long across the seat.

Cal gripped Theo's shoulders and squeezed them. I wondered why, if he was so upset, he was driving instead of Cal or me.

"Alright," Theo said gruffly. "Go cuddle your woman, not me."

Cal laughed but I caught Theo's eyes in the rearview mirror. Theo nodded and an understanding passed between us. No matter how together he seemed, Cal needed me.

I scooted to the middle and buckled in before grabbing Cal's hand in mine and resting my head on his shoulder. His muscles relaxed as he traced calming circles on my hand. We were silent the entire way. Once or twice, I thought of starting a conversation to break the tension, but both men had their mouth set in grim lines, like they'd fall to pieces if they opened them.

We drove to the old Crawford farm, down a rutted dirt road, past the farmhouse to a large barn that had seen better days.

Poppy and Aiden stood in the field, still handcuffed together. She'd swapped her Grinch slippers for an enormous pair of work boots that were obviously Aiden's. Theo slammed on the breaks and threw the truck into park. He exploded from the driver's seat so fast Skye jumped and barked.

"What's going on?" Theo shouted, stalking toward them.

Cal ran after him, and I opened the passenger door to help Skye down.

"Greetings, Theodoros," Aiden said, lifting his arm, and by extension Poppy's in the air. "A little help Cal."

"What the hell are you up to?" Cal asked but laughed.

Aiden reached into his left pocket and pulled out a pair of handcuffs. "Your choice, Pixie. You can be handcuffed to me or Theo."

"Why don't you play with each other," she said, and turned her face away.

"Sorry, Poppy," Cal said snapping the handcuff to her right hand.

"You don't deserve my sister," she said.

"Don't I know it," he said. "Theo?"

Theo blew out a breath and stepped close enough to be snapped into the other cuff. "You really don't understand triggers, do you, Aiden," he said.

"Key to this set is in my pocket," Aiden said, holding up the arm connected to Poppy.

"Aren't these things universal?" Cal asked.

"This pair is for kink," he said, looking at the arm attached to Poppy. "The other are the kind correctional officers use."

"Man, you really don't get triggers, do you?" Cal said, unlocking the cuffs that bound Poppy and Aiden together. "You could have at least put him in the fluffy pair."

"Rowan," Poppy said. "Are you sure you like Cal? He's giving off mad creeper vibes. And his best friend is a lunatic. Not you, Theo," she added softly.

A smiled tugged at Theo's lips. Cal glanced at Theo and patted Aiden's shoulder. The bond between the three of them, forged in so much pain, brought tears to my eyes.

"Good job, you've made Rowan cry," Poppy huffed.

Cal's attention snapped to me, and he hurried to where I stood with Skye, his forehead scrunched with worry. "I know this is weird. But I think Aiden was right to bring Poppy. If you think she's uncomfortable, I'll make him give me the key now."

I shook my head. "She's only fighting because Theo didn't ask her himself. She wanted to come."

Cal nodded and pulled me into a hug. "Thank you, for being here. For being you. I wish Logan could have seen us together."

"Me too," I whispered.

He stepped away from me, his face anguished. "It's my fault he died. I was the DD that night, but I got trashed after Avery broke up with me."

"Bullshit," Theo shouted. Poppy jumped, jerking the cuff that held them together, and Theo softened his voice. "I was the one driving. The accident was no one's fault but mine," he told her.

"Stop being such a fucking martyr," Aiden yelled. "As much as you'd like to take all the blame, Cal and I have just as much guilt as you do. Logan was sitting in the backseat behind you, Theo. If he'd been wearing his seatbelt, he would have walked away like you did. I'm the reason he wasn't buckled in. So go ahead and claim the accident as yours, but Logan's death is on me."

"Neither one of you should feel guilty," Theo said.

"You went to jail for a year," Cal yelled. "You're a convicted felon. I ruined your life, brother. I ruined Aiden's. Everything happened because I broke my promise to drive. No matter what you say, Logan would be alive today if I hadn't."

He drew in a stuttering breath, turned to me, and fell apart. He sobbed into my shoulder, pulling me so close I could feel every thud of his breaking heart as I rubbed his back. I couldn't imagine holding so much guilt, so tightly for ten years.

Across the field, Poppy gripped Theo's hand as silent tears ran down his face. Aiden stood alone, staring at the barn. Skye took off toward him, bumping into his legs. He knelt and rubbed her head.

"I love you, Caleb Cardoso."

Cal squeezed me harder and sank to the ground, pulling me into his lap. "Thank you," he said between sobs.

For loving him? For telling him? For giving him something beautiful in this moment, this place? It didn't matter. We didn't need words. Not anymore. But that wouldn't stop me from telling him I loved him every day for the rest of my life.

EPILOGUE

Cal

TWO MONTHS LATER

The last time I attended the homecoming game, I was crowned homecoming king. This time, I sat in the bleachers beside Rowan and cheered as Chris took the field. On my other side, Aiden clapped so hard his hands had to sting. Despite watching college and pro games for years, neither of us had been able to return to Spartan Stadium until Chris's first game of the season.

"Kid's on fire," Aiden said, shaking Rose's shoulders when Chris caught a difficult pass in the second quarter. She had her hands over her eyes. Though she came to every game, she was too nervous to watch. Aiden had taken to sitting beside her and narrating the entire game like a sportscaster. So far, Chris had no idea his mother couldn't bear to watch him play.

"Stop being dramatic, Mom," Poppy yelled on the other side of Rowan. "Your baby is fine."

"If you were out there, I'd be doing the same thing," Rose shouted.

"If I was out there—"

"Go, Spartans," Rowan shouted.

Theo took a sip of his soda, trying to hide his laugh. He and Poppy were still just friends, or so they said. Rowan and I were doing whatever we could to push them together: Romantic double dates, gentle nudging, outright exasperation. So far, nothing had worked.

"Was that a first down?" Lauren asked in front of me.

"Yep," Cammie said beside her.

"But last time it was closer to that woman in the red coat," Lauren said. "Not the entrance to the bathroom."

Aiden groaned and opened his mouth to speak, but Cammie turned and shot him a glare.

"That's a good observation," Cammie said. "It changes. Each time the team takes possession, they have four plays to gain ten yards."

"Ah," Lauren said. "Too bad they don't paint the lines on the field like they did in that game we watched on TV."

"For fuck's sake, Lauren. Those aren't real," Aiden huffed.

Cammie and Lauren both turned and glared at him.

"Language, Aiden," Rose said. "Leave the girls alone and tell me what's happening."

On the next play, Chris got taken to the ground in an assisted tackle by two huge defensive linemen. Rowan, Cammie, and Lauren gasped, and Rose's hands flew from her eyes. She stood like she was about to sprint down the bleachers to check her son for boo-boos. Aiden gently pulled her back to her seat.

"Remind me to stop by your shop and send my mom flowers," he said, trying to distract her. Chris popped up, and everyone breathed a sigh of relief.

"You owe that woman a trip to the Caribbean for watching you play as much as you did," Rose said, rubbing her chest like it ached. "Why couldn't he have joined the track team?"

"Because talent and passion like his are rare. You'd never want to hold him back, right?" Aiden said.

Rose shook her head and covered her eyes as Chris joined the line for the next play.

Rowan rested her head on my shoulder. I pulled her hand into mine, rubbing the finger where I hoped my ring would be in a few hours. I took a deep breath, trying to calm my nerves, and caught Theo's eye. He smiled and whispered something to Poppy who laughed so hard she snorted.

"What's so funny?" Rowan asked.

"Theo asked what Mom was going to do if Chris went pro," Poppy said.

Rose groaned and pressed her face harder against her hands.

Aiden smirked, knowing damn well they were sharing a laugh at my expense. Everyone but Rowan knew what was happening after the game. Lauren and Poppy had helped me pick out the ring, and I had to tell my two best friends and Cam, if for no other reason, than to brace themselves for the utter mess I'd be if Rowan turned me down. I'd asked Rose for permission, and she'd yelled at me that her daughter made her own decisions, before pulling me into a hug and bawling on my shoulder.

At half time, Lauren glanced at her phone and frowned. "Sorry, y'all. I've got to run. Wyatt is having trouble with the espresso machine." The new full-timer at Karma moonlighted on Aiden's crew and could fix about anything, but Rowan didn't seem to question the text.

"I'll go with you," Cammie said, standing.

Lauren smiled at her and said, "That'd be great."

Rowan frowned. "You're both still coming back to the house later, right?"

"Of course," Lauren said. "You promised me victory cake."

"Just cake," Aiden said, rubbing his forehead. "Don't jinx it."

"I'm calling it victory cake to manifest a win," she snapped back, linking her arm with Cam.

"Poppy outdid herself," Rowan said. "She recreated the entire stadium with different figurines of Chris if they win or lose."

"I can't wait," Lauren said, touching the shoulder of the couple beside her. They stood and let them pass.

Red Blossoms Bakery had taken the special event industry by storm. In addition to baking sweets for Karma, Rowan and Poppy had become the most in-demand cake makers in Southwest Virginia. They were already discussing moving their operation from Rose's kitchen to a commercial space next year. Aiden even offered to help them find a place he could convert at cost whenever they were ready.

"Aiden, what's happening?" Rose asked, sounding distressed.

"It's half time, Mom," Rowan said. "Rest a minute."

Rose dropped her hands to her lap and let out a relieved breath. She seemed more worked up than usual, and I wasn't sure if it was because she knew how much a win today meant to Chris and his team, or if she was anxious for what came after. Maybe she was worried Chris would be upset that I'd chosen today to ask his sister to marry me, stealing the attention from his victory. I didn't know much about manifesting, but Lauren seemed pretty damn sure, so I was going with it.

It'd seemed romantic at the time. If Chris hadn't wanted my help with football, Rowan would have dropped me as her PT before I got a chance to know her. I'd chosen this game because Rowan was my home now. Damn it, I should have talked it over with Chris.

I pulled out my phone to text Cammie and call the whole thing off, but Aiden shook his head at me. I slid my phone back in my jacket and did my best to distract myself with the game. In the third-quarter, Rowan started squirming in her seat, and I shifted my worry about the proposal to her pain, rubbing circles on her lower back. We'd continued to work on building her core strength, but some of the injuries from her life before me were difficult to heal.

Aiden was right. Chris was on fire, and the Peace Falls Spartans took the win. The entire stadium erupted in cheers, and Rose put her head between her knees.

"Maybe I should tape him and make you watch after," Aiden said rubbing her back. "Exposure therapy."

Rose straightened and shook her head. "No, I'll know he's ok if I see him after the game. I'm doing better. I didn't even cry this time when they tackled him."

"You did great," Aiden said, kneading her shoulders like she was a boxer about to hit the ring for eight rounds.

"Let's go," Rose said. "All this screaming is fraying my nerves more."

My nerves went into overdrive as we climbed down the bleachers and made our way to the exit.

"Shouldn't we say hi to Chris?" Rowan asked.

My heart stopped. Chris would be tied up with his team for at least an hour. I couldn't take Rowan back to her house before he was finished or he'd miss everything.

Aiden let out a loud whoop, and I turned to see Chris heading toward us, covered in sweat and dirt and smiling from ear-to-ear.

"I almost cried when you made that catch in the second quarter, kid," Aiden said.

"You were amazing, honey," Rose said, hugging him. Poppy and Rowan did the same.

Chris held out his hand, and I pulled him into a one-armed hug. "Chris—" I started.

"Somebody set off a stink bomb in the locker room," he said with a smirk. "I'm going to walk home with y'all to shower and give it time to clear out."

"Ah, man," Theo said, slapping my shoulder. "Remember that time you and Aiden set off that stink bomb in Glenn Cove's locker room."

"Allegedly," Aiden said.

Rowan looked at me with a shocked expression. "You did not?"

I wanted to throttle Theo until I realized he'd distracted Rowan while we passed the entire Peace Falls football team headed to the locker room without Chris.

"I'm a changed man," I said, taking her hand and kissing it. "Amazing what the love of a good woman can do."

She shook her head but smiled. By the time we walked to Sullivan Street, my palms were sweating so bad I had to drop Rowan's hand before she noticed how nervous I was. Luckily, most of the town was still celebrating at the stadium, so the street was quiet as we approached Rowan's house. If I had to stop and shoot the shit with the neighbors, my heart might explode from anxiety.

"Oh good," Rowan said, seeing Lauren's car. "Guess the machine wasn't that broken."

Just then, Cammie walked from the back yard with Skye. My parents stood from the porch swing and walked to the railing with Lauren, who was filming us with her phone. Cammie unhooked Skye's leash like we'd practiced, and she ran toward us wagging her tail with a ring box attached to her collar.

"Hey, baby," Rowan said, kneeling and opening her arms.

I knelt beside her, ready to ask the most important question of my life when my beloved dog ran past us barking her head off.

"Squirrel," Chris shouted, taking off after her.

"We've got this," Aiden said, sprinting after him.

Theo froze on the sidewalk, looking from Rowan and me to Skye. "Come on," Poppy said, grabbing his arm and tugging him to her hearse.

Rowan stood like she was going to join them. I caught Rose's eye. Usually, I'd be running after Skye myself, but I couldn't wait another minute to ask Rowan to marry me. Rose grabbed her daughter's arm. "Chris is catching up to her now," she said, pointing.

I stood and turned. Sure enough, Chris and Aiden had gained enough ground, I felt confident they'd have her soon.

Rose gave me a pointed look. "I'm going to set out the ice cream, so it's soft enough to scoop," she said. She linked her arm with Cammie's and dragged her to the porch where the others were waiting.

"What's going on?" Rowan asked.

I dropped to my knee again and pulled out the ring from my pocket because as much as we practiced, I wasn't trusting Skye with a diamond. Rowan gasped and her eyes filled with tears.

"I love our family and friends, but I'm kind of glad I get to do this part without them because you are my world. Rowan Eloise Stevens, would you do me the honor of sharing your life with me?"

"Yes," she said, dropping to her knees and throwing her arms around me. I slid the ring on her finger. My parents, Rose, Lauren, and Cammie ran toward us clapping. A moment later, Chris and Aiden returned with Skye.

"Come here," I said, holding out my arms for Skye to join us.

"Couldn't you have waited two minutes," Chris huffed.

"Did you plan for the dog to take off?" Aiden asked, frowning at the ring on Rowan's finger.

I shook my head and opened the box on Skye's collar where two pitted cherries rested inside. "I know they're not chocolate covered. One, I couldn't find the ones you were talking about, and two I was afraid Skye would somehow eat them. But I had this whole speech planned about how I wanted to spend every moment with you, the happy, the sad, and the ones that were a little bit of both, that I would eat those disgusting cherries with you whenever you visited your dad, but suggest you make them yourself because if anyone can make something delicious it's you."

Rowan put her face in her hands and wept. Chris looked from the cherries to Rowan, utterly confused. But my mom, Rose, and Lauren wrapped their arms around each other and started sobbing. Even my dad looked a little choked up. Cammie and Aiden seemed as baffled as Chris, but they were both smiling.

Poppy's hearse screeched to a stop behind us, and she ran over. She glanced at Rowan's hand, the ring box, and then threw herself into Theo's chest as he climbed from the passenger seat, her shoulders heaving. He wrapped his arms around her and rested his head on hers.

"Is it a good thing they're all crying?" Chris asked. "You said yes, Ann, didn't you?"

"Yes," she said, lifting her face from her hands and laughing.

"Well," Aiden said, clearing his throat, and I swear the man had tears in his eyes. "Time for that victory cake."

We headed toward the house, my arm wrapped around Rowan. One by one the others went inside, leaving us alone on the porch.

"I love you so much," she said. "I can't believe I'm going to be Rowan Cardoso."

I bent and kissed the words from her lips. Nothing had ever tasted so sweet.

More from Hannah

Can't get enough of Rowan and Cal? Sign up for my newsletter for a bonus epilogue of their wedding day.

Visit https://BookHip.com/ZTNMQQV.

If you enjoyed *For You I'd Mend*, you'll love the rest of the Peace Falls Series.

Book 2: *For You I'd Mend* Available October 10, 2024

Book 3: *For You I'd Bloom* Available January 7, 2025

Letter to Readers

Dear Reader,

I hope you enjoyed Rowan and Cal's story as much as I enjoyed writing it. This book began as a dare, specifically a challenge to write a romance in one month. Though I've read and loved romances for years, I lacked the moxie to chain myself to my laptop and write one.

Many authors write full novels during National Novel Writing Month in November. I told myself that some year, I'd find the time. But let's be honest, as a mother of school-age children, that time would never be November. My kids have an entire week off at the beginning of the month, not to mention Thanksgiving break, and the ramp up to the holiday season. It will be a good eight years, if ever, before I could dedicate that much time to writing in November.

During one of my weekly zoom meetings with two writer friends, someone suggested we all try to draft a novel in January. Why January? I, for one, like to burrow into my house for the entire month, avoiding the cold while I recover from all the glittery holiday magic. I confessed to my friends that I'd always wanted to write a romance novel, a very different genre from my usual work. One of my friends had a partial draft of a paranormal romance she wanted to finish, so we dragged our third friend along for the ride.

I expected to be very busy that January. I didn't expect to love every minute of it. I fell in love with the characters, the story, and the thrill of writing something I couldn't wait to read myself. In short, I was hooked. By the end of January, I had a full first draft and knew I'd finally found my place as a writer. Poppy and Theo's story formed in my mind even before I finished this book (and believe me, there were many drafts to follow the first). I can't wait to share it with you.

I appreciate the time you've given Rowan and Cal's story and would love if you'd leave an honest review.

Thanks for reading!

Hannah

P.S. Please keep in touch! For news and exclusive content visit https:// hannahjordanauthor.com and sign up for my newsletter.

f facebook.com/hannahjordanbooks/

instagram.com/hannahjordanbooks/

Acknowledgements

To James Carpenter and Gerri Mahn, thank you for issuing the challenge to write this book, and for your steadfast support through revisions, rewrites, and bouts of mental anguish. To the RWA Romance Author Mentorship Program, specifically my mentor Jeannie Watt and co-mentees Claude and Melyssa, thank you for your invaluable feedback and continued support. To my sister friends, Wynsor, Laura, and Malina, thanks for sticking with me during my awkward wallflower years and every year after. I could not have written this book without the love and encouragement of my husband, who has championed my crazy ideas with unwavering enthusiasm for over two decades. I launched this book on our twentieth wedding anniversary because everything I know of true love, I learned from him. Finally, to my daughters, you hold in your hands proof of what can happen when you dream big and persevere (but don't read beyond this page for at least ten years. Even then, you might want to spare yourself the ick since there's a lot of sexy stuff written by your mom. You've been warned.)

About the Author

Hannah Jordan grew up in the Blue Ridge Mountains of Virginia but moved to South Jersey after falling in love with her complete opposite. She's got all the advanced degrees of a "serious" fiction writer but only smiles when she's writing romance. She lives with her husband and two daughters in a picturesque town outside Philadelphia where she enjoys reading in all genres, especially the spicy ones, and confusing people with her half-Southern, half-Northern accent.